Enemy Force

Enemy Force

by

John-Antoine Nau

adapted into English by

Michael Shreve

A Black Coat Press Book

Introduction

Not very much is known about this unstable, voluntary exile.

John Antoine Nau was born Eugène Léon Édouard Torquet on November 19, 1860, in San Francisco, California and was thus an American citizen. His father had emigrated from France to California around 1845 and became a naturalized citizen. Attacked by typhus in 1864 he died leaving a widow and three children behind. In 1866, the family returned to France, to Le Havre, where his father's family lived. His mother remarried in 1870 and, when the future laureate was 17 years old, they moved to Paris, where his mother was originally from, to complete his education.

Nau always had a desire to write and in Paris, he found an outlet and sympathetic friends. He was associated with the club of *Hirsutes*, the circle of *Zutistes* and the club of *Hydropathes*, predecessors of the surrealists. He collaborated on the journal *Chat noir* in which he published his first poems. But his family worried about his future and got him an office job; he failed miserably. He had other plans and other desires.

To escape the middle-class ennui, in 1881, at the age of 21, he boarded a three-master as a pilot's assistant and sailed to Haiti and the West Indies. Later, he became Assistant Commissioner on board the ocean liner *La France*. After that, he traveled to Colombia, Venezuela and New York before returning to France to search for his literary fortune.

After returning to France in 1883, he married Henriette Dieudonné in 1885—33 years of travel would follow, which never exhausted their curiosity or love for each other. For their honeymoon, they went to Martinique, planning to settle there, but family obligations forced them to return to France in 1886. He would never return to Martinique except in his writings—it seduced him and became his inexhaustible source and treasure, real and imaginary, for his poetry and novels, as we can see at the end of *Enemy Force*.

In France, his lifelong wandering began. He lived in Piriac-sur-Mer, Les Sables d'Olonne, Le Lavandou, Pontoise and Carteret and spent winters in Spain, Malaga, Soller and Barcelona. Between 1899 and 1901, he was in the Canary Islands, Orotava del Puerto and Lisbon. From there he went to Huelva (where he finished *Enemy Force*) in 1902.

On December 21, 1903, a group of writers gathered in Paris (and what writers!—J. K. Huysmans, Octave Mirabeau, Léon Daudet, the brothers Rosny, Paul Marguerite, Lucien Desclaves, Elémir Bourges, Léon Hennique, Gustave Geffroy) and awarded *Enemy Force* the first Prix Goncourt (by a vote of 6 to 4). Edmond de Goncourt had stipulated in his will that they would crown a prose work of imagination to distinguish and support a young literary debut full of promise. He rested in peace that first year. Even if Nau was 43 years old.

They searched hard for information about this mysterious author who was only known for a very few exotic stories published in *La Revue Blanche* (*Enemy Force*, his first novel, was published at his own expense and was a flop). Since he did not send his book to critics to be reviewed, no one seemed to know who this outsider was. In fact, his taste for the incognito even caused some critics to deny his very existence. They finally tracked him down through his brother and a friend. He was living in Saint Tropez at the time and did not even return to Paris to pick up his prize money.

In 1906 Paul Léautaud said, "The Prix Goncourt has really only been given once—the first time to Nau." And years later, Joris-Karl Huysmans (who was not easily satisfied) would say, "It's still the best one we ever crowned."

He gained some fame…for a few weeks, months even, but in the end, the event did not make a big splash and he soon returned to distinguished obscurity, following his inspiration, writing at his will and publishing as often as he could.

In 1906, Nau set off for Algiers where he stayed for three years. The death of his mother in 1909 called him back to

France. He stayed briefly in Paris and then went to the Côte d'Azur. From there, he moved to the Island of Beauty, i.e. Corsica. It would be his longest residence in any one vicinity. He lived in Cargese, Zicavo and Porto Vecchio where there is a street named after him. During the First World War. the couple moved back to France, first to Rouen and then to Tréboul, where Nau died in 1918 at the age of 57.

This brief biographical sketch hardly sheds light on Nau's genius or personality. Even his name reflects his strange, obscure nature. It was said that he was called Gino by family and close friends and thus his name—pronounced the same as "J. Nau" in French. Others suppose that it is a mixture of his American birth (John, the English form of his grandfather's name) and French heritage (Antoine, the name of his great grandfather) together with Nau, a name from the Loire valley meaning "vessel" in Catalan and showing his love for the sea. Others again say that it is in homage to the Haitian poet Ignace Nau. Perhaps it is all or none of the above.

He appreciated the wandering life, leading a marginal existence (like the protagonist of his novel) as close to the sea as possible, refusing "normal" social life to pursue his interior dream. He continued to write his entire life, but slowly, carefully and never with never a thought for profit. He was reputed to be a wild character and the best of company when he was among friends (mostly writers and artists of the places where he lived), but cold and retiring among strangers. Many of his writings contain autobiographical elements: the people and places he describes are those that he actually encountered.

When he died he left a pile of unedited manuscripts. Many of his books remained unpublished until long after his death, even until today. This is the first English translation of any of his books.

Michael Shreve

Bibliography

1897: *Au seuil de l'espoir*—poetry (On the Threshold of Hope)

1903: *Force ennemie*—novel (Enemy Force)

1904: *Journal d'un écrivain*, translation of Dostoyevski (A Writer's Diary)

1904: *Hiers Bleus*—poetry (Blue Yesterdays)

1905: *Le Prêteur d'amour*—novel (The Love Lender)

1906: *La Gennia*—novel

1908: *Vers la fée Viviane*—poetry (Toward the Fairy Vivian)

1912: *Cristobal le Poète*—novel (Christobal the Poet)

1914: *En suivant les goélands*—poetry (Following the Seagulls)

Posthumous Publications:

1921: *Thérèse Donati, moeurs corses*—novel (Therese Donati, Corsican mores)

1923: *Les Galanteries d'Anthime Budin*—novel (The Gallantry of Anthime Budin)

1923: *Pilotins*—novel (Apprentice Pilots)

1923: *Les Trois Amours de Benigno Reyes*—stories (The Three Loves of Benigno Reyes)

1924: *Poèmes triviaux et mystiques*—poetry (Mundane and Mystical Poems)

1929: *Archipel caraïbe*—stories (Caribbean Archipelago)

1933: *Lettres exotiques* (Exotic Letters)

1949: *Lettres écrites de Corse et de Bretagne* (Letters written from Corsica and Brittany)

1972: *Poésies antillaises*. Illustrées par Henri Matisse (Antillean Poems)

ENEMY FORCE

Foreword

I hope readers who are about to discover *me*, or rather *us*, will not want me to be immediately committed to Sainte-Anne or any other lunatic asylum.

I collaborated on this book in only a very limited way. *Enemy Force* is really the work of a semi-lucid mental patient whom I visited often, for many years, and who, just before his death, charged me with publishing his work after I had "revised" it.

I thus altered only a few details; but the core remains perfectly insane, even though it might seem coherent. In my humble opinion, this is what makes it a rare and interesting work for open-minded readers.

I must add that, in my life, I have never seen a mental institution even similar to the one that the *real* author describes. I visited many of these establishments, I talked with many psychiatrists, nurses and guards, but I can swear that I never met a Doctor Bid'homme or a Célestine Bouffard or a Le Lancier or a Barrouge or an Aricia Robinet.

I always saw the demented men and women treated with care, or at least with proper attention. Once again, this book was written by a "reasonable" lunatic, although that's open to interpretation.

My natural, even notorious, modesty, which I hope the public will have occasion to appreciate in the near future, forces me to offer one final piece of advice:

When, in the course of reading, you come upon a well-written passage, a subtle expression, a sentence revealing intellectual sensitivity or higher morality—in a word, a beautiful soul!—feel free to attribute those passages, subtleties, sentences, etc. to me.

When, on the other hand, you are shocked by low or vulgar style, confused or banal ideas, scenes that are indecent or downright offensive, passages that drag on, platitudes, etc.— blame those on the rotten lunatic, the nasty lunatic!

I am all the more noble and generous in saying this since I have recognized the poor, dead mental patient's work as being 99% of the book.

Huelva, June 28, 1902
John-Antoine Nau[*]

---

[*] Asterisks denote footnotes by the author. Numbers denote endnotes by the translator.

PART ONE

I

What a strange awakening! Of course, I recognized the room, but it felt like it had been months, maybe years, since I had last seen it!

These polished walls of yellow timber had once been familiar to me. But why were they padded six feet high with huge, thick mattresses covered with gray sheets that looked like wagon tarps?

The golden light of morning seeped through a large window with poorly fitted bars.

Getting out of bed and looking out the window, I was sure that I would see a big, white building, gleaming as if it was made of stucco; a vast garden rigidly planned by some modern sub-Le Nôtre [1] and a kind of wooden tower [*] ribbed with thin, slatted strips.

And yes! It really was there! And I recognized, in the distance, the fiddle-backed hill of groves; and closer, the flimsy, small, light gray bell tower that the greenery caused to look slightly pink; and on a reddish knoll, the solitary elm that looked like a giant. How could all this scenery seem to me as if it was both a familiar sight and a vision lost in the waves of time? It was a strange contradiction that troubled and confused me: Had I become old without realizing it? Had I slept forever and a day? Was I, indeed, a really ridiculous, really horrible *Sleeping Beauty*?

These stupid ideas crushed me with such heavy sadness, such leaden *pesadumbre*[2]—as the Spanish would say—that I wanted to forget it all again.

---

[*] I found out later that it was a dry kiln.

I went back to bed, lay my head on the pillow and closed my eyes... Come to me, O wonderful, beguiling dreams, or divine unconsciousness!

...*Cllacck—fffrrrt*... A harsh noise—authoritative and menacing, you might say—froze me to death. I barely had the courage to peek out from under the covers and I was not comforted by what I saw: a gaping hole in the wall above my head and two very pale blue eyes staring at me—ferociously, I imagined. But right away, I was ashamed of my cowardice. I sat up in bed and cried out in my most intimidating voice:

"What the heck are you doing here? Why don't you let me sleep and go spy on someone else?"

The hole in the wall was quite large. A face with a look of compassion poked through—a face with strange, pale eyes punched into it, with a thin nose sticking out like a parrot's beak and a long, drooping moustache, yellower than the walls. The mouth opened, twisted into an ugly grin baring golden-brown teeth—a little gapped—and uttered these words:

"I *dint* mean no harm and I'm glad to see *yer* better. If Monsieur wants *sumthin'*, I'll go *git* it *fer* you."

"Give me something to eat...anything! But first, can you please tell me what I'm doing here?"

"In a *minnit*... I'll *es*plain it all to you..."

The man closed up his "puppet show" and left.

Ten minutes later, I heard bolts grinding and the heavy swoosh of a big lock.

The man with the pale eyes and the yellow moustache entered, jangled his keys, pushed the door closed and came to my bed carrying a plate.

"Here's what you asked *fer*."

"Thank you. And now, are you going to answer my question?"

"Right away... First, Monsieur, you *otter* eat."

"Good. What more could I ask for? Look now! Talk to me! Where have you stuck me? I can tell I'm not in prison: there are locks, of course, but..."

"No! Monsieur did not run into trouble. He only ran into bad luck. You *been* sick, very sick…"

"Then I'm in a hospital?"

"That's it—without being…"

"What, then?

"It's a hospital for unwell people… like Monsieur."

"A… mental hospital?"

"You can call it like that… sometimes—if you'd like."

A painful shiver ran down my neck, then all down my spine.

"You mean to say that I'm in a lunatic asylum?"

"Oh! You have a way of *e*splaining things! But don't beat *yourself* up, it's not one of those charity sister houses where you rake up *clargymen* in every closet… Here it's free, It doesn't belong to the State or to the *Claricals*; it's the establishment of Doctor Froin."

"And where is it?"

"In Vassetot, of course! You know that!"

"But I have relatives here!"

"'Course you do! It's the other Monsieur *yer* cousin who *brung* you here t'other day! He said like this that you were walkin' around in Dieppe [3] *kinda* unwell and he *din't* know what to do with you. Don't say I told you who! It's forbidden here, but seeing that *yer* so calm an' nice…"

"Ha! I'm not surprised that Roffieux is mixed up in this! Anyway, you're right. I'm very calm and I'm not the least bit angry with that… individual. But you said 'the other day'? How long has it been since I was put in this room to… cool down?"

"The day after tomorr*er* 'll be two weeks."

"You're sure that I've never been here before? I feel like I've stayed here in the past, within these very walls, but it was centuries ago…"

"Yes, they say it feels like that. It's the *ideers* you have because me, who's stayed in this place ten years, I've *not never* seen the likes of you, Monsieur. *I can raise my right hand to that!* But, you know, that's how it can happen: *they* bring a person here, by coach, *fer* example; *they* introduce him to the Director and admit him. Then, just like that, *they has* to pay a visit to *someun* who'll *wartch* over him. The Director goes too. And it doesn't matter that the *person brung* is upset; it's an annoying visit *fer* both of 'em. The person will wait and have a rest. *They's* a little tired, *'cuz* they's unwell, they has a little *egzitement*. It'll *git* better, but they has to deal with it carefully. Only *they* may git bored in the Director's office, that isn't a *perty* room. Then, *they* bring him to a place where there's a very beautiful view and *illustred* journals—that's perty good for a little *rezdence*: the person looks out the window, *grines* away in the room… *They finds* everythin's nice and proper. But after this, *they gits antsy* and when t'other *esplains* that they can't go back to *git* him, and the Director's invited him to spend the night in the establishment, thoughtful like a friend, the person wants to take off, then they stop him, then they *gits* angry, and they has… an anxiety attack. They put him in bed—they stays there ten or twelve days, sometimes *egzited*, sometimes sleeping. When *they's* better, they remembers a little of what they saw the first day, but it seems far, far away. There's nothing like the *egzitement* to make time seem long…afterwards, because during, it doesn't bother 'em."

The man with the parrot beak was not as absolutely idiotic as you might think at first sight, or hearing him talk. He had just told me, I understood, in his sometimes stupid and awkward, but fortunately considerate way, how I had been admitted to Doctor Froin's establishment. In his brief account, and especially in his final explanation, I could even glimpse a small dose of rudimentary psychology.

But no! He was a moron because he told me that I had been crazy for almost two weeks. He should have figured out how to keep me in the dark about that for a while. I could have thought…what? What could I have thought?

In fact, I was the moron! What could I expect from a poor devil stupefied by his environment after being raised in country of cow patties?

Whatever the case, since he was obviously taking pity on my misfortune, it would have been wrong to turn him against me—he had a big mouth that could be useful if I needed information…

My memory was coming back to me a little: yes, the mysterious ways of Roffieux, Dieppe, the coach, the arrival at the "Establishment," my cousin leaving for the bogus visit, even my anger—I remembered all this in a fog. But I had to feed the conversation if I wanted to stay in the good graces of my guardian. More than anything else, people like him hate the silence of so-called proud people, middle-class jack-asses—(damn! I must have looked middle-class to him). So, I asked the first question that came to mind:

"What about Monsieur Roffieux? My cousin? Have they got any news from him since he drove me here?"

"Ah! He came five days ago, last Monday, he left *haf-hour* later, very upset. He said like this that he *wuz* very worried that Monsieur *din't rec'gnize* him and that he'd come back *mebbe* next Monday, day after tomorr*er*."

Here, a new idea crossed my mind: a crazy idea, for sure. I remembered speaking with the Director, but it seemed that, after a few minutes, he underwent a complete transformation. At first, tall, fat, maybe around 60, he suddenly became young, average height and weight, his graying hair was dyed brownish-red. Only his voice didn't change. I confessed this strange feeling to my guardian, being very careful to translate it so that it didn't sound too crazy.

"No, no!" the man with the weeping moustache replied. "Our hospital doesn't have two directors. Here's the deal: the *Boss*, Doctor Froin, the only boss, hired an assistant, as they call him, from around Franche-Comté,[4] where he's from; a kind of little monkey of a doctor who has the same *agzent* as the *Boss*, imitates his talk and all his *espressions*—a keister so fired up to show he's *sumthin'* that he's always on the heels of the *Boss* when there's an admission. He's like a little 14-year-old sick boy, messin' things up to impress 'em grown-ups and make *hisself* look important. When ol' Froin turns his back, he's the one who plays director, goes around mumblin' things, *gits* all worked up. He's not imitatin' no one then! If Monsieur was tired by his trip, he'd have been *confusioned* and not known just *when the little one broke off from the big one*, and kept talkin' in the same way as the *Boss*, but with less *ameni-ty*. Me, who's used to it, I *rec'gnize* both their voices with my eyes closed. The little one, Doctor Bid'homme, is a lot more hard, more *iss*olent, while old *Boss* Froin's more maj*is*tic. But new people like you, how would you know the first time?"

"Is Doctor Froin a nice man?"

"He's got a warm heart and he's a good talker. They say he's scientific like a museum. Anyway, he's good for the patients. He doesn't bother 'em, not even enough as his assistant tells from behind his back. Yes, Doctor Bid'homme, he's always on about how's there's not being enough *despl*ine here, that the less un*copra*tive patients walk around too free in the gardens, that he's seen 'em talkin' with the women near t'other building. And somewhere else, in Doubs, he worked in a hospital where it was all serious like, where the *almost cured din't* even move from their ward. Sometimes, they were shut up in the rooms; sometimes, they were in recr*a*tion in the yards, but the doors only opened for *the real world…*"

"You don't like this Doctor Bid'homme very much…"

"Like *bronchites* and frostbite! As soon as old Froin leaves, he *aggrevates* the whole shop from head to toe. The nurses of t'other building die of colic *ever* time they see him without the *Boss*. Us others, it *ain't* so bad, but it's *likit*. Sometimes, we flip out all the same."

"He's really a little fiend?"

"Lissen, I'll tell you like I'd tell no one else *'cuz*, really, you're a very dec*in* and reasonable patient…"

A new shiver ran through me and it was not a very nice feeling.

"Yes, I'll tell you. I can tell you like under the *sil* of confession as if I was a *Clarical*, but never repeat to no one what I'm *gonna* tell you now—seriously!"

My guardian's face looked mysterious and alarmed. He leaned forward and whispered in my ear:

"Doctor Bid'homme, you want me to give you my *judgmental* opinion, well, I think he's a Goddamned!"

This blasphemous qualification undoubtedly meant something awful to him. This one word must have carried oceans of horror, be the supreme insult, blackened forever, because the pale-eyed man yanked at his moustache and looked very sorry for having risked so much by opening up like that.

"I'm tellin' you," he concluded, "that I'd just as well never talk about that again, *never, never*. And why? Now, you know everythin' and I'm askin' you to say ab*z*lutly *nuthin'* about it."

His emotions got the better of me. To sidetrack his anxieties, I asked him politely to take away the two plates that were on my bed; one still had a cold cut on it, the other a chunk of Swiss cheese. My guardian put the first plate in the drawer of the night table, and the other, he put up—or rather locked up—on a shelf in the cabinet next to an empty cup, a knife and a fork. He came back to the bed, satisfied by the completion of a well-done duty. He pontificated a little:

"We *needs* to have some order. It's not a good system to let everythin' get messy, then you can't find *nuthin'* afterward! Oh, I would never accuse you, Monsieur, of takin' the dishes of the Establishment, but *agzdents* happen so fast!"

He looked at his watch and his voice changed.

"OK. Now it's seven o'clock. You'll be *gittin'* a visit from Bid'homme soon. When the service isn't messed up, he always starts here, in the wing of the *special* cases. I'd rather meet him in the hallway. There's plenty of room there—Bid'homme's quick on his feet."

With that, he made a fine exit on the tips of his gigantic toes and waved a bunch of warning signs that obviously advised me to be discreet, sensible and extremely careful when dealing with the horrible little doctor.

II

Some accident must have *messed up the service* because my door hadn't clanked for two hours when I heard a cheerful but rough voice that I recognized!

"Leonard! You Pig! Driveller! Where are you dragging your filthy espadrilles? Ah-ha! There you are, you little screw-up! Open this lair for me right now or else..."

New music of locks and bolts!

The massive door was shoved open and, standing there, was a little gentleman in a black suit, frock coat and all, decked out in a white tie, slightly yellowing, but topped off with a Boyard hat [5] and all booted up with spurs on his heels and a riding crop in his hand.

He had two viciously buoyant eyes, brown eyebrows,—like toothbrushes,—a big red moustache,—like a scrub brush,—and a motley red and brown beard, trimmed into two very distant points. His short, straight nose—straight meaning horizontal—seemed to aim his nostril cannons at something about 50 feet away; and in spite of his bushy beard, his jaw jutted out atrociously, ape-like, too bulky for the size of his head.

He came in and threw his riding crop on the chair.

His relatively high, wide chest, going all the way up to his shoulders, was completely flat in profile and stiff like a plate of armor. His thick, short legs could have belonged to a well-developed 12-year old child.

He breathed heavily when he walked and reeked of cigars, drugs and horse droppings. Watching him rub his hands together, wink, chuckle to himself and at the same time keep flapping his jaw, his ferocious jaw, and wrinkle his ugly, bristling brow, it was easy for me, especially after Leonard's advice—since it was Leonard—to see here the perfect brute who was playing the good boy for the moment:

"Good God! They'll nab me again on horseback some muddy day!"

He talked to the wall, the window and the trees in the courtyard. He pretended that I did not exist—although I caught him staring at me when he came in. He went up to the table, fumbled with the books on it pretending to look for something, examined the marble of the cabinet... Since I was so intrigued by him, I watched everything he did, but his little act—if it was an act—lasted only a minute.

He suddenly turned on his heels and marched over to my bed. He was standing there less than three feet away from me, staring into my eyes and he fired off a burst of laughter:

"Ha ha! So, I must seem very funny to you for your eyes to be popping out like that!"

His throaty, booming voice sounded assertive; he stretched out certain syllables as if to really emphasize that they were of the utmost importance and that he was not using them haphazardly.

I couldn't help making this stupid remark: "Funny, maybe, but not too surprising, pretty common really. Before talking to you in the Director's office, I had already met you in *Tales of Hoffmann* [6] and other books like that."

His eyebrows looked like two arched brushes about to take aim and attack.

"Go on! You haven't recovered as much as I thought! And you don't remember seeing me after we spoke in the Director's Office?"

These last two words were tinged with bitterness. I had hurt him by reminding him that he was only the second in command.

"No, I don't remember..."

"Too bad! But it's exactly as I thought. And how are you feeling this morning?"

"Pretty good."

"Have you eaten?"

"Voraciously."

"It's about time, because these last few days we couldn't get you to eat much at all."

"I've thought about that. It's all in the past! What worries me now is the immediate future," I asked him impatiently, "and how much longer do you plan to keep me here? If I was crazy, I'm not anymore. I'm still a little weak, but that's all. Could you fill me in on this?"

Bid'homme's eyebrows bristled more and more. "It wouldn't be so hard for you to speak to me a little more politely, but I will answer categorically: you will leave this hospital when I…when *we* consider it the right time to let you leave."

"A lot of good that does me! Of course, you have no intention of keeping me here under lock and key forever. I am completely reasonable and present no danger to anyone."

"You are still quite excitable and quite nervous like everyone in your situation."

"What do you mean by that?"

"I mean, like all alcoholics."

"What? Did you come here to insult me?"

"Hey! You're starting to annoy me and get on my nerves! Can you insult a drunk, a *boozer*, by calling him a boozer?"

It took everything I had to keep my cool and answer very calmly, "I am ready to admit that I have been guilty of a few excesses. Until recently, no matter how it might seem, I could hold my own. I've always been a big eater and drinker, but I guarantee you that I never had any problems because of my…intemperance before going through these hard times lately. Anyway, it seems to me that a doctor is supposed to cure, not injure. When I leave this place, you can give me some advice…as politely as possible. Your rights stop there."

"You're getting on my nerves! Maybe I'll put the gloves on!"

"Great! Let's just suppose for a minute that you had a right to speak to me like you did… Can I ask you who has been kept up-to-date on my situation?"

"You're asking me questions again! The world is upside down!"

"No doubt! It's you who should have been asking some questions before taking at face value what Mr. Elzear Roffieux, my illustrious cousin, decided to tell you. I remember very well that he was the one who brought me here."

"And finally you harass me! You're getting on my nerves again! If you know who it was, why are you asking me? And since you're making me lose my temper, I will tell you again that, when a patient is in your situation, it doesn't really matter what he thinks. Especially when it comes to a patient who thinks he's a *po-ette*, who's been rhyming for years, who's had a hundred jobs under his belt and keeps going back to his paper scratching! The family's opinion carries all the weight."

He had found an argument—decisive in his view—that filled him with such joy and self-esteem that he straightened up like a little rooster and spoke to me from on high, if I could say this about a gnome like him.

(This bad joke belongs to Leonard who, in spite of being scared of the little doctor, was curious enough to enter the room two or three times during the visit—for his duties, he said.)

Bid'homme's eyebrows shot up toward the sky, or rather the ceiling, and his voice clamored in triumph:

"Did you commit yourself to us for treatment? No, Monsieur Philippe Veuly delivered you into our hands. So, I owe explanations only to him."

He gloated. There was really no reason to, but he gloated.

"Doctor Bid'homme, I am too polite to tell you what I think about such an argument."

"Think what you want, that's how it is! And besides, I'm wasting my time here. I have to go and see other patients who are a little less insolent and bull-headed than you. However, I don't want to have come into your lair for nothing. You are very excited…" (was I to be hounded forever by that hideous word?) "Leonard, you gave him some wine or coffee to drink this morning, didn't you? We'll get rid of all that: nothing but watered wine and herbal tea from now on! Ah! If only I were fully in charge here! Let's see, is it in Vienna, Brussels or Copenhagen? Well, there's an excellent hospital for people like you. They drink nothing but plain water there, water, water, and more water! And personally, I would make this water healthy, but with a horrible taste, a taste…of…scum! That would teach the filthy drunks! But they're still too sentimental in Europe!"

I should not have lost my patience again, but I could not help it. I shouted at Bid'homme, "So when will there be hospitals for psychiatrists? If I knew of one, I would immediately write the director a letter of admittance for you! You, too, need treatment, if you call this a cure!"

This time, Bid'homme was angered for good and totally forgot his position.

"*Ach!* Pig! You really get on my nerves! I've seen plenty of drunks in my life, but never a boozer as foul and revolting as you!"

Then, satisfied to have "told me off in no uncertain terms," he nobly headed for the exit. He grabbed his riding crop on his way out and used it to slap the dust off his boots. I was foaming at the mouth, literally. He opened the door and his grand body disappeared when—I don't really know how it happened!—the plate that was so conscientiously put away by Leonard in the drawer of the night table shattered noisily against the thick door that was turning on its hinges. The drawer was open and I was barefoot, in my nightshirt, out of bed in the middle of the room, all shook up in a fit of rage.

Bid'homme hooted, "Leonard! Pig! Driveller! Come here right now!"

My guardian was not far. He came, terrified, his pale eyes wide open, his long moustache weepier than ever. Bid'homme followed him in, pushing him and swearing like an ex-priest. "In the goddamn holy name of…" all kinds of things! There was a good two minutes of these holy names, more profane than holy since I heard him talk a lot about children of loose women, about hotels where mothers of a sad progeny found their bed and board under the tolerant eye of the police, about high priests with uncivilized tastes, about insects and fish, about old heifers, etc.

Bid'homme turned the color of a blue-tit plum! The flood of angry eloquence was filtered down to curses and the dwarf finally shouted, "This swine here! You hear me, Leonard! You're going to chuck him in the bath…and no hot water! The other tap! First of all, he reeks!" (I hoped this diagnosis was wrong). "Yes, he reeks, the pig! When he's calm and disinfected, you will take him to the courtyard and onto the grounds (standard procedure!) to tire him out, wear him down. You will make him walk at least three hours and be sure to show him the Violent ward where we'll put him if he starts up again!"

The notion of a cold bath sounded pretty nice, but I pretended to be outraged by the gnomic doctor's tyranny. I wanted him to think I was as terrified as I was furious. That way, he would later decide, for sure, to always punish me with the water torture. Bid'homme obviously did not like baths, if I could judge by the grayness of his collar, and I only had to yell a little loudly for him to feel the inquisitor's joy by dunking me in a bath as often as possible.

So I howled, "No cold baths! Goddamnit! (It was my turn). It'll kill me! It'll give me Crop Sickness! (This strange disease popped out by chance, I really had no idea what it meant.) Help! Murderer!"

My wishes were fulfilled. The savage sadist made a bunch of sniggering, devilish grimaces before telling Leonard his plans: "And then you will desalinate this sardine every day. And when he annoys me, it'll be two soakings. Ha ha! I have him now, the filthy bugger! And we'll try the shower if he gets on my nerves too much!"

He left in an indescribable state of jubilation.

III

I took a wonderful bath, too quick really, but Leonard thought it should be cut short "'cuz you don't want yer blood to be *luged.*" He mumbled something else about the *estremities* and *cerebral congections* while helping me get dressed. I had never had a butler, so I was a little embarrassed by his assistance. When I was finally dressed, we went to visit the courtyards and the grounds.

Leonard took me out of the bathhouse by a different exit. We followed a kind of hallway with an open ceiling between two low, white structures, like school buildings. We stopped before a medieval-looking door, covered in iron, fitted with a lock as thick as four Quicherat [7] dictionaries. My guardian took out a bunch of keys, bigger, I was sure, than they used back in the days of the Bastille. He chose one that could have shattered the pavement and the door opened almost noiselessly.

We were in a large courtyard with tall, thick trees, surrounded by an asphalt exercise track. In the middle of it, a little lawn bulged out, bordered by baskets of pretty, iridescent flowers, like a chain of oval medallions.

Groups of three or four people, pretty calm and neatly dressed, were circling on the exercise track, like schoolchildren at recess, talking quietly or thinking deeply between what they said or heard. They paid no attention to me. They seemed to be above the daily cares of life, only concerned with investigating certain thoughts that could be—when need be—not always—communicated between them, but that might be misunderstood, or at least distorted, by the average intellect of people from a more common environment. They were as serene as Hindu fakirs.

"Ah! Them!" Leonard confided in me, "They're the cream of the crop! We don't hear much of a racket from them. Or, well, it's only when you *sarch* for it, *porvoke* em! I'm not saying there aren't times…but in general, there's no one more

24

distinguished. So you, Monsieur, who is much less an idiot than 'em, much nicer, much more lively, would not be good company *fer* 'em; you'd give 'em some days with *yer egzitement.* (Again!) The only trouble with these good people is that, for some of 'em, things change and then they have periods of black sickness. Oh! When that *gits* 'em, there's nuthin' but nuthin' to do! They're bad trouble then! Not too mean, you know. It's not like the black sickness that I'm gonna show you somewheres else. Over there, there's no bad more dang*a*rous. It's only that I don't see 'em now, the good ones, y'know, but hard to satisfy, and who don't like other people. They don't come by here too much, even though they belong to the courtyard. They prefer the little garden with less space that's over behind there, next to that little room they use as a club, a *sarcle*, they say. There's only five of 'em in all. We call 'em the *Philzophers*, *cuz* one of 'em was a knowledged and practicin' doctor; two were lawyers; another did acting on stage and the last one, the most annoying one, they say he wrote *pootry* columns and some adventure stories for the newspapers and things…"

"Ah, a colleague!"

"…You wanna see 'em? We gotta *git* over there."

Certainly I wanted to see them! I thought I would get along better with them than with the nutty Mahatmas for whom I was too *egzited.*

This time, no closed doors and no locks. A big room on the other side of the yard. We went across, bothered by the bitter scents that sickened me a little. It was the mess hall of the "good apostles" of the first division. But a breath of heliotrope and reseda drove off my uneasiness. We took a gravel path lined with two rows of fresh bushes. Narrow flowerbeds perfumed the air. Twenty feet farther, we climbed the stairs and entered a room that seemed less wonderful to me than it did to Leonard. It was clean enough, but even though it was very large, it had only one table and a few chairs.

Five gentlemen, quite proper, as my guardian pointed out to me, stood up with extraordinary politeness. I answered five greetings and shook five hands—held out very graciously.

Four of these gentlemen sat right back down and in unison invited me to do the same. They looked very dignified, though a little tired. But the fifth remained standing and, taking me by the arm, gently forced me to take a trip around the room, as if he wanted to show me the bare walls, the frayed carpet and the chairs scattered around.

When he figured that I was familiar enough with the cracks in the stucco, he led me to a chair, carefully dusted it off with his handkerchief and asked me—properly—to have a seat. Then he took a chair, sat next to me and started chatting like a host trying to break the ice, to put the newcomer completely at ease:

"I hope, Monsieur, that you are only visiting this hospital—clean and nice enough, as a matter of fact. I am sorry for you if you are staying here—and for the same reasons as these gentlemen and I."

I answered that I was afraid that my stay at Doctor Froin's might last at least a few weeks.

"Ah, Monsieur, I am very saddened by this. I fear some hard days are ahead for you. Even more so since you are, I am sure, only mildly afflicted. I am a doctor myself, Doctor Magne... (he bowed) ...and I know how most of the diseases that require hospitalization work. I have been able to observe my friends here present and myself, and I have found nothing positive. Oh well! I am sorry that my colleague Froin decided to keep you here, because he is not often wrong... Sometimes, however..."

He had a strange smile and a mysterious wink that I took for symptoms of his mental state.

I asked him in spite of myself, "So, you are aware that everything isn't...working normally in you?"

"Certainly, even though that charlatan Bid'homme exaggerates childishly when he claims that the five individuals whom you see here are stark raving mad—and let me tell you that this is not how doctors should really speak to patients. It is rather obvious that the functions of our brains are not always normal. Isn't that right, my dear friends?"

His four companions nodded eloquently.

"…We have, for example, observed the following phenomenon—among one another—and each of us in ourselves: it often happens that we, against our will, even though we really try to stay still and quiet—often say and do things that prove, beyond a shadow of a doubt, that the speaker or the actor is in a period of *very mild* insanity. That's one little thing out of a hundred. Secondly, the troublesome Doctor Bid'homme gave us the great pleasure—I am not being kind by saying this, but too bad!—he gave us the incommensurable pleasure of coming down with a fever that was not very dangerous, but that kept him in bed for a few days. So, for a little while, we had no visits from this foul-mouthed, fickle, wicked, little imp. All five of us enjoyed a brief period of freedom, positively exquisite, but mine was spoiled by a frightful obsession: more than anyone else, I knew it was ridiculous, unlikely and idiotic, but I became obsessed by the idea that, if Bid'homme were to end up on death's door, it would be up to me, and me alone, to administer his last rites! Mind you, it never entered my mind that I had received the Holy Orders, or that priestly garments might fit me any better than a lifejacket on a shark! But, when I couldn't think of anything else, I was constantly tormented by this grotesque vision: myself, Dr. Magne, still bearded and wearing my best suit of English cloth, this tan jacket and green and lavender tie whose elegance and fine taste you—yourself—may have already admired—but now covered with a transparent surplice; a Dr. Magne whose preaching gestures and rambling homilies would amaze and then comfort the little scrap of an ape-like man balled up in his blankets.

"The worst thing is that I had made up my mind that my good comrades would not have to watch my *detestable derangement*, but I couldn't help playing out the whole scene in front of them. They were good sports about it, but not very thrilled. I saw Bid'homme as I see you. I even imitated his looks, at first fierce, and then blessedly pious. I preached to him more and more zealously, and tried to force my friends to admit that the awful little doctor was really right in front of our eyes... At the same time, I was ashamed and told myself that I was like those children who play war or pirate and are *almost actually* present at the defeat of their imaginary enemies or the capture of a purely imaginary ship. And there was a miserable Latin text that was absolutely necessary for me— and I could only remember the first two words of it: *Et nunc... et nunc... et nunc!*[8] For the life of me, I couldn't remember the rest, and you would have laughed at how irritated I became. I only got over my ghastly obsession when Bid'homme graced me with a morning visit, back on his feet, more courteous than ever, and calling me those sweet but mysterious names like 'big dardlet' and 'phelsumer.' By the way, I have to show you a cartoon of Bid'homme. It's not a very good drawing, but it's entertaining, and I made it. I'll go get it."

Doctor Magne left after royally, magnificently, bowing to his companions, to me and to the walls—especially to the walls. Right away, one of his friends got up and sat in his chair. He was in his 50s, a little gray, clean-shaven; his pale, shiny face was sanded smooth. He had bags under his eyes— big, bulging eyes, half-hidden by his cockleshell eyelids. His nose was huge and so boldly curved that it made me think of a peninsula. He constantly held onto a kind of naval officer's cap that he fanned himself with from time to time. He was charmingly polite, though more casual than Doctor Magne.

"My friend," he said to me, "you are new in this hospital, which is both glad and sorry to have you. You seem full of wisdom and insight, but it would be helpful if a weathered pilot of these scrubbed and polished waters—but with plenty of treacherous reefs—were to brief you on some of its particularities. You already know what we think of Sir Bid'homme: he's a monster with a barely human face. But there are other perils here, apart from those that come from rascals like that. Certain dangers threaten you that I think you are not, as yet,

28

aware of... Even your good self might frighten a good mind in less than a minute..."

I reflected that Leonard had been right. I had to be pretty dangerous for this man to notice it after less than 15 minutes with me.

"...Always keep your cool when dealing with, say, our dear Doctor Magne. You saw him: we try to make him happy; we agree with everything he says. Doctor Magne is our friend; he's a very valuable man, but he worked too much—way too much—so that his brain became anemic, and now he's under the weather, as the fellow countrymen of my dead friends, Richard the Lionheart, crown bearer, and Jerry Nastyswine, bookmaker, might say. He's sick, but he knows it. Unfortunately, he really wants the four of us—victims of misunderstandings and family ploys—to be in the same state as him. Since he's the best and most noble being on the entire Earth, we put on an act so as not to worry him, but from here on out, you have to know that he's the only one of this little suffering group who is really afflicted with what I refuse to name... So you will deal with him appropriately, won't you? If, my friend, you have something to say about him, take me aside and tell it to me—only me, A. Desbosquets, dramatic artist, starring—as I'm sure you already knew—in the role of Cusenier in *The Dangers of Distillation*, a wonderful play by the great poet Noilly-Prat[9]."

Having put his mind at ease, Monsieur A. Desbosquets completely forgot I was there and went to talk to Leonard, who was standing by the door. He criticized him for this and that, for his jaw, his accent, the neglect of his indecent moustache, his inability to walk with his toes pointed out; and he told him—kindly—that he would never make a good leading man. I believe you, A. Desbosquets!

I missed the rest of the conversation because, while the good actor was carefully cooking his sentences with criticisms spiced with kindness, another member of the group, a young man who looked Chinese, with a face like raspberry jelly, stumbled up to me.

His naturally yellow complexion was complemented by bright threads of broken veins, more purple than red. He had thick hair, a receding brow, jutting cheekbones, narrow eyes whose dark pupils seemed more polished than alive, a barely visible moustache the color of dead leaves, a little salt and pepper beard that was worn out like an old carpet, a long neck with an Adam's apple stuck in it like a huge walnut, and shoulders like a scrawny old horse which did not fit with his thick, short chest and his pot belly. He was knock-kneed and bowed legged, with kneecaps shaped like coconuts.

He also borrowed Doctor Magne's chair, blew cigarette smoke out his nose, and took his turn to tackle me. His language was less elegant than the other two; it was hard for him to speak, which you could put down to shyness. He was dull and awkward. He seemed horribly unhappy and sorry to have come over, but there he was. He had to *march on*—and he did so heroically!—death in his soul.

"Monsieur—finally yes!... Monsieur... I don't like to *jaw* about brothers... absolutely not! But I have to tell you that Desbosquets is a lot more... absolutely... oh, I'll blurt it out... a lot more... absolutely *cracked* than our friend Magne. Absolutely yes!"

He wanted to be frank, to open up, which he constantly regretted, because he knew that he would be clumsy and mocked; he felt ridiculous and it was killing him. But his need for some honest self-indulgence gnawed at him, and he spit out his slang and his absolutelys—'absolutely yes!' and 'absolutely no!'—which made him think he was revealing the *deepest depths* of his soul.

He continued. "Maybe they told you about me—yes! I know: bing, bang—mechanics! Absolutely yes! A hack, they must have told you..." (Aha! I thought. So it's my colleague the poet!) "...and the worst trouble, right? That's Leonard—yes! Ah! When I'm a little...bing, bang...mechanics! I guess—grumpy—I don't say... but there's not an ounce of meanness in me! Disgusting, this awful problem with talking, but the mechanics, you know—because it's the mechanics—

no way! Do you want me to tell you my name? Ah! Totally unknown, my name, but don't want them to mangle it mechanically when quoting it to you: Oswald Norbert Nigeot. Don't say Numskull—no!—Although my verses!... Ah! Damned mechanics!... A bonehead, a stupid bonehead, bitten by the morbid mania to write—and the slander of the old students of the Polytechnic! Oh! To write! Terrible trade for the poorly gifted like me who are... bing, bang, not mechanics! And angry at the mechanics of words. Polytechnic pigs manufacture words; so, poor hacks can't use them. Ah! Even this is mechanics!... And drunk on it, Desbosquets too, very drunk! Obviously you see it: Cusenier, Noilly-Prat, why not Pernod? It's awful for people like him and me! See, you know—liquids are scarce—but thanks to the guards' hatred of Bid'homme... and thanks to old Froin, too good, don't believe in any bad— but can you call that bad? He lives with the Heaven of...mechanics...of...bang...of derangements, no! I want *arrangements*, not *derangements*!"

Mr. Nigeot seemed very proud of having successfully (?) completed such a long sentence propped up by only one "bang" and one "mechanics," but in spite of his satisfaction, he was scared of continuing less elegantly and he got all tangled up in a run of bizarre expressions in which the hated Polytechnicians and the bings and bangs (not to mention the absolutelys) got so out of hand that I could not understand a word of what he said.

Anyway, he soon interrupted himself. "I'll...bing! I'll let you go. Here... mechanics!... Get it—he's the least stupid of us all, absolutely yes!"

The ex-doctor had returned, looking thrilled, smiling, sweeping his big, brown beard across a thick piece of paper.

"Here, Monsieur, please tell me honestly what you think of this cartoon. Let's not talk about the drawing, which is childish, but the picture's funny, very funny; I say this proudly."

Funny! No, I didn't think so. Although Doctor Magne did not think so, personally I found it very skillfully drawn, but funny?

A Bid'homme, an eerie likeness, but like a wild animal with a devilish grin that was ferociously exaggerated, was busy digging around with one of his blessed spurs in the skull of a scalped and drilled patient. It was a horror, a horror! Absolutely yes! as Monsieur Oswald-Norbert Nigeot would have said.

I pretended to think tthat I found his imagination wickedly funny, even though it scared me. Nigeot, the ham Desbosquets, and the two lawyers whose silence astonished me, all came up quickly to take a look. This work, which in some way was revenge, fascinated and amused them. Doctor Magne had a pretty strange little smile on his face, too. I began to feel something different, maybe more uncomfortable than before: was he crazier than I had first thought?

But then, he stopped smiling, his eyes looked brighter, more gentle, more serious than ever; you could almost say that they were compassionate.

And he sounded completely different. "Now that you've had your fun with this cartoon, let me tell you that it has its sad side...This little doctor, such a tyrant with his patients and such an abusive brute—well! I'm afraid his role is going to change—and maybe soon. You still don't know him very well, even though he's probably played some tricks on you already. But I have observed him for two years, more and more carefully, (It was strange and a little scary, wasn't it, that this half-crazy doctor would monitor the man in charge of his care?), and I have noticed some major changes in him. He's always been mean and nasty, but before, when he still had full use of his faculties (Yes! Surprise! But you'd already guessed it. I'm only telling you what you already suspected.) when, I say, he had full use of his faculties, there was some method to his madness; today, he's completely lost it. He'll get worse... Study him and tell me if you don't agree..."

Just then, Leonard politely excused himself from the excellent Desbosquets and reminded me that, according to Doctor Bid'homme's program, I had to *exharst myself* in the gardens and grounds.

I left with my monitor after goodbyes and handshakes with the three talkative gentlemen and the two close-mouthed lawyers.

They ended up being even more courteous and distinguished than when I arrived. Obviously, they enjoyed the little games of social politeness a great deal; it was a kind of sport to them, and maybe rehabilitation too. They wanted people to say, "These gentlemen here are not what the vain public thinks they are. You can be locked up, of course!—rightly or wrongly—without losing an ounce of dignity. We know these gentlemen have problems—and yet! Anyway, the minor mental illnesses that they're suffering from—as you claim—don't *degrade* them at all; these are not *ordinary* patients."

IV

I was so preoccupied with my new friends' ideas and with the strange prediction about Doctor Bid'homme that I did not pay much attention to where Leonard was taking me. I heard him, like in a dream, turning some locks and suddenly, we were in a courtyard pretty much like the one with the "Mahatmas," the blessedly unconscious whom my guardian asked me to leave alone in their troubled beatitude.

The only difference was fewer flowers, maybe, and a shabbier lawn.

Here, too, the residents mostly walked around in small groups; they were decently dressed and, for the most part, looked peaceful; most of them chatted calmly among themselves. However, I started feeling that, in this new environment, something strange and disturbing *had to* happen sometimes. I could already see some things that were not quite normal. What was I saying? There was a small, dry old man, with a bird-like, clean-shaven face, scampering along next to us, lifting up his leg and swinging it around, high stepping like a Turcoman horse. He was humming a weird little tune in a minor key that he kept interrupting to growl a twangy "Pwack! Pwack!" that started to get on my nerves. Could I say that it scraped against them? That would be totally absurd, and yet...

"Oh! That one," Leonard said when he saw me wincing, "can't *git* him worked up! When he's mean, he's like a *chide*. They put him to bed when it lasts too long—that's all. He's a ex-mayor who was rich and partied too much. He used to have himself a good time at all the county fairs, and when he went home, when he was tipsy, he made three or four girls *git* in his coach. You know what I mean! Sometimes, he dumped one or another just anywhere, on a pile of stones, *fer* example. But he always *brung* back at least two to his house. And, imagine, he was running the town for 20 years! When they thought about it, it was like they said that they'd had *'nuff* of 'im every five years. But they were used to him, and some people had a personal interest in keeping him mayor. Well then! Ah! Damn old Marical! And he's the one who married everyone! Gives you the *wullies*! He's a special case like you, in the same building, *yer* next door neighbor."

Marical went by again—this time hopping around like a June bug. His pasty eyes had a blank stare, but his mouth was screwed up into a bratty smile. "Pwack! Pwack!"

He was already long gone.

Another loner went by. He looked like a Roman emperor touched up by Daumier.[10] He was calm and proud; he would have made a wonderful picture if he could have stopped his strange obsession of bitingwith his beautiful teeth a wool rag that he took out of his pocket every two minutes.

Leonard *barnumized.* "That's a former *clarical*—really a bad small town priest. who was more Jesuit than Archdiocese" (Ah-ha! So they defrocked him, even if he did not want it; that must have taught him!) "He got it in his head that he *wuz* the Antichrist; well then, he used to smoke his pipe in the *cemteries* and dance on the graves, chewing his handkerchief whenever he dropped his stubby pipe. That seems funny, doesn't it? They had an investigation and they found a collection of little wired *skeltons* in his trunk. Then he said something like this: 'As the Antichrist, I review the Last Judgment on the 23rd of every month and I need more stiffs!' Oh! It was dead certain, they packed 'im up for here, especially after he hollered out like a badger in church one Sunday while the real priest was preaching and he started sermonizin' a bunch of filth to keep his boss from talkin'. Sometimes, too, he hid *in back of the doors* to scare the old bigots. It was me they sent to *git* 'im. He wasn't easy either; I's forced to *restrim* him…"

Leonard pronounced "restrain" "restrim" but I completely understood the meaning of this verb with a Turco-Bosnian ending. I felt like a wicked, cold breeze chill my skull and ruffle my hair. And the pale-eyed man continued:

"And when he got here to old Froin's, what did he eat? but handkerchiefs! It ruined the Treasury, which is less generous than the Doctor, *'cuz* unfortunately the guy's under the heel of *senurities* set up like a Company, as he tells it. Well then. there's this guard they told to give Marangot—the old vicar—pieces of old underwear and jackets to chew on. It's all the same to him, and the Treasury don't pipe up anymore. Well then, he's mean, that one, sometimes, like a *brizzly*. He's told them that has the 'black sickness' I told you about; he was too slick with his stories of the Antichrist."

"Leonard, have you ever lived in Paris? Sometimes you don't sound like you come from Dieppe: *stiffs, dead certain, pipe up, slick…* If it weren't for your lovely, local accent, I would say you were from Belleville or Charonne."

"I almost married a lady guard from t'other building who was a *Parisienne* from… Clichy-Levallois[11] where her parents, as she told it, were swimmin' in it. Things were movin'—movin' fast…"

He clicked his tongue and looked naively smug. "Sure *'nuff*, she shot herself in the foot with a dishwasher who stole from the Treasury. Even if they never caught 'em. Well then, it's like fate: every time there's someone from Paris, it's me who's put in charge of 'em. You learn words like that, you know! Well then, it's up to you now. I'm sure that, since you're from there, you'll teach me some new words, too, without meaning to, and I won't be remembering the nicest ones"

"You flatter me. But… Good Lord! What's that?"

An old man wearing a big wool overcoat, despite the heat, and a kind of gray fur fez hat, went up to a window, grabbed the bars and started dancing like a big bear in a zoo. He was grunting quietly, but sometimes thundered out. He was a spitting image of Martin.[12]

"That's old Mabire; used to be a notary—even if he had problems with his feet."

I hoped for the sake of the young Parisienne that this little joke was not hers—but just when I was about to ask Leonard for some information about old Mabire, I heard the sound of a galloping horse. I turned around and saw a scary-looking fellow pulling up in front of us.

He had wild, blinking little pig's eyes, a large hound's nose, whose nostrils could each hold a good-sized hazelnut, dull purple skin, if you could call it that, and a big, disgusting, seal's moustache. He wore a flat cap on his head and had draped a starched blue smock over his bird-turd colored suit.

While galloping along, he dragged a little toy cart tied to his huge thumb, which was bent and blackened with hair. He stood there silently for a minute before he saw us looking at him, then he took off again, walking this time, tugging his string as if he were leading a stubborn horse by the bit. While walking away, he sang, or rather yelled, a tune that sounded like that unforgettable melody *The Mender of Pottery* and *Purcelai-no!* as well as that other excellent song *Chair Stuffer! Chair Stuffer!*[13]—but with a much faster rhythm: "Onward little rabbits! The cabbage! The trumpets! My father was hanged!"

"Ahh! That's Jean Jouillon, the prophet, making his rounds. He has his frenzies, the animal! Today, he *figgers* he's a little brat who's laughin' in the streets with his little car. Before, he was goin' round with vegetables, chicken or little knick-knacks; another time, he was an *agrobat strick* by prophecy. They say he worked as a street peddler, a fruit and vegetable seller, and even a gymnas*iarch* and barker at fairs. Here he comes, watch out! He has the damned sickness of kicking you in the ass—with all due respect—when you're not looking. It's happened to me, even once in front of a visiting lady—that put me down bad. Oh! For every r*a*peat offense, I *restrim* him, what's called *restrimin'*. And well, he r*a*peats again, ever' chance he *gits*. He says it comes from his father, the one who was hanged—If you believe 'im."

As if to prove Leonard right, Jean Jouillon snuck up behind my guardian and stalled, then sent his boot to the appropriate target; fortunately, it was dodged.

"Wait a minute! I'm *gonna* give you a treat!" Leonard clamored.

The prophet-acrobat-vegetable seller-street peddler was left in the lurch, but kept his guard up—and surprised him. He looked so incredibly kind, so unbelievably divine, that a saint would have hated him instantly, like any incurable little brat.

He was not about to give up his act.

"What's up with you, my man?" he made nice. "You think I was *gonna* give you one? No! No! It's not part of the game anymore. I just wanted to have a little pow-wow with you and this fine friend of yours. Hold on, look at this! Here comes the damn seizure that's plaguing me."

He fell on his face and wiggled like a worm. Some drool spilled out of his mouth and he roared, "Name of names! See the prophet, the damn prophet! I'm gonna tell y'all the present, past, and future and whatever comes next. I predict for 1859 (it was 1897) the Battles of Sorferino, Palostro, *Palikrao*[14] and all the trembling. Ain't I a good prophet? Was I wrong? Didn't it happen like I said? Hold on: I'm gonna show you the Battle of Sorferino."

He got up and galloped around for a minute while we kept an eye on him. He rattled like an alcoholic, "I'm MacMahon, Bolivar, Garibaldi and all the boys of the Coup d'État. In front of me are the Aurstrians, the Hollanders and all that band! Behind me, my troops are laid out like toy poodles. On my left, my artillery, on my right the *Gloury* and the Star of Honor. Long live the Republic and the Emperor! Onward, Hussar hats and African Huntsmen! Let's capture the Malakoff tower and the Summer Palace! That's it! It's no more far than that, to the bayonet! Never a frame-up with us! Garnadiers, I'm happy with you, you bunch of calves! 'Gin a little cannon and gunfire to scetter the last vertiges of the Corsacks! Boom! Enough for now! It's done! The French are great and generous, they always spare the dead! I excuse them for everything and I *decrate* them like all my regiments. We're all brothers, there's nothin' like being stuck together in a dogfight to love each other after. Now, there's no more dead! I respect you all! Amnesty! Everyone into each other's arms or I'll stick you in the sick bay! Now that's war, school of good feeling and good heroin'!... Ah! Coward Kabyle! You're spittin' prunes at me!..."

He fell back down.

"Shove me in the silo before I start dying: they'll shoot me after. I'm dying! I'm dying! But happily since there's Badinguet[15] bringing me the Cross of Public *Ens*truction encrusted with diamonds, the baton of the Major General and whatever comes next—in the big chest with padded lining. He rubs it on his coattail to make it *sheen*. He's crying! I got a tear of the Emperor up my nose! I die happy! Long live France! Argh! Ha-ha! It's okay, since I said argh!..."

Jean Jouillon reenacted the whole grotesque battle and whatever comes next. He pranced around, charging with a bayonet and even climbing the Malakoff Tower, he positioned his cannons, protected the devastated enemies from his army, decorated his regiments, the Cossacks, the Austrians and others, embraced the world, accepted the chest, polished the diamonds and kissed the hand of the Emperor. He died in the end! It was none too soon!

We moved away quietly because Jean Jouillon seemed slow to get up, but we had not gone ten feet when Leonard leapt up like he had been shot by a catapult and grabbed his rear with both hands.

"The swine hit the bull's eye this time," he bellowed.

And my guardian took off after him, but the prophet had a good head start and, when Leonard came back to me, humiliated, down but not out, angrily rubbing his bruised hemisphere, the crazed Jean Jouillon was prancing around again on the other side of the courtyard. The toy cart danced wildly at the end of its string and the ex-peddler acrobat and vegetable seller shouted out a new song: "Green peas! Rutabagas! Fresh Guano! Sugar dogs! Here's the tripe-monger! My father was hanged!"

V

Leonard's anger did not last forever. He screwed up his face so that one of his eyes looked like a baby's twisted belly button, raised the other eyebrow up to his hairline, swelled one cheek like with a huge plug of tobacco and caved the other into a dimple…in which he could hold a bar of soap. Then he said:

"He'll pay dearly for that at the *pher*macy, but I'm not there t*a*day to do the pig's shoppin'. First, we best follow Doctor Bid'homme's orders."

We started walking again and were about to leave the prophet's hunting grounds when we were accosted by a beanpole, in his 50s, skinny, bearded and important-looking, who said to us point blank that he was nice, a good boy and all that, but he would not put up with them offering up his head.

"What's eating you now, Loiseleur?" Leonard asked.

"You know where my wife is, you little sneak—and you're hiding her to throw her hot on my heels at the worst possible moment. I won't have time to protect myself and the harpy will make a scene like she always does—to destroy me!"

He stopped, looked me up and down and seemed satisfied, but a little snooty. He patted me three or four times on the head like they used to do in the *Belle*—and melancholic—*Epoque*, 25 years ago, when my nine-year old ragamuffin skull, totally round and bald, polished clean like a dessert plate (in the senile words of my grandfather, who was an enemy of Merovingian hairdos), made the old family friends and even the school principal—the kind-hearted, serious, hypocritical creep!—drum on me with signs of friendship like that.

And Monsieur Loiseleur continued, talking to me now, "You are not old enough, my boy, to know what a woman is. I mean a legitimate woman, a spouse, as the lawmakers and sewer workers say. Well! My boy, it's a puke green spoonful of a disgusting dessert. What am I talking about? I'm making a tragedy out of something so good. To understand me, you need to be cured good and quick of Love and Life, the two deadly diseases that follow each other and vice versa. I'm not exaggerating. It's even worse than that, and more annoying because a legitimate wife generally lasts a long time! It's like a cornucopia of itching powder wrapped up in sacks and smelling of lavender, a brew of Ipecacuanhua that breaks you down a little everyday without finishing you off, a bunch of bites by big parasites and red ants, a pack of poisoned nails lying there all the time, pointed up, boy, under your ass! Ah! Wonderful invention, marriage! Listen here, I was in the Bridges and Roads; I loved the Roads! I wanted to invent velvet rollers to level them and I dreamed of paving them with nougat instead of gravel! I adored the Bridges. I would have trimmed and decorated them, if I could have. But no bad jokes when it came to something serious; I was a model employee! Well! My awful wife gave me such a hard time and made me so disgusted with everything that they had a hell of time—and strong guys!—getting me out of the dive bars where I spent my paychecks playing dominoes and ended up getting drunk any old time of the day or night. I've been led astray by her though I'm a road surveyor! (Oh! Oh! That was a good one!) I can't even look at a pile of gravel or even a painting anymore, and if my brother bums and boozers count on the bridges I helped build to find shelter at night after their heroic absorptions during the day, they might just as well go talk to Old Scratch, down there in the hole, as everyone knows. Here, now, on this lovely country property—just between us, I still had no clue about the name of this charming place! But I pretend it's a holiday in order not to ruffle the feathers of my distinguished friend Doctor Froin—Oh! I don't give a good goddamn about what that Monsieur Bid'homme might think!—on this, let's say, lovely country property where I am proud to be spending a few months or maybe years—I've tried to go back to my first loves. With the few things I had at hand—a scraper, a salt scoop and some pieces of wood, my boy—I tried to draw some cute little roads, to dig some nice, artificial rivers with no excuse for existing except the craftsmanship needed to make them exist. Let me say right now that any beetle could have swum across them with no trouble... But it was like I'd watered the inside of a violin. I don't give a f...—excuse me—it wasn't a slap in their face, my boy! Then what? I'm here like a fallow deer, just eating the slop of that the bossmen shovel out—excuse me!—that my kind hosts serve, sleeping in these four-poster beds that are as uncomfortable as they are —perhaps—imaginary, dragging even more imaginary spats on paths that someone else—gardeners (!!)—not I—designed and, the rest of the time, playing the fool, as an old, very respectable lady used to say, who was my grandmother's friend and who knew Madame de Genlis![16] Oh! If I get hold of my legitimate wife again, I'll feed on her eyelids and nostrils without a drop of vinaigrette! But she's the one who'll catch me first, the dreary wench! I'll leave you. I can't go on. I don't want to think about my bitter, painful marriage anymore!"

"And he *perty* much always talks like that!" Leonard giggled. "There's more like him, too!"

A grunting bear made me jump. Mabire had let go of the bars of the window and waddled up to us. He looked at me straight in the face, put his hands on my shoulders and continued his little dance, growling scarily a few times. Then, whining a little, he whispered sadly to me:

"Glum sight, eh? These poor folk I've been so severely punished to live with! A lot of cruel, devilish obsessions like you saw in Loiseleur, an old friend of mine. He doesn't recognize me now, but the two of us used to be very close at Saint-Valéry; me, a government official, him working for the Bridges and Roads. Poor folk! Yes, poor folk! Often messed things up, got too drunk, and always had to take it out on some family member. If married, nine times out of ten, they bawl out their wife. Ah! Go figure! Nerves always affecting each other in marriage; anger, rage, punches, bitterness! Can't explain it myself! I passed the bar, but didn't study the sciences. It's something... magnetic. And then, basically, believe me, came the *Enemy Force* that made me a bear, a miserable bear, made me totally crazy, too! And not out of charity... Ah! My wife, so good!"

He left, grunting and crying. His fat, hairy cheeks trembled hideously and scared me.

Somewhere else, and with someone other than Leonard, this simpleton that I am, who knows a lot about the miseries of the human species, might have been hard-hearted enough to laugh at this old bear. But here I was, not too ashamed to show I was touched.

My guardian was naturally less sensitive than me—he was blasé, of course!—and just shrugged his shoulders. Then he monologued. "Some guy, that old Mabire! And he loves his wife, he does! He may be the only one in this place who's suffering from that sickness. If he only knew it was his old bag—the old trash!—who stuck 'im in here! You know, he was harmless. It was I who's got him. I know 'im... And his old bimbo who said he was like a *line*, a crazy tiger, and that she wouldn't brung 'im here like she wouldn't brung 'im stark naked to a police station eveb if they paid 'er. I was scared to death of her—true as gold! They made me come with t'other boy, good for *restrimin*, but what they call a boy! That's 'nother thing, but it's not for me to say! Ah traaageeedy! I found 'im grunting very gentle-like, dusting off some little ivory toys on a shelf. He asked me if I'd come for the *succession*, which was nice, and told me to sit down, poured me some wine and *escused* himself for toasting with an almost empty glass, *'cuz* that morning had shut him up and he could only have more in the afternoon; and he *beggared* me to *esplain* myself. I gave it to 'im gently: that he was *espected* close by, about a will, by a friend who'd sent me with an old beater and two horses and for proof, I had with me the friend's nephew, who was the guy with the *bicex*. He *din't* do *nuthin'*; he just asked for his hat and gloves. He said, 'I don't need any gloves but them there,' and he put on the handcuffs I'd brung, just in case. 'It's nice,' he said, 'to bring me a pair. It'll save me a pressing.' And then, he tried to kiss his wife, he pecked her eye, telling her not to worry, that she was a good old girl and a bunch of reasons like that. And the filthy old poison, who was purring quiet and twitching her eye, said, 'Watch out, he's a bad one, a panther, a *leotard*; can you put a muzzle on im?' And the only mean thing that Mabire said—and I really think it was a kind of joke—when the door was closed, was he asked me to *whip the driver*. Now, it's been 18 months and he's still playing the same dirty tricks on everyone. He scratches, dances, growls, sometimes like a real bear, but always snickering or whimpering. Never angry, never *fow* words. He's an old turtle when she comes. She makes a scene, yells, says the man's *ruenin* her and she wants them to take less care of him so it costs less. She says, rightly, it's true, that they're not here to have a good time, to live it up. Ah! If only he knew, the poor old guy, but he wouldn't believe it if you told him."

VI

We entered another courtyard. Leonard was talking to me but I was not listening. I was haunted by a strange vision aroused in me by something old Mabire had said: *The Enemy Force.*

The picture was hazy, but terrifying. I could only make out a murderous grin and huge, white claws... And yet, I was terrorized by the hideous idea that was hounding the old bear's brain: *The Enemy Force*!

Could there be, in fact, an occult power, baneful and hostile to the human species, tirelessly on the lookout to torture our limited intellects that are lost in a mysterious world of which they know only a few appearances? And I was intoxicated by this absurdity because I was scared of it!

Yes, the *Enemy Force* existed. It often took hold of me, penetrated me, invaded me, because, all of a sudden I saw terrible, dreadful things, *whose elements were not in me* and that no word in the human language could translate...

Oh! The *real* Universe is nothing but terror and horror!...

Come on! It was only a hallucination! Leonard was talking to me and I heard—I understood—what he was saying. But maybe the hideous traitor had only gone away for a minute—to come back soon?

"No! Take a look at this courtyard," Leonard grumbled. "Have you ever seen anything more filthy and more *fow*? Uh oh! Are you getting...sick... again?"

"No, No! It's nothing, Leonard, it's over now."

"Good! You were looking kinda funny... But take a look at that muck!"

The ex-fiancé of the young Parisienne had exaggerated a little. The very small courtyard was really just covered with leaves. Half a dozen very active patients were climbing the trees, stripping them bare and making it rain.

Some guards were scolding them just for show. They looked like they were having fun and, between warnings, they commentated like sportscasters.

"Hold on, looky there, François! Anquetil's up another branch. None's *lydder* than 'im; he's in shape, the old bugger!"

"*Wun't* say, but Dumoreau's solider. He's *bottomed*."

"And Pageot there! He's loaded, hand*er*capped, as they say. He's got one of 'em, the firecracker!"

"Good goin'! There's Paillard, gonna break his *nick*. E's done it this time! To Hell with 'em! I'm *gonna* call one of 'em Doctor-types or the Boss-Gerd!"

"Get down, you bunch of sons of monkey bitches! Now, *dun'* make me come up there, Chanteburne, or it's *gonna* be trouble *fer ya!*"

"Go on, make me *larf*, Beuzeboc! He's a funny one, he is. He's lost the lead now... Beat 'im, Anquetil! It's like the runnin' of the bay t'other day at the turf* in Dieppe!"

"*Wanna* slid down from here, for fu...n's sake!"

"Watch out! There's Doctor Bid'homme!"

Right away, all the climbers came tumbling down from the branches faster and faster. The guard—François—had been brilliant enough, or stupid enough, to mention the local bogeyman.

Since the fearsome little creature was nowhere in sight, the patients looked at one another and, "could've got nasty" as Leonard said, already primed for *restrimin*.

Beuzeboc went up to François rolling his big, stupid frogs' eyes, kicked at him but missed, slapped his thigh, quickly put his hand on his groin wiggling his pinky, then raised it up straight, fist closed, thumb aimed upward and going around in graceful circles. Then looking nobly moronic he said, "Come on! This is *fer ya*. Ya're just a liar...and I'm *gonna* knock ya!"

---

* Race track.

But at that very moment, there sprung out from a door or from the ground—I do not know how which!—like a jack-in-the-box—Bid'homme (This time, for real), all tiny and grotesque, but frightening, like a huge insect: "What's this, by God! I'll give it to you now!"

The leaf pickers huddled on the ground; you could not see them anymore. But we were surprised to see Bid'homme rush up to the guards and threaten them with his whip.

"Aha! You bunch of ragstools, barbalots, sputkins! (Always his use of strange epithets!) By God, I believe you made my best men sweat, my elite *freaks*, my first-rate subjects, incurable for everyone but me! I'll cook you in Robert sauce, you bunch of pissaloofs, gloafers, crastypots!"

I said *we* were surprised, but the guards seemed less impressed than I by the genial runt's extraordinary behavior.

François got over it quickly and said, maybe out of respect, to Bid'homme:

"But, doctor, these bad practices are what's making salad of the trees! We'll be *crastypits* if you like. You're the boss and we'll always accept the reasons that'll come out your mouth with mindful consideration, but you've *gotta rec'nize* like us that it's no good seeing grubby bakers like 'em change the courtyard into a *pal* of garbage. 'Tween you and me, that's the *legal* side of discipline when it comes to cleanliness. And then, there's the health of the trees that we're responsible *fer*, like the same of the monkeys."

Bid'homme calmed down. "Well spoken, Rhadamanthus! I didn't see the damage done. You will serve them nothing but *their due* for two days. No pure wine or cider, you understand! And boot them in the rear if they start up again. Ach! Spending your wonderful youth in Froin's can with these cocklestains—It's getting on my nerves!"

It was always getting on his nerves! He looked at us again for a second. His eyes were sparkling with wicked joy and they blinked, blinked fast, fast, like a monkey's. He puffed out one of his cheeks and pushed it back in with the pommel of his riding crop, puffed out the other, repeated the little exercise three or four times, then let out a booming click of his tongue that sounded like he'd uncorked an empty wine bottle.

Then he noticed us, Leonard and me. His smoldering rage flamed up again even worse:

"What the Hell are you doing here, you thousand bums of fifty thousand barrels of bird turd! Pig! Driveller! I told you to tire him out, to exhaust this disgusting Veuly, and I find him here like a bump on a log, feasting his eyes on this show like at the Grand Theater of Baume-les-Dames! Make him sweat for me, the bastard, and don't dawdle!"

Maybe I had come down with the prophet Jean Jouillon's sickness! Leonard held me back just in time. I had already broken a plate that morning and I was just about to turn red again, which would have cost me more than buying a whole pile of Old Rouen[17] ceramics. My guardian took me away as quickly as possible, drowning my anger in a sea of words. He dazed me, diverted me, *changed my mind*. When he saw me less *egzited*, he told me that Bid'homme had seen nothing, but without him, Leonard, I might have had one of those incidents "that the Inquisition and an earache were nothing compared to!" Then he shook his head and got a strange look of rare insight, of disillusioned experience or philosophical resignation:

"That miserable Bid'homme," he grumbled, "I always figured him to be *perty* odd. But after what just happened, I'll swear on a burnin' stove that the poor Monsieur Magne was right: Bid'homme has *sumthin'* not natural. Was he drunk just now, the rabid guinea pig? Or else...?"

To get his mind off the distinguished psychiatrist, I asked my guardian about the courtyard that we had just visited.

"Oh, that one!" Leonard answered. "That's the last one. After that, there's *nuthin'* but the ward for the totally stubborn or mele*rn*cholic with the *meler*mania of *sucide*—the ones bedded down in the infirmary and the Agitated wing in the third building. Them in the courtyard we've left have crises all the time. (There's the black sickness again!—big time!) They

48

were having fun just now, but don't come see 'em in the eve-nin'! The cells are not shows! You know, the guards can only let the doctors come close: it would upset their watch, right?—people coming to hang around there, for curiosity. Can't have distractions! Each of 'em sits in a little hallway just big enough to stick a chair in, and they keep watch on two cells through barred windows on both sides. It's a bitch of a job. I did it six months and I still have *crickin* in my stomach all day long. There were times I dreamed of 'em at night—The Agi-tated—they ordered me to bring you there, but I'll just show you two of 'em who are *kinda* funny, '*cuz* the others!... It wouldn't be nice of me to make you see 'em: there's some-thing that can crazy a man all of a sudden—an *egzited* man. I'll obey orders, but keep you safe. We'll go through the grounds on the way over."

In a new corridor we met two *inoffensives* who were moving around all over the place, from the superintendent's room near the barred entrance at the end of the gardens all the way up to the Visiting Room.

"*Inoffensives*," Leonard repeated, "yes, that one who's coming first, he's sick. He crazies all the time, but he never has a nasty crisis; the other one is *sane*, but not inoffensive! I'll tell you right after they go by."

But the sick one stopped. He called out to my guardian, "Leonard, old man, it's awful! The administration of this place is absolutely useless: negligence, dereliction! I would even say: ruthlessness! You know I'm scared, nervous—and you've left the electric main in my room broken for a week now; and I, who am scared like a six-month old baby, go to bed every night to the roar of thunder as if I were living the high life."

"That's great, Charlemaine, we'll bring in a *larcksmith*."

"No joke, eh, Leonard? And then I want to tell you: there's a big night bird that craps in my chimney every night. Yesterday, I let loose the thunder at it, but like a mousetrap for lice, it didn't give a damn. He shrugged it off it with a peck of his beak and came back to bother me some more. It unplanked a chair and busted my barometer. So, along with the locksmith, send me a carpenter and an *optical engineer*. I'm a corporal, you know! And if you don't walk straight, I'll throw you in the brig for eight days on a bogus charge. Colonel Froin will double the penalty, you can count on it."

This Charlemaine seemed very gentle and childlike. His still hairless, fat face was totally round. Round were his big, clear, naïve eyes and round was his chubby mouth, topped by a plump little nose. He looked like a healthy baby. Even when his words were threatening—quite innocently—he still looked friendly, open and dazed. He shook Leonard's hand and continued his endless stroll in the establishment of *Colonel* Froin. From his deep jacket pockets, he took out a paddle and ball and walked slowly down the hall, playing like a little boy. The small rubber sphere sometimes struck one wall, sometimes the other, and bounced back on the swinging paddle. All of a sudden, he threw his toys out the window.

"Oh! He'll find his toy when he's a mind to," Leonard assured me. "There's a method to his madness; he always knows where he tosses his stuff."

Charlemaine rummaged through his clothes again and pulled out some tops, a billiard ball and a shaving brush that he threw into the yard by another open window and went back to his pockets—real stores!—that, this time, coughed up a trumpet and a gigantic pair of black glasses. He fitted the specs, put the trumpet—thankfully almost soundless—to his lips and disappeared down another corridor.

The second stroller, the *sane* one, as Leonard had said, had waited patiently for Charlemaine to finish. He came up to take his turn. He was a fatty one, young too—22 or 23 at most—with a sneaky, mean and dirty look. He seemed (I'm going to wade in contradiction) both ashamed and cynical. He examined us arrogantly and worriedly. His voice was muffled, with a thick accent:

"Leonard, you know I hate informing, but I've seen too many dirty tricks this morning! I know who stole the wine from the dining hall: it was Topsen! He's hiding two liters in his jacket every time he leaves the table and goes to drink them in the toilet. I caught him today! Socaux, from the second courtyard, broke a geranium just to do it... And then, afterward, they'll say it was the guards who destroyed the plants again to offer bouquets to the nurses for free."

He meant something by this last remark. His looked harder and even shiftier, if that was possible, and his fiendish eyes drilled into Leonard's pale pupils, who seemed embarrassed.

"Goulin, who is not allowed to smoke because it gives him fits, always finds a way to get cigars that he lights up with the kitchen fire. Jollot was found drunk again—not from the house alcohol, for sure!—but drunk like a hostess in the Visiting Room when the young Mortebranche ladies came to see their brother around 10 a.m. Legourd and Bucaille were fighting behind the gym; Anfry and Thieullent told me so. I came across Cibourrier just as he was chatting up a fat nurse—you know, Celestine Bouffard—chatting... I'll say no more! They were under arbor B, the *bush*, as they call it, and you know that Cibourrier isn't supposed to leave his courtyard. Things are looked after so badly here! He would have had to slip out the door that the guard Crochon forgot to close when he came back from having a few drinks with Lenient on the main road. Crochon brags about going to drink with the IOU whenever he's bored. Colboc, the gimp, who had garden privileges, did some lewd and dirty things in front of two female patients who also had privileges... Ha! You know, Leonard, write all this down! Don't cover up for a single one of these delinquents; because otherwise, I'll complain! You should note down all the infractions. When I happen to report on these nasty fiends, I don't want you to miss one of them! The filthy pigs!"

"*Happen to*," snickered my guardian when the nasty-eyed young tub o' lard was far enough away and grunting like Mabire, stepping like Marical, and then prancing like Jean Jouillon. "Happen to! He'll sit around for hours without saying a word, and then only spew about other people's business! You know why? 'Cuz Bid'homme palms off tobacco vouchers, *Moellaga* wine or over the counter phermacy from the

Treasury for the slackers who squeal. *Hafta* give the list to Bid'homme!—he doesn't have it!—and *tomorra*, I'll see Auzoux—that gross lardbutt who's a real pain in the... ears—comes to sweeten the pipes of the Administration Corporal or wet his gullet with wine from the Islands or with Anti-Scorbutic... (!!)"

"He's really ugly..."

"Make no mistake about it. There's no one more gross."

And my guardian told me very briefly the story of Auzoux.

According to Leonard, this patient hated his partners in misery and would be better off in prison than in a mental hospital. He was no sicker than an assistant *Sectary* of State or a Franciscan brother or all the *claricals* of the rich, what?! He was a *well educationed* child of very wealthy country farmers. He got upset when one of his cousins married a rich girl he fancied, so he set fire to the newlyweds' house hoping to roast them. Fortunately, he only burned the house. Then the family seized the opportunity like wildfire and worked the system so cleverly that the Court declared the fat arsonist not responsible for his actions and committed him to the mental hospital where the too kind Doctor Froin classified him right away among the inoffensives.

"That beats everything!" finished Leonard.

This Auzoux acted as if he did not know where he was anymore. He was very nice with Doctor Froin, hoping the good man would sign his release and certify that he was cured. And, in front of the guards, he imitated all the other lunatics in order not to pass for a criminal but "for a *poo* little Gentleman who had trouble with his *poo* little head!"

"Yes, he copies ever last one of them," repeated Leonard, and after thinking about it for a minute, he sneered, "He can't even find *sumthin' oreginal*, the bas...he's as flat as wet hair!"

"OK. And what about the other one, Leonard, the little Charlemaine? You said you'd tell me about him..."

"Ah! The '*poo* boy!' He's got a sad family! All of 'em are very nice, but flipped out like old shorts! Can you believe that his father, who was a grocer in Cany, and filthy rich, died here almost five years ago. The Saturday the boy came—it was after his military service that it got him; they hazed him too much in the barracks—that Saturday, two years ago now, his sister started to go crazy and I brung her here through the back door, as they say, Monday the *fiteen*, at dinner time—we had legs in vinaigrette and beans of lamb, that day if I remember right, *mebbe*! He's got a brother who was *barreled up* with us 18 months ago: he's in a cell, the *afortunate*! And it looks like, one of these days, we're gonna see the mother too—she was the father's first cousin. There's neighbors' complaints *fer ya*! *Mebbe* it's I who'll go buckle her up, the sad sack. I'm more caring and more arranging than the others. They send me if they can, in cases like this. So Charlemaine's gonna have his whole family in the hospital! And everyone brung by me!"

"Does he see his brother and sister?"

"His brother! Of course not! In the cells, they can't be riled up, as you probably figured. Charlemaine is a funny one. His sister... only sometimes! She's kinda *purty* to look at. Some days, they know each other, others, not! Then they call each other Monsieur Digard or Madame Retou, Mademoiselle Thiel or Old Alleaume—or they don't even want to chat. There ain't no *kin* to explain it. It makes you shiver! Well, the sister's nice, like a lady of Dieppe or even Rouen. A little too skinny, but very classy, always clean like a bleach ball. And she's *educationed*! She knows *pootry*, riddles, organ music! Everything! I'll show her to you. They let her go pretty free. No more meanness than a six-day old calf!"

Charlemaine's story sent chills down my spine. The fate of this grocer's family was tragic, Shakespearian! I felt sure, too sure, that I would see the poor, baby-face boy's mother soon. Destiny was calling her to Froin's establishment. Ah, I would swear to it!

But Leonard *changed my mind* again. We were in the large garden that I had recognized that morning from my win-

53

dow, and when my guardian saw me lost in thought, he cried out, "Hey! Monsieur Veuly, looky there, you know it now, yer *winder*!"

Ah! That it was! It was framed with a pretty wisteria vine that I had not seen from the inside: blue wisteria, blue ideas!

And here was *the other building*, gleaming with stucco exactly like ours.

"Speak of the Devil..." Leonard whispered quietly.

A ravishing face, both cheerful and dreamy, was leaning on a windowsill between two bars.

"Well, there you go, Charlemaine's sister: Madame Letellier," barnumized my guardian. "She's not bad even if she's a little bony!"

Bony! Brute, get out of here! Madame Letellier was graceful and delicate like a dream form in a pre-Raphaelite painting.

Her skin was pale pink, smooth and floral. Her eyes were black, like you've never seen—even among the most beautiful mulattoes of the Antilles—black eyes that suffocated, that *killed* everything around them, eyes of night that were passionately, paradoxically bright. Those eyes! I felt like I was turning into a moth! And the sister of the colorless Charlemaine had hair like an Arab or Hindu woman, not really black but blue, like the hair loved by the god Baudelaire, who celebrated it so wonderfully. Her exquisite mouth was red like hibiscus flowers. This grocer's daughter was enchanting, like a princess from the Thousand and One Nights, enough to drive you crazy.

We were walking by her window and I slowed down; I could not get enough of her. Suddenly, she called out to my guardian, who was obviously popular at Doctor Froin's. Her warm voice was almost song-like and captured me, cradled me like sensual music.

"Leonard! Celestine locked me in here by mistake and I forgot my little mirror on the garden bench by the greenhouse. Would you go get it for me? I need it for a magic spell... No! The gentleman doesn't have to go with you! You'll make him run, won't you? I wouldn't want him to get all out of breath for me. He's not an old friend like you!"

Leonard was flattered but nervous. He looked at me out of the corner of his eye; I pretended to pay no attention. Then he said, halfway reassured, "I really want to, but it's *dangarous*. But I *gotta* say, it's wicked hot and I won't be but ten minutes over there. I don't want to kill Monsieur Veuly and I'm gonna sprint! It's not time for Bid'homme to come over here... but... get away from the window, Monsieur Veuly, there are some mean nurses."

I went over to a flowerbed after making up my mind to go back to the beautiful patient as soon as my mentor was out of sight. Good! He was going around the building. I saw nothing but one of his huge, well-shod heels...

I wanted to look at my oriental princess again. What calamity was she suffering... Well! What about me? I was practically reasonable today, but how would I be tomorrow or next week? It seemed that I had been nice lately! I was so glad to be in an establishment as badly kept as Doctor Froin's! Anywhere else, I could never have been cheered up, even for a short time, by the sight of such a beautiful woman.

I went back and already the ravishing patient with the Hindu hair and the fantastic eyes of tropical night was talking to me:

"Well, don't just stand there, Monsieur Veuly. That's what they call you? Monsieur Veuly? It's just for show, isn't it? So, come over here. You're in disguise, aren't you?... You're here to free a prisoner... Maybe like me? I *recognize* you. That's why I sent Leonard to get my mirror, which I don't need. Don't you usually have a kind of golden armor, a flying horse on fire, two spurs like lightning bolts and a sword that is a ray of the Sun? I bet you like it in the *Niebelungen* when you're not in *Jerusalem Delivered* or *Rolando Furioso*—I also know that you thought of Baudelaire's women when you saw me for the first time and of the fairy Pari Banou, of Scheherazade and of Nour Mahal who has her Taj in Agra where the peacocks are made of living gems more beautiful than those of Delhi—which were only the priceless work of a goldsmith—,or in Agra where the roses sing, breathing out their dawn and twilight scents. Oh! Twilight brings me back to Baudelaire! What blissful twilights in his verses, even the dark ones—you know! that one with toads—but especially those mysterious ones, like *Hear, my dear, hear the gentle night that walks!*[18]

"But no! He was solar, he was god! You're surprised that a meager princess of Travancore in southern India near Ceylon, a second-rate Persian princess of Firouzabad, the city of jasmines with blue domes, like eggs, stretching up into the sky, that a pathetic princess of burning lands shining with thick greenery where the old abandoned capitals of the first sultans of Java rise up, that a princess who lived in Cany, in a grocery store, before marrying a ghastly African wizard who was changed into a middle-class lord because of his crimes, that such a princess could have read such things. But you don't know that my father was a wizard, a good wizard, yes! who transformed almost inedible, base materials into gold and who gave me everyting. In Cany, where the charmer Louis Bouilhet was born and where the great Flaubert[19] used to come, I had a library that was the envy of the Comte de Sauvemare's daughters and the Marquis de La Haye-Bolleville's too. And my father let me become a fairy sometimes, and sometimes the empress of Borneo. I was also all of Shakespeare's heroines and even that friend of Gustave Flaubert, that Madame Bovary whom you loved so passionately and whom you still cry over..."

Can some poor insane women see right through men who are also suffering?

I am no hero. I have to admit that just the idea of doing something brave, no matter how absurd (which would be an extenuating circumstance), really gets my goat. So princess Letellier's imagination had some holes in it, but it surprised me that this princess of all the zones of the Orient knew that when I saw her for the first time all of Baudelaire's India and all of the Supreme Poet's exotic lovers flooded my memory.

56

She was such a darling, the poor little lunatic, so adorable! You would probably say I was thunderstruck. But it was nothing like that. I was not dazed. It was not hard or violent. Those few minutes were wonderfully long. Little by little, I felt a sweet, sweet embrace! I was lifted up by the bright, captivating beauty of that princess whom *I loved*—see, I did not dream of lying to myself about it—but I was not completely lost. I was fevered, but it was not a *devouring fire*, as the old cliché says. I was drunk on the flowery perfume of paradise.

And the wonderful princess continued: "So, come over here! I want to see the face of a real knight. Good! Just as I was expecting: you're not handsome, not at all! But powerful people like you don't need to be good-looking. A fire burns in your eyes that is more attractive than a thousand hunks."

My poor eyes! Was it only love that was burning there? Wasn't madness in their fiery stare?

I was more scared than ever of the *Enemy Force*—If I was going to forget that I loved her, the Exquisite One! Oh! If a new fit was going to throw me back into the abyss, back into the bitter flood and drown my only happiness, which was to love her!

She seemed a little impatient: "But you're so cold for a hero! You haven't said a word! Tell me quickly that you love me! I want you to love me! I can't give myself to you like this from the very start—a woman!—But am I not doing you a huge favor by asking you to say it? Isn't it a good sign? Come on, quickly! Tell me that you love me!"

"Oh! Yes! I love you"

"Ah! You've really said it! And I've changed my mind. I don't want you to say anything else this first time…"

She stopped suddenly, in a panic and more beautiful than ever. "Quickly! Save yourself! I hear Leonard. Come back soon, some evening if you can! They don't watch me very closely in this dungeon!"

My guardian found me farther from the window than when he had left. I was carefully rolling a cigarette with my back to *the other building*. When he had given back the little pocket mirror, he looked a little wry—my guardian—and scolded me in a friendly way:

"Well what? Monsieur Veuly! You get the jitters around *purty* women? In *yer* place, dressed like you are, all wrapped up in a nice suit cost more than 40 bucks, I would've *took* advantage to *kinda* compliment the little lady while the idiot Leonard was playing deer on the run. Oh! It couldn't be easier—even here where there aint no filthy guys and gals *accept* Bid'homme and two or three nurses!..."

"Ah! Mmmmmonsieur Leonard! Are you saying that Doctor Froin's institution is like a... house of ill-repute and that (here, I choked) Ma...Madame Letellier has had affairs, that you know of?"

"Well, really! Hella common sense! That's a bit much! You're too hard, really! Is that how you thank me? Next you'll be calling me a pimp! Mebbe you're gonna offer me some money, but I guarantee you that I would... ditch the dough! Ah! Tragedy!"

I could see that he was sincere. I had really hurt his feelings without meaning to. He was very upset but softened up—willingly:

"You gotta treat people with some respect! And yeah, I'm gonna tell you *everthin'* to make you feel guilty: you know why I said I'd do it *fer* her? 'Cuz Madame Letellier never looked at no one—she's sweet but afeared like a little pigeon—with all due respect. She made eyes at you, but I figured it was *fer* a bit of distraction—with *nothin'* ugly coming out of it, of course! What do you want? It takes all kinds, but it ain't her fault! If she was in her right mind, *mebbe* she'd choose others!"

And that was the end of Leonard's revenge as he twisted his great rag of a moustache, feeling proud of himself. It was so easy to see that he was hamming it up—and not in a mean way—that I could not hold it against him despite his nasty rudeness.

But when did my princess want me to see her again? Would they ever leave me as free as she was in this institution? I knew Leonard closed his eyes from time to time, but would he go so far as to forget to lock my door, on purpose or not—*preferably in the evening*? Should I feel him out? Could I come up with some great excuse to fool him... or not? (Simply a matter of form!)

It worried me, but did not get me down. I clung to hope!

VII

In the gardens, the patients looked peaceful and glum—mostly country folk who were watched by a few guards while they took care of the rosebushes, picked vegetables and pruned the vines.

Farther on in the open field—would I ever have believed it if I did not see it with my own eyes?—there was a huge stone wall that looked like the Great Wall of China. And a squad of inmates was baling weeds. Another troop was digging a ditch whose purpose Leonard could not explain to an ass like me. I thought it had something to do with irrigation… I've always been so good with practical things!

We kept walking, but did not reach the wall—I was completely exhausted, just like the nice Doctor Bid'homme wanted. The few days of fits had busted my legs. Leonard noticed it.

"Well, that's enough for today, and anyway, it's almost time for dinner. You *wanna* go back?"

"On the bus if we can!"

"Oh! We'll have a little break near the Agitated like the doctor ordered. That'll loosen up the strings in yer hams. Not too long and you can *mess* in *yer* room. And we'll take a shortcut."

On the way back, we followed a path of brooms and elders, silver hail and a heady rain of gold. We came to a large quad surrounded by bushes. In front of us was a brown brick building that looked like a prison. The windows had huge bars on them and were all closed with metal shutters, except for two in the middle. We went up to the two cave-like black holes.

Something swarmed in the darkness. We heard hideous laughter and angry grumbling and then saw two gruesome living beings that you would have thought—if you did not know any better!—were huge and hideous apes. They were dressed in rags that barely looked like clothes and that were all the same color, dirty yellow.

One had a diamond-shaped face: a triangular forehead, wide cheekbones—bulging!—and pointed!—and a sharp chin like the tip of a spinning top. The other had a totally round head, monstrous, like fat Dutch cheese: Odilon Redon[20] would have loved both of them.

The first one was wearing a kind of ancient Tyrolean (?) hat whose ragged edges were maybe an inch wide; the second had a straw hat that looked like an open snuffbox with a broken cover. The Agitated on the right had an evil laugh that bared his stumps of tarnished nuggets; the Agitated on the left foamed with rage. The laugher started dancing, doing somersaults and dancing again, like a circus ballerina; then he jumped up and down, tirelessly, saying "Opa! Opa!" and guffawing. He smiled less and looked satisfied, almost happy. He obviously thought he was funny and was playing nice, but all of a sudden, he started yelling, rolling on the ground and jumping back up. He kept yelling and jumping and then finally fell down on the floor of his cage and wiggled around in a kind of epileptic fit. After maybe 20 seconds, he got up and started dancing; and the whole time he was scratching himself and smiling absentmindedly. The furious one climbed the bars of the window, tried to spit on us, shook the bars, moaned and groaned and his eyes looked like they were going to pop out of his head. He tore at his rags, scratched his face until it bled, howled and cried in frustration—at not being able to bite us, to wring our necks and tear off our skin. He aimed his claws at us; he choked; his face turned purple, almost black!

"OK, Leonard! Now I've had enough of looking at these monsters! They're hurting me. Not to mention that us being here is not good for them. These crises must wear them out. When they're alone. they can hide in the corner, curl up and go to sleep, or whatever, but they'll calm down. I'm getting out of here!"

"Good! Good! Let's go," my guardian said very seriously. "They're very gentle, almost proper. It's the others I don't wanna show you, no matter what Bid'homme says. The others, ah! They're nightmares! If there's any like them outside of here, they're only found in jars—and drowned in alcohol—again!"

Just then two young, buxom nurses passed by us. The two sad anthropoids whinnied—literally—like horses and threw themselves against the bars—then tore off some of their clothes, seized by an exhibitionist rage, and slobbered and roared.

The nurses ran away and Leonard finally agreed to get away from the awful scene—so sad that it was almost not disgusting.

I was so tired I hurt. I felt like needles were stuck in my kidneys and I was dragging along gigantic lead balls hanging from my ankles...

Finally, finally!! I saw *my* building! Leonard opened the door; it felt like there were 500 or 600 stairs instead of 20. I fell into a chair. I ate and drank and did everything they wanted; I would have swallowed dung and acid if they would leave me alone afterward, free to go back to bed.

VIII

I slept a long time. My room was no longer lit by the great golden flame of the warm hours: a ray of weak topaz, from very far away, danced on the varnished wood; my drinking glass glimmered like a huge diamond prism with a thin veil of gauze...

The big key must have turned in the lock because I heard an iron echo in the room again! Then, I heard the second turn of the *keystone*, as Leonard called it. I saw the thick oak door shake—a gentleman whom I did not recognize at first walked through, a smiling gentleman in formal clothes—God forgive me!

There was a false note however. The elegant socialite was stuffed into knee-high riding boots with spurs—blinding boots that looked clownish with the white vest and coattails that made him look like a swallow, and the top hat held out like a bouquet of flowers.

He looked like a ringmaster at a circus about to present a trained horse. The stovepipe was, maybe, too much, but the result was the same.

In spite of the newcomer's exquisite grace, pleasantly pudgy gestures and Japanese greetings, I had to recognize Doctor Bid'homme. Then, the socialite jumped on top of the table, sat down comfortably with his boots on the armchair and started whipping his leathered calves with a riding crop that appeared out of nowhere. Despite these glitches in his venerable behavior, Bid'homme's polite language fought the good fight against professional protocol, which is known everywhere from the French West Indies to Pondicherry, and from Zuydcoote to the Isle of Bourbon:

"My dear Admiral," he began (even though in the merchant marines, I never got above the rank of passenger), "I am lucky enough to be the herald of my excellent master, Froin the First, king of this establishment and all its dependencies. He will enter your rooms at 6 p.m. If he doesn't come earlier to pay his respects, it's because a… picrocholalgy of the left calcaneus (???) has hobbled him. Now, I must go and tell the other honorable dignitaries of the imminent visit of our ruler."

He galloped off—of course—shaking his riding crop and squeaking his boots. I had no more doubts; Bid'homme the Friendly, like Chopard, was in some ways a rival of the prophet Jean Jouillon. We were in good hands, we "freaks" of Vassetot! And I got scared thinking about my little princess!

Anyway, the dangerous psychologist had told the truth on his diplomatic rounds, which were, I am sure, not his responsibility. Ten minutes after his horse-like exit, Leonard unlocked my door, looked at me in secret partnership, pursed his lips like he was blowing on hot soup, stretched out his arms, hands flat, like a hypnotist and hissed rather than spoke:

"Pfuuuuutt! Here's the big boss!"

Then he backed out bowing low and ever so slowly.

Suddenly, I was looking at a tall, fat man in his 60s, with a kind, honest, fatherly and open face. It was Doctor Froin; I recognized him.

He spoke with the same voice and the same accent as the gallant Bid'homme, but more softly and more friendly. Leonard was right.

"Well, Monsieur Veuly, this morning I was happy to hear that you were feeling better. I'm sorry that I didn't come to see you earlier, but I wasn't able to make my rounds until now. I had a bad attack of rheumatism that crushed my left leg all day long. I'm still having a hard time dragging myself around, but it's better now."

He did, in fact, limp. He sat down in the armchair wincing in pain.

I went up to him and said, "I hope your pain will go away completely," and I added automatically, "Rheumatism, isn't it? Monsieur Bid'homme said something about a weird illness with a strange name."

Doctor Froin looked surprised. "Oh, Monsieur Bid'homme, Monsieur Bid'homme..."

He was just about to tell me something, but he decided against it.

I was more reckless and said as coldly as possible: "Monsieur Bid'homme is crazy, and possibly dangerous, as you probably suspect already."

"You're right to tell me what you think, but don't be fooled by appearances. Monsieur Bid'homme is very, very eccentric, very weird, but that's all..."

But I saw him shiver, and it was not due to his rheumatism. He continued very calmly, without the least concern in the world:

"Don't forget that my colleague..." (he paused here) "my colleague *Doctor* Bid'homme is here to take care of you, and you should trust him completely. Doctor Bid'homme likes to surprise his patients... for excellent reasons... which I understand. His attitude and behavior are part of his game; you have to know that. But for now, it's you and not my assistant that concerns us. I think you shouldn't be feeling... nervous... anymore."

"No, Doctor. I like to call a spade a spade. I think I had an anxiety attack, maybe a brief moment of insanity, or just a high fever—whatever. But you can be sure that it's over with now."

Doctor Froin looked at me carefully. "I, too, have my ways—and they work—usually."

The doctor was obviously worried, like any good man tortured by his conscience. I knew exactly what he was telling himself: "What if I'm wrong? What if this patient who is locked up only suffered temporary insanity! What if he only had a case of nerves or high fever that was quickly cured? What right do I have to keep him here if he's as sane as I am? He spoke freely about a possible moment of insanity. A *reasonable* lunatic would have been scared of tipping his hand by even saying the word. What should I do? And if he became dangerous again outside my establishment? There have been stranger cases!"

I was sure that I had read him perfectly, even more sure when he said, without any warning, as if he had actually spoken what he was only thinking:

"...And besides, one of *his*... excuse me! one of *your* relatives is coming on Monday—the day after tomorrow. We'll talk to him about it and maybe, my God! yes! Maybe your treatment will last a little less time than I thought... Do you still feel upset or angry? Do you still feel like you might want to hurt someone, Leonard or me, for example? You see, I'm talking to you as if you were all better, as if you never had any problems, except a little nervous breakdown, cleared up already and forever; as if you didn't need any more treatment!... No? Nothing against Leonard, nothing against me or against anyone else?"

"Against you, Doctor! How could I have it in for you when you're so nice to me? Against poor Leonard, who does everything he can so that I don't get worked up, so that I get along here as well as possible? Against anyone else? Well, that's another story! I have to say that I can't stand that quack Bid'homme. Of course, I feel sorry for him—as he deserves— but I am tired of seeing this ridiculous fool, who should be put in a straight-jacket, intimidate, act like a tyrant, rant and rave, yell and insult everyone. He should be washed with Niagara jets until he bursts, which would not be a great loss to humanity! That Bid'homme! Argh! Him, yes, I hate! He's a constant danger to the patients, whom he knows nothing about, and whom he might kill with his stupid brutality! Why don't you lock up this dangerous lunatic, Doctor—or, at least, send him back to Franche-Comté, to his family, if they agree to be responsible for such an evil creature and keep him tied up 24 hours a day?"

What was I saying? Doctor Froin looked different; he shrugged his shoulders sadly. I saw him—his mind was made up now: I was a monomaniacal madman with delusions of persecution. All my ideas, all my preoccupations and all my anger, was focused on Bid'homme. I was acting exactly like someone who was crazy. I would keep saying that he hounded his patients and hated them all—me, first and foremost!

His doubts about his assistant might even have been erased by my angry outburst. He could blame it all on my madness.

I tried desperately to redeem myself, to save myself. What should I do? What should I say? Wouldn't I be *cleverer* to tell him everything I was thinking—however uncomfortable it might be? I cried out—as *unloudly* as possible:

"Doctor! No! Don't write me off like that with a flick of your hand. I know what you're thinking; you think I'm obsessed! Don't deny it: I'm sure of it! But it's nothing like that! To show you I'm not the least bit deranged, let me say that I was a little hard just now—even though I hate your colleague Bid'homme, and think he's dangerous and harmful to your patients, I have absolutely no problem thinking about other things. Why, today, I thought about a thousand things that had nothing to do with him. Do you want me to tell you about waking up this morning in this room? About what went on inside my head—pointing out the difference between the sane ideas and those that are still a little...off? Do you want to be sure that I am not sneaky or vindictive, like most of the mental patients? Well! You just told me that my relatives are coming on Monday, but you didn't say whom, probably because you were concerned about making me angry. I'm going to tell you: it's Roffieux—the one who brought me here. I swear to you that I have no hard feelings against him. I can honestly say that he is close to my heart, but if I leave Vassetot, no harm will come to him from me, I guarantee it. I will do what any good man would do in the same situation: I will go as far away as possible. True enough, he disgusts me and I don't want him to have any more control over me, but it would never enter my mind to play a dirty trick on him!"

Doctor Froin was impressed by my speech. But he still had his doubts: lunatics are so unfathomable! But he slowly gave in as he considered the terms of my plea. I saw him barely nod his head. He could almost not help smiling. He got up—with some trouble—shook my hand and concluded:

"Come on! Let's go! Everything seems absolutely ship-shape; this will have been nothing. You had a little vacation and that's all. Eat well, don't tire yourself out walking in the gardens—with or without Leonard—I'm telling you—read something light, Alphonse Allais, Shoomard, Courteline, Franc-Nohain or Mark Twain—I'll send you something later—go to bed early, don't get up too early, and your vacation won't last long."

And it was at this very moment that some obscure enemy *crouching inside me*—since when?—chose to twist around and shake my nerves, to force me to vent anger that I didn't feel, that I didn't want to feel, to make me yell and dance and then convulse like the two Agitated in the brown brick building!

I had been completely honest, sincere and frank—and now it was no longer true! I hated Bid'homme and Roffieux! I wanted to *bleed* them, to *do them in*—and I shouted this out as clear as day! And I didn't want to hate them and I didn't want to shout out—and I clamored more loudly than ever!...

I was sure that a terribly hostile being haunted me, a cruel being that had *settled* in me, a dreadful being that tortured me to force me to roar and writhe around like someone possessed...

There was a moment of semi-calm and I begged (so absurd it was disturbing!):

"Doctor! Doctor! Save me! I'm *inhabited like a wormy fruit*!"

PART TWO

I

I must have gone out of my mind again and into a coma.

When I came out of my devastation, I was in bed, buried in my covers up to my nose. I was not alone. Sitting by my bed, lit by the dancing flame of a candle, Leonard was busy cleaning a sturdy bowler hat—so faded that it was almost white—that looked like the dome of a mosque. The harsh smell of benzene perfumed the room.

My guardian looked wise and determined, like a student putting the finishing touches on some asinine homework that the good professors of old always included in their collections of nonsense known as honor notebooks; he looked so stupidly self-satisfied and preoccupied, blinking his eyes and sticking out his tongue, that I almost broke out laughing.

But I suddenly remembered my stupid behavior and I was heart-broken. Ah! I really knew how to take advantage of Doctor Froin's good intentions! It was just when the he was beginning to think I was cured that I kicked off a new performance! Triple brute that I was! Couldn't I go suddenly crazy and be terrified without being an idiot and unable to hide it in any way?

But it's always the same old story! I saw clearly enough—with the help of Magne and others—what I had done. The *reasonable* or *semi-reasonable* lunatic who only had temporary crises would be on the verge of committing some hopeless stupidity, would do all he could not to do it... and he would see himself doing what he should not do, hear himself saying what should not say... He would not be able help it. He would be a victim of that *Enemy Force* that Mabire was had mentioned.

I was dying to know what Doctor Froin thought of me. I coughed, turned over, threw off my choking blanket—sounds of alarm—and then called out, not very loudly, "Leonard!"

My guardian, who was very carefully rubbing the top of the pale felt cupola with a wool cloth soaked in benzene, groaned and looked at me.

"Leonard! What did Doctor Froin say?" I asked. "Does he think I'm ripe for the shower after that attack?"

"No! He told me that you were too emotional for a man in *yer* state, that you'd had a kinda of... *Lisa...Lucy Nation...*" (I knew it!) "but that it wouldn't last; that it was too stiff... No! He didn't *espress* it like that. He said that it was too *philomenal* to *irrigate* the brain; that he'd never seen anything so *morvid*; that he'd heard of it, but that was all; that the calm was *gonna* come back and I could leave on assignment tomorrow; that whoever was around, maybe François, could take care of you until I get back, you'd be quieted down. That's why I'm *furbishing* my bowler."

I was angry at Doctor Froin's insight, but the hallucination—if it was indeed a hallucination—was still there. I was sure that *I was not alone inside myself.* How could I explain what I felt without sounding ridiculous? I was haunted by an unbearable presence—even though the *being* was not torturing me like it did during Doctor Froin's visit. I guess it had been quiet for a while, but now it spoke. Can I say that it spoke? It did not have a voice! But it *suggested* words to me... strange words that translated its thoughts. And I understood very well what it commanded—when it *communicated* to me the following:

"*So, ask this... idiot where they're sending him on assignment?*"

And I automatically asked my guardian, "And where are you going, Leonard?"

"I am in charge of the delivery of Mother Charlemaine, as I was *especting*."

"At Cany, then?"

"No, the poor woman was scrappin' with her neighbors and they *din't* take too kindly to it. She got *afeared* and *warlked* to Villiéville where she's got a relative. She got there only in a shirt *'cuz* the bit of slip that was dancing on her butt don't count. She made another wild scene and her relative wrote here right away to get rid of her—wouldn't dare drive her here himself."

"And when are you leaving?"

"Tomorrow morning at 5 a.m. And so that's why my clean *lid*. It's almost midnight. You should sleep. And me too. Good night, Monsieur Veuly. I'll bring François by before I leave so you won't be alone if you need something *nessary*. You want me to *let* the light?"

"No, thank you, Leonard."

Alone! He had no idea that I had company. Maybe I would have preferred another, but beggars can't be choosers.

I should not have refused the light. Suddenly I felt childish and thought I would have been less scared in a lighted room than in the pitch black where my guardian had left me. Scared? Yes!—scared of the *Being* that haunted me and might talk to me again.

In fact, I had barely closed my eyes when I glimpsed something hideous *inside me*—hazy and unclear—but hideous—and the invader *suggested* these words to me:

"*What a surprise, eh? You've never seen this, a man inhabited like a wormy fruit? That's a good one! I bet you're going to think I'm the Devil and try to exorcize me! Bonehead buffalo! Sad little calf! That's not how you will get rid of me, come on!*"

I asked him *mentally*, "Well, who are you and what are you doing inside me?"

"*I'll explain it to you when you are able to pay attention. Do you understand me? That's the question. But tonight, you are tired and sick. Sleep! Otherwise you're going to enjoy suffering. Oh! I'm not sensitive. I don't care much about your well-being or your pains. But you'll tire me out with your stupid complaints and, what's worse, is that I might end up suf-*

71

fering too! We only have one nervous system for the two of us."

"You'll keep me awake. You're hostile and you bother me."

"*Me, hostile? Because I talk to you like you deserve? Why do you think I'm your enemy when you can be useful to me? Sleep! I won't bother your dreams. They are of little interest to me.*"

The... *Spirit* that... possessed (?) me spoke in a very levelheaded, very respectable tone. He could have been a professor... let's say, a professor of Psychic Science, only wanting to perform an experiment on a subject. This interests him, that does not. So I could be useful to this disembodied gentleman on vacation inside me—like for a research article! He interrupted my thoughts:

"*Come on! You can rationalize some other time. Sleep! You're a moron tonight. If you think you can distract me, you're wrong. Right now you've got the most f***ly boring brain I could imagine!*"

The *Being* was not respectable for long! He had very *bad style*, as a proofreader friend of mine would have said, and added, as usual, "He has dirty words in his mouth." He was an *impure spirit*.

Anyway, I was not scared at all. What seemed so awful to me just before, now seemed to be only a light fog, almost clear in the darkness. I did not see the green and red lights that were certainly the eyes of the... *ghost* that only I could see. The *Being* was bored to death of my mental life and was taking a rest. I was just dozing off when...

...an awful racket broke out in the dark night that was loaded with electric radiation. An infernal howling came from somewhere close to our building—maybe—yes, certainly—from the women's building!

I heard desperate hootings and dreadful howls followed by shrieks that drilled into my ears and even my bones—that entered my marrow—meows that roared.

It stopped for a second, barely, and then started up again louder, more painfully and more frenzied. My heart was torn apart; I was frozen in a cold sweat; my limbs were paralyzed; I thought my teeth were going to shatter each other. I too was going to howl!... Then the hatch snapped open and I saw Leonard's face like the first time. A jet of yellow topaz light, sequined with bloody jewels, splashed the glistening wall in front of me and my guardian spoke, very calmly and clearly amidst the sinister hullabaloo:

"No need to get upset, Monsieur Veuly! That's the ladies opposite who are feeling the storm... If I *din't* have the car, I wouldn't give two cents for my bowler. Tomorrow, it's *gonna* be a flood!"

I knew all too well, Leonard, that it was the "ladies opposite" and even, for a minute, among all those jarring yelps, I thought I heard a little cry that was more delicate and lovelier than the others, but maybe also more furious and ferocious, that had to come from my adorable princess. It was finished; I could not sleep after that: She, too, was a howler!

"*All of them are howlers!*" kindly answered the *Being* inside me. "*I recognized her, your good woman!*"

"Animal!"

"*Don't insult me. Do you know how I recognized her? Painted in your brain, my friend, and beautifully painted—no other way.*"

"So tell me! Since you've decided to continue the discussion without my asking this time, will you please explain why you chose me instead of someone else to harass with your bad jokes? I would like to know who you are and where you come from. You can be short and to the point since I'm so stupid tonight!"

"*Oh! Being scared didn't clear your head—far from it!*"

"Will you tell me already?"

"*I'll say again that you won't understand a thing... But since you insist, I'll give a little lecture, very short. You need to lie down, only for my own sake—like I've already told you, I might feel the pain if you hurt your nasty carcass.*"

"It would have been very easy to leave this nasty carcass alone!"

"*It wasn't totally by choice that I blessed you with my company... Well, do you want explanations?*"

"That's what I'm waiting for."

"*Listen then: I'll be quick. I'll give you the details later; for now, nothing but the run-down.*"

"Go on then!"

"*Good. Maybe you know that your planet of mud is not the only inhabited star. There are worlds superior to yours— quite a few. Inferior ones, too—almost countless. There are happier and unhappier ones; but all of them are not organized according to* human *ideas—earthly, if you'd like. Thus Tkou-kra—the star I come from—or planet rather, since it belongs to a solar system, the red star you call Aldebaran—yes, you do call it Aldebaran, I see this in you as clearly as the stupid idea you have of it—so, Tkoukra, my planet, has a population pretty much the same as your globe. Although most of the intelligence is more advanced there than on Earth, the people are meaner, as you might say; the conditions of life are much more dismal, more rudimentary and savage. For example, many of us have the gift of second sight, not innate but earned by hard work, and the will to know our future, at least for our lifetime on Tkoukra. On the other hand, we can't protect ourselves against bad weather, and we never have enough food, except at certain gruesome times that I won't talk about until you're more used to me. Right now, you would be horrified by me—you're still not so crazy about sharing your body with me! Anyway, I can't say I'm one of my planet's elite, but since I had enough education—you might think it was hard to get when you learn about my fellow elders—enough education, I said, and skilled at farseeing across space, and, on the other hand, I didn't trust the Creator's plans regarding my future— he might figure it better for me to try out another existence even more miserable and at the same time more intellectual—I promised myself to conquer or to* swipe *a little temporary but immediate happiness. I knew about Earth telepathically... Of course, there are many better and more beautiful worlds, but how could I put up with them? In those worlds, the Souls are too serene and strong, or too brutal and vicious for me. Earth suits me best. After countless trials and errors, I managed to release my* astral body—*as your Mages call it—and flee across the Ether, abandoning my inert, material remains to the glacial winds and the hard, thankless soil of my planet. I hope that another spirit on an even sadder vacation will use them and suffer less than in his old body on an even more intemperate star. That's the first generous wish of the Being from Tkoukra!*

"*When I arrived on Earth, or better said, when I floated into the atmosphere of your planet, I searched a long time for what I wanted: a body to steal—oh yes, to steal!—for I wanted to use a human organism alone, by myself, after sneaking inside, thanks to a blackout or a kind of wandering off of the owner's Soul. That's how the inner spirits you call Elementals are taken away. Unfortunately, except for a few carnal boxes of very high Brahmins or western mages who threw me out right after they came back, I found empty cabins only in the filth. I'm being crude, but accurate. Do you see me in the body of a hysterical, anemic, sorrowful, whimpering old woman, living only out of habit or stubbornness, or in a neurotic whose body would be nothing but a keyboard of suffering, or in an invalid, a future candidate for the cemetery?*

"*I resigned to share. So, all across the Earth, even among the freaks like you, I met no soul as stripped of energy, as sluggish, as* wrecked *as yours...*"

"You flatter me, but you exaggerate…"

"*A little. Maybe my search didn't last as long as I said; but as far as mental debility, you were just right. Plus, your body wasn't in too bad shape, far from it. Psychological problems, so be it, but not a penny's worth of infirmities. Nice financial expression—between parentheses—that I dug out of your mental inventory. I think you're a good enough boy and figure that we can work things out together. And, you're so sluggish, so* vulnerable—*your name Veuly, certainly fits you well!—that I'll be less mean to you than to someone else. And that's enough for tonight, isn't it? You now know who I am, where I come from, why I've* rented a room *inside you. And I'll tell you that I'll move out only when I find something better. I want to study life on Earth and enjoy it as much as possible; and the* lodging *you offer is a last resort, nothing else! So, there's still hope for you... Whoops! You don't know my name—what can I tell you? Yes—here it is, in the harmonious sounds of your music box: I am* Kmôhoûn. *And I've already told you that my sub-Aldebarian planet, invisible to your telescopes, is called Tkoukra... Now, good night!"*

It was incredible, I was able to fall asleep despite the shrill cries that demolished the walls of the building across, turned it into a huge cage howling in the darkness. The gloomy cacophony must have lasted a long time because I felt like it tormented me even in the abysmal depths of sleep.

Then, all of a sudden, it was morning, gray-blue break of dawn, and Leonard entered my room with François, my substitute guardian.

II

Despite the threats of storm the night before, at 7 a.m., it was such beautiful gold and sapphire weather that I decided to go and see the gardens again.

I would go past the window of my princess. If I could say two words to her, my heart would be blooming during the whole walk; or else, I would wait and the plants and the grounds and the fields imprisoned by walls would be made beautiful by the hope of talking with her on the way back.

I must have dreamt the night before. There was no *Kmôhoûn* from *Tkoukra*; and the women's building was quiet, or if someone could not hold back their screams—ah yes! there it is again, that inhuman clamor!—at least, *she* did not cry out. I was probably just a little crazier than usual and enjoyed scaring myself, terrorizing myself. Lovely work of the demented! And Kmôhoûn from Tkoukra! That was a good one! What an imagination! I discovered planets and became an armchair Le Verrier[21]! How ludicrous!

"*It's not so bad,*" Kmôhoûn answered very quietly. Now I could recognize his psychic voice, angry or calm. "*It's not as ludicrous as that, since I'm still here and very happy to see the excellent health of our carcass. Hey! Isn't it great to get rid of the absurd 'How are you?' between us, which is even said on Tkoukra!*"

Even though I meant what I had said about sharing, I felt like a goner. From now on, I was going to be watched, spied on, by this being of a different and, maybe, terrifying species. I could not escape into myself anymore. I would no longer be alone! The last refuge of an abused convict, of a beaten dog, would no longer be a refuge for me! There would always a *presence,* even if I were dying of pain!

Oh! I wanted to escape from Kmôhoûn of Tkoukra—just for a few hours—a few minutes!

"*Ha! It's very easy,*" Kmôhoûn answered. "*Do you want to take a walk outside yourself? I'll help you out. You don't have to say a word. This is not your refuge today. You can use anything as a refuge! You only have to leave your rags behind. You can bet that, after so much trouble finding the secret of astral body cruising, I am not stupid enough to forget it. You'll be able to leave the man from Tkoukra, go see your princess and stay with her as long as you want. Whenever you choose to come back to your prison of flesh and bone, I'll welcome you with open arms. See, I've thought about it and I don't want to monopolize. I'd rather give up a little corner to the rightful owner; or else, he might make my existence unbearable by always fluttering around and twittering, 'I want to come back to my house! Give me back my stoop!' I would never have a second of peace. So, you don't have to worry about going out. When you come back, I'll be more polite and more thoughtful than any doorman—I won't leave you waiting on the street."*

My Kmôhoûn had really made incredible progress in a short time. He had carefully read the chapters of earthly life in my brain: he knew about doormen! But it wasn't about that. If I wanted, I could spend a few hours near my princess without any guard getting in a huff. Wouldn't I be invisible to everyone but a Yogi? But what if Kmôhoûn was lying to me? If he ignored me and left me wandering in space? Who cared! I was already so tired of him that I believed that I would have no trouble giving my body up to him. I would leave it behind to forever haunt my princess, who would be good and friendly company. I would even realize the beautiful dream of lovers. I had suffered so much lately, anxiety had changed me so much, that I was starting to think that my passion was completely platonic, ideal—and so much more wonderful for it. I would certainly have made the good storytellers of *Gil Blas*[22] laugh if they heard me rambling.

In any case, I made it very clear to the Tkoukrian, "I only want to get away for a few hours."

"Oh! I see what you're brooding over! You don't think very highly of me, but I won't hold it against you. Go, my friend, you'll come back to me sooner than you think. You

78

don't have a strong soul like mine. I'll be ready and waiting for your reentry. *Do you want to leave right now? Good! The best way to free your spirit is like this: Will very strongly to escape your body. OK, you have to know how to will, to will in a way that you can't explain; some beings discover this secret in themselves little by little. But you're not there yet, my vulnerable Veuly! I'll have to help... a lot. Give me something to think about—use what little will you have to do this: dream of somewhere, like the other building, and desire very strongly to be transported there..."*

It was easy, all my dreams flew there... But what did I suddenly feel? Was it a shameful, shattering fear, a nameless fear? Was it a furious joy? Was it an exquisite, almost fatal pain? What did this Kmôhoûn do? I don't know, but hell broke loose and I thought I was dying...

...And there I was—leaping again?—flying?—over the garden. Not really leaping or flying, I didn't have a body anymore, but I could see and hear just like when I was incarnate.

Almost at that very second, I saw my princess in her bed, her eyes rolled upward, her pink face turned peach, her delicate white teeth bared—like they were grinding—and her bluish lips stretched into a wild grin. She was still beautiful, but almost frightening! Doctor Froin and a female guard were talking at her bedside:

"Ah! Doctor, you know how it is! Every time there's shrieking at night, she's like this the next day. T'others get better right away. At 2 a.m., they made a hellish racket, but true as my name is Celestine Bouffard, at breakfast time you'd've seen 'em like a *far*-engine, red and smiling and hungry. But Madame Letellier has one of them crisis that takes all day to get over. It's not that she goads herself more than t'others. She *don't* shout as much as her friends, but it's true that when it hits her, it makes you *trimble*. It's sharp as a *shank* and makes like there was a saw runnin' down your spine..."

"Auber's music makes a very famous baritone..." I discovered the gracious Bid'homme sitting in an armchair, hidden until then by its high back and the sensational hips of Celestine Bouffard. (Celestine Bouffard? Didn't she have something to do with a story of libidinous trysts and arbor B told by the arson Auzoux?)

Aha! This time I saw Doctor Froin get angry:

"Monsieur Bid'homme!" he scolded, "you might as well go tell your jokes somewhere else. You're stupid and tacky…"

"What do you mean?" snickered the booted psychiatrist.

"I mean, leave right away. I don't need you anymore."

Bid'homme, dubbed the Friendly, was thus dismissed and rode his whip to the door while jangling his spurs.

"What have you got on your feet? Have you gone mad?" Doctor Froin blasted.

Bid'homme answered as the immortal Ubu had done with a single word made up of three consonants and one vowel[23]… but quiet enough that the Director could pretend not to hear it. He kept watching his assistant:

"And a riding crop to boot! And you're prancing! You must be drunk!… Coming to a patient's room to play horsey! That's the last straw! Go and wait for me in my office… No! Go to bed! You can give your excuses later!"

How did I witness this whole scene that obviously scandalized the outstanding Mademoiselle Bouffard whose contralto voice moaned, "Aah! At Doctor Froin's! Such stunts like that! Where're we headed? Everthing's upside down!"

How could I have even paid attention to all this nonsense when I only cared about the woman I loved?

She was still pale; her eyes rolled, crazed; her nose was pinched and deathly pale; she sneered a little! Abomination! She would have been… almost ugly… to anyone but me! The director fussed over her, lifted her head onto the pillow and applied the smelling salts while Celestine Bouffard patted her hands.

She woke up suddenly and looked around. Her beautiful eyes were still wandering, her whole face convulsed; she didn't look like *herself* anymore.

"O Doctor!" cried Mademoiselle Bouffard, "What's wrong with her, the *po' li'l* Madame Irene! Good God! She's changed! What a tragedy!"

"Be quiet," Doctor Froin said dryly. "She will be back to her old self before evening!"

But the blow was dealt: Irene—(it was thanks to Mademoiselle Bouffard that I learned her name!)—Irene was about to cry. She grabbed the small mirror that was kept in arm's reach and looked in it with terror:

"Oh my God! I'm hideous! I don't want you to look at myself anymore! Oh! It's awful to see myself like this! I want to hide! Oh… especially… the one who's going to free me… he can't see me like this… I would lose him! My only friend, the only one! For pity's sake, go away!"

"It's best to leave her alone a minute," Doctor Froin gave in.

After what she had just said—(was it me she was talking about? Was I the friend who would free her? Or had she invented some weird knight whom she thought she met everywhere? It did not matter!)—, I would have felt heartless spying on her despair, even if she did not know it. I would come back later; I would give her time to get better.

And when the nurse followed the Doctor out the door, I left the room—without thinking—through the wall—because there were no more material obstacles for me. I let myself go, floating at random… and soonm I was far from Vassetot. Such absolute freedom scared me; I did not know what to do.

But I felt that, if I was not so abysmally sad and had the slightest bit of spiritual energy, nothing would have been easier than to reach, in no time at all, the beautiful countries that I always dreamed of seeing, gliding over the bright blue Oceans to the bays surrounded by palms and flowery forests. But because of Irene's troubles, I dreamed only of what could *mentally* bring me back to her and I was not very surprised when I saw that I was again floating above on the road to Villiéville that Leonard had taken that morning to fetch the mother of my little princess.

I went slowly or quickly as I pleased, and even though I had no organs, I saw and heard more clearly, I could smell the fields and hedges more vividly than I could in my bodily prison.

Leonard probably took the old route, the shortest one. In fact, just as I was about to pass over an old covered carriage dragged along by a wheezing horse and driven by a drunken coachman, I recognized my guardian's noble head sticking out of the door window. He looked furious; he was red like the setting Sun and swore loudly and a lot. When he had blasphemed enough, abused enough, shared enough of his indecent idioms and Cayenne[24] expressions, he started speaking again more normally and I understood why he was angry:

"When I think that it was me who came to *git* you *yesserday*, old booze-hound corpse, you and *yer* bell collar, I *wanna* turn me and you both into nursemaids for roasting pigs. When Doctor Froin said to me, 'Take the establishment's coach,' and I *says*, 'No! I'm *customed* with Robidor and his hack; it's the only car in Vassetot *builded fer* the sick.' Ah! He's great, Robidor! Come at 5 a.m. drunk like a pig—or like a pack of *wile* beasts!—I can understand a stiff one under the belt in the afternoon, but at 5 a.m.! He breaks the axle of his *willbarrow* and *rapeers* it with a rope. He fails this and throws me in some cow patties and with his mule of a horse that has feet of lead, he makes me go half-mile an hour! Damn son of a b…ad woman, *git movin'*!"

Robidor stayed quiet. Only one time when my guardian shut up to catch his breath, he murmured, "C'mon, Leonard, *live* me be at last! I *sheen* you drunkerer than me. Did I make a big deal of it?"

Leonard finally pulled his head back into the carriage and started brushing his pale bowler with his coat sleeve; he spit carefully on one small, unnoticed stain and rubbed it with his handkerchief. Then he took a newspaper out his pocket, wrapped his hat in it, picked up a tarpaper case and a thick string, took out a kind of chestnut picker's helmet and gloved the skull. Then he monologued:

"This is a delicate hat. It can stand two or three hours of dust but not a half day… I'll put it back on to go into Villié-ville, but why should I ruin it in Robidor's old junker? I'm sure he hasn't swept his *polstry*? Who's it *gonna* matter to anyway? I'm *gonna* look good *fer* three windows and the backside of a driver in the Lord's slammer?"

The rocking and rolling of the carriage became so gentle and cradling that Leonard thought he was in a rocking chair and ended up sleeping.

At least an hour went by. The driver also slept, saluting the pony's rump and the road, deserted until then, that was lined with tall trees hanging over piles of rocks and livened up with gray houses. The slow nag walked caught a whiff of familiar stables and began to speed up, but still in no hurry. After the gray huts came big houses of redcurrant brick with blue slate roofs, undoubtedly the homes of respectable financiers, and the horse stopped scraping the hard cambered roadway with its shoes. It pulled up behind some hay carts that barred the road and, a little embarrassed by its worn-out bit, fat like a girdled whale, it began to lurch slowly.

The fat driver woke up, rolled painfully to the back of his seat, put his arm through the window and shook Leonard awake yelling, "Hey! My old prison guard! We're at City '*All*!"

While Leonard was rubbing his eyes, fixing his hair and putting on his hat, the coachman spoke again like an objective observer:

"I seen plenty of horses in my donkey years, but nary a one who could've been a chauffeur. This guy here always knows *perty* much near where we're going. Course, he's *oppo-o-sed* to going by these cart-driving pimps, but ya know, there's nary a horse who'd go into the gutter. Not 'im. He spies the inn at *15* feet and tells *hisself*, 'Don't bother makin' *oreginalities* when it's only a hair's breath away. And '*cuz* there's some lettuce, I'm *gonna* eat a bit!'"

"Ha! The broken nag!" Leonard replied. "It's a special kind, like its master."

Robidor seemed flattered, even more when my guardian added, "*Lissen* up: you're gonna put away your caravan and *yer* turkey here at Angu-Postel. Me, I won't be long at City *'All* that'll tell me where Mother Charlemaine's relative is livin'; gotta be *perty* close. I'm gonna tell the chap that he's gotta wrap up his cousin and make her *decin' fer* when I come to pack her up on the spot in three hours. Yer animal can't go back before then, right? He's spent like an old balloon. So in 20 minutes or *halfor*, I'll meet you back here. In case you sober up, we'll have a drink or two; then we'll eat what there is, then coffee, a gloria[25], an after-dinner and one fer the road if *yer* in control. Then we'll load up and it's off back to Vassetot. We won't be much later than 9 a.m. since it's not more than a three hour trip fer a pony younger than 39. And you see, I count double *fer yers* who looks worse than boot leather. Don't give a damn about the oats either; it's Froin who's paying!"

My guardian didn't even have to worry about going to City *'All*. When he got out of the carriage, he met the top official of the town, an elephantine countryman with a blue nose and hairy nostrils and eyes so incredibly sly that it must have been hard to keep them looking like that all the time.

Leonard called out to him, told him his little business and got the necessary address: "in front the biggest manure pile over there, next the *navgatin'* area," and he headed for the huge heap of designated filth.

He knocked at the door of a dirty but pretentious house. A young, chubby-cheeked maid—not at all pretentious but dirtier than the house—grumbled that "he *wuz* in the nick," because Frederic had "gone to come back." Frederic himself showed up soon, an old country gentleman, puny, cross-eyed and dazed, and dressed up like a hunter from some comic almanac or a cheap postcard.

The dining room was cluttered with all models of guns, game bags, powder flasks, etc. The owner of this cynegetic arsenal was not warlike at all. Even though he was older than 70, he had the hairless, pitiful face of a scolded little child. His squint eyes looked like a dead rabbit's; his lips trembled when he spoke with false sophistication; the little hair he had, planted like stubble on starving land, stood on end:

"You've come to take my cousin off my hands," he sighed. "She's a very dangerous person and I'm sorry to say she has questionable habits. Her branch of our family in Cany has not received as much scholaring as us others raised in Vil-liéville. That's the reason, I'm sorry to say, for her *sickning* behavior that's not very good for the *familial*. The doctor-physician-obstetrician of our *locusality* should have *phlibos-tomized* her the day *afore* yesterday. Yes, Monsieur, this woman here is *Tadmerlain* in a skirt…"

Leonard interrupted to ask him to pack up some clothes and things for the future inmate and he told him about the schedule.

"In three hours, my dear sir! I'm very disappointed! I was thinking you would *transmit* her right away and it'd be no problem! She still has plenty of time to start dancing—that's the nice way of putting it, my good sir!—and to *porphyrize* my furniture and injure my body, which she has already threatened with *issaults* and other violence."

My guardian explained the situation: a tired horse, a driver still getting over a fit, no coach to rent at Villiéville…

"I see! I understand," the crestfallen hunter answered, "but I sympathize with my own problems. I won't breath a *sight* of relief until this demon has *crossed over the horizon*! But at least you can stay with me until you leave for Vassetot? I'm about to drop. Look at me, me, a man of my age, so harm-less that I've never *esterminated* anything but innocent ani-mals, me, armed with a deadly revolver in my belt!"

Indeed, a "bulldog" shined all silvery against his flat belly. He forced himself to whisper, "And do you know why I've been holding this gun since the night before last? The crazy woman wanted—ah! My good dear man, should I say it?—she wanted to steal my honor!"

The old Nimrod shuddered again.

"But I can't just dump the driver who is supposed to eat with me at Angu-Postel!" my guardian said.

"Well," Frederic answered, "bring him to feed here: it's on me! but for once, I won't die!"

Leonard rushed out to look for Robidor, who had not waited to have a lot more than his two glasses, and a second drunkenness had cured him of the first. O homeopathy!

"Who'd *thunk* it," my guardian muttered, "but that's really what was keeping him going, damned Robidor: he was drunk, but not enough!"

The fat coachman, whose stomach was a real warehouse, did justice to the meal. Moreover, the three sitting at the table got along perfectly, even though they all talked at the same time. Frederic went on about the malice of hares, "filthy beasts that have no respect for the best marksmen," while Leonard talked about the common depravity of "nuts who were more smart and *obstinate*," than the others. Robidor could not stop telling the tale of dung. In his long experience, it was a touchstone. He had seen some extraordinary ones, but they were always signs of the habits, personality and abilities of the subject!

By the second course, Frederic was impressed by his guests; at dessert, they were in such perfect harmony that they spoke like they had one voice between the three of them.

Coffee was served and the master of the house uncorked a bottle of cognac. The party was really taking off, each of them having a great time talking to themselves, when an incident happened, just like in the House or the Senate. The door of the dining room cracked open and a small, wrinkled head peeked in, an old head, bronzed like Cordovan leather, with strangely brilliant black eyes that seemed familiar to me. The party was not paying attention, so it disappeared and came back again two seconds later on top of a very skinny body that floated in a black, grease stained nightgown and a drab petticoat.

Frederic looked up and yelled, "*Aye!* There's my cousin!"

The old lady—that tigress!—shuffled into the room and begged, "I'm hungry too! And you've given me nothing to eat!"

Frederic turned green and screamed like a skinned animal, "Robertine! Come quickly and help these men!"

The maid entered—kitchen side. Leonard and the driver were already standing up.

I was expecting a violent showdown when the allies went up to tame the old woman, but she only repeated, "I'm hungry too!"

The maid giggled. "Are you a nincompoop, Monsieur? She ain't so wild! I'm gonna take her with me and give her *sumthin'* to munch on."

"Nothing from my table!" Frederic groaned. "She'll gobble up all my food and I'll have nothing left for tonight! Make her heat up some of yesterday's potatoes with a bit of soup. Nothing else! She'll be the ruin of me, a crazy old woman with an appetite like that!"

Robertine took the old woman by the arm. She was crying, but calmed down when the simple young girl promised "to stuff her chock-full of good things."

"You understand," Frederic continued, "I can't set gold dishes on silver plates for a crazy old woman who doesn't have a penny to her name anymore. Of course, she had her means in her time, and fat like a millstone. But bad management, vice, craziness, and maybe drink, ate away most of her capital. This crazy family's guardian—a notary[26]—is sentimental…" (Oh! A sentimental notary! A crocodile that gets a muzzle, then!) "…and insists that his *pupils* be treated like a senator's cousins at Doctor Froin's. This comes to… to… terribly expensive, all those private rooms and so-called *fortifying* diets, *ekcekra*. I'm sure it's far more than their actual income. Yesterday, I had to buy her two of Robertine's used but still good outfits that she'd put out for spring-cleaning. It cost me ten francs, hard cash! Will I be reimbursed for that?"

"So, her bags?" Leonard asked curiously.

"She's got an old shirt and Robertine's outfits that she isn't sporting today."

"Well, Doctor Froin will fix it with the family guardian."

"I'm counting on it. I've done enough. All my money is already spent... poorly... I've even given up the idea of marriage in order to save money! So you understand!"

They drank their cognac. Frederic recorked the bottle and measured the level of the liquid by making a little mark with a glasscutter. Then he locked up the bottle, but I heard him mumble, "The *larksmith* is useless *taday*."

It was almost 3 p.m. Robidor went to Angu-Postel to harness his horse. Robertine brought the bags. Mother Charlemaine started worrying.

"Doesn't she have a hat or something?" Leonard asked. "We won't get to Vassetot for awhile and it'll get cold!"

"She owns a shade hat, I *racolleck*," Frederic answered. "You could wrap up her crown in her scarf if it gets too *refergerated*."

Ten minutes later, Robidor came back with his whip around his neck to tell them "the beast is in the litter."

Robertine wrapped Mother Charlemaine's head in a sort of black wool towel that had obviously been too close to dripping candles. Leonard courteously offered his arm to the good lady. She whimpered and wanted to know where they were going "like that."

"We're gonna go *fer* a ride in the coach," piped my guardian.

"Not with these men I don't know," the crazy woman protested. "There're trap doors in these cars and they throw old women like me out 'em. I'd rather go see the tin birds on top of the barn. They sing like harmonicas!"

"That's where we're going with the *carge*, up a windy road," Leonard whispered.

"Is that right?"

Mother Charlemaine took two steps, halfway reassured. Robertine said goodbye, slapping her on the back in friendship. Frederic took a deep breath. But the poor woman suddenly turned around and started crying, as if she felt it in her bones:

"Aren't you going to kiss me goodbye, Frederic? Twice, so I might come back later?"

"Get *outta* here! See how she starts up again with her nonsense! See how she's *gonna* torture me again with her wicked ways," Frederic shouted. "Stop her. Look at me here. Isn't she ugly enough for 60? I used to know pretty women her age who you'd say were young girls. And looking 90 like that the rotten witch attacks grown men! Aren't you disgusted with yourself, Eulalie? No, Madame! You will not kiss me! It would feed you full of perverted ideas!"

"Perverted ideas!" the unfortunate woman burst out. "How can you say that?! Me who only loves frizzy sheep and carrier pigeons!"

Frederic's modesty must have been pretty sensitive! How did he get it in his head that this sad old woman could ever threaten weak virtues? The eroticism of this poor dried herring Eulalie did not seem the least bit Senegalese up to that point!

Robertine must have thought the same thing because I heard her mumbling a kind of protest:

"Sure *'nuff!* As if she was a naughty one! No pity for a *skelton* like that! If virginity was redeemed, old Frederic could be afraid of *olders* than *youngern*, the old goat!"

But we were already on the street. Leonard went to the car and was going to help Mother Charlemaine get in when… *fffffftt!* the crazy woman slipped away, hopped to the side and took off toward the dock. Robidor and Leonard ran after her, soon followed by Frederic, who had quickly armed himself with a dog whip. The old girl still had strong legs and made a job of it for the three runners hot on her heels. But she made the mistake of going on the pier: no exit! She ran around in circles, ducked and dodged, and was about to be grabbed by Leonard, when she got the bad idea of throwing herself in the water. I saw her jump, I thought she was lost; but we (she and I) had not considered the boats lined up along the shore. Two fishermen, who were busy unfolding an old sail from its yard, had turned around at the sound of the chase and—literally—caught her in mid-flight.

They heaved her onto the pier. Leonard and Robidor grabbed her and, without too much *restrimming*, carried her wiggling around to the car, where they plopped her down on the bench like baggage. And on the road!

She was a little wet despite the skill of her saviors, who couldn't stop the hem of her skirt from taking a little bath. With her dress stuck to her legs, Mother Charlemaine looked even skinnier, longer and more unreal. I saw Frederic at a distance, out of breath but full of joy, rubbing his hands in delight and Robertine shaking her fist at him.

The crazy woman cried and—after sitting still for a minute—made some devil's music, as my guardian called it:

"Where's we goin'? Where's we goin'?" She struggled, but was held tight in Leonard's fist. Doctor Froin's recruiter finally got a bright idea that he should have had earlier:

"Where're we going, my dear woman? But to see your son and daughter who are staying with friends."

"*Shudda* told me so!" the crazy woman shouted. "I was scared of being taken away by the police, *respec* to a piece of sausage I stole from Frederic '*acuz* I had the knife rounds in my stomach. I know what they do to thieves! They put the red irons under their pits and cut their hair with pliers…"

"So your cousin *din't* give you nuthin' to eat?"

"Oh! He's very nice, but he doesn't like hogs. He told me so. So I *din'* say a thing when he gave me a few little bread crumbs and I sought my life in the corners. Course, Robertine gave me stuff, but he *larked everthin'* up. Well, not *everthin'*, since he left the sausage under the kitchen table—a slice, that's all, and not all that good!—and then a old piece of lard next to a pair of boots in the shed, and then a half a smoked herrin' in the yard, near the chickens. But I stole it, the *po'* Frederic, and it wasn't good!"

The way back was hard. The weather, which was so nice during the day, had turned bad around 5 p.m. It rained and Leonard put his bowler back in the newspaper. It was summer, but a bitter cold, which I did not feel but I sensed, seeped in through the cracks of the carriage: The vehicle was old and coming apart; the wood doors were rattling; the top should have caved in. Mother Charlemaine shivered in her wet dress and my guardian was in a foul mood. Later, when night fell, it got worse. The trees that marched past the windows looked like monsters and terrified the crazy woman; water began dripping into the crazy old junker. Big, icy drops sprinkled the head and hands of the old woman who cried out in shock. The splendid bowler did not stay protected; the newspaper was soaked. Leonard started swearing again and Mother Charlemaine started weeping again. They passed through a village with its blurred red lights. Dogs were barking. Robidor was refreshed by the shower and decided to hurry his horse up a little. The carriage rocked like a boat on a stormy sea.

Finally, at around 8:30 p.m., they went through Vassetot and the hack stopped in front of the gate. The driver got down from his seat and rang the bell; the gate opened and the dreary chariot rolled down a wide gravel path.

Robidor and Leonard unloaded Mother Charlemaine, squashing her between them, and when they crossed the lobby—being close to the Head Office affected them both—they suddenly pretended to be struggling like a couple of gendarmes bringing in a boy who stole some prunes. Rolling their wild eyes, swelling the veins in their forehead, huffing and puffing like they were exhausted, they dragged their "dangerous" prisoner, dazed by this sudden frenzy, into the director's office. Doctor Froin—long since bored with this childish act—just shrugged his shoulders:

"Come on, Leonard, go easy on the lady. You'll end up pretending to brutalize her, which would not be keeping with the spirit of the game—well played too, I might add. Hold on, Robidor, here's what I owe you. You can go."

The fat driver left after a school marm's curtsy.

Bid'homme was standing near Doctor Froin, but a Bid'homme once again transformed, a Bid'homme without boots and without a riding crop, serious and respectable—a little overdone, maybe—a psychiatrist for *The Graphic* or *Le Monde Illustré*[27]. His voice was even harsher and more assertive than usual when he interrogated Leonard about some "observed irregularities," but his politeness toward the patient was perfect. Old Froin was obviously pleased with the behavior of his assistant whom he watched with a fatherly eye.

"Is it true that I'm *gonna* see my children?" the crazy woman asked.

"My God, Madame," Bid'homme tromboned, "let me point out to you that it's a little late this evening for that. But, first thing tomorrow morning, I will be glad to bring them to you myself in your room. I understand a mother's impatience!"

You would have thought you were at L'Ambigu.[28]

And after Doctor Froin had reassured the poor woman, even cheering her up, but probing her without her suspecting, Bid'homme escorted the new inmate very chivalrously to set her up nicely in her room in *t'other building*.

But he had barely got her there, and turned her over to a nurse, when he met the head female guard in the hallway and terrified her by telling her awful tales of savagery that made Frederic's cousin a cross between a cannibal from the Dahomean Amazon and a worshipper of the Phoenician Baal. He added:

"You're going to weaken her for me, calm her down, by purging her over and over again. And if she makes a racket, give her the diet, the shower and the jacket—you know it!—the wonderful jacket!"

The guard was all shook up and did not know whether she should enter the room of the shocking lunatic who was already in bed and calmly watching a burly nurse hang up her wet rags.

And should I enter the other room, farther away, that I ran away from this morning? Yes! I wanted to see *her* before going to rejoin in what was, by all rights, my body, the hateful Tkoukrian Kmôhoûn.

Irene was sleeping in the golden pink light of a small lamp. She was beautiful again, more beautiful than ever. Mademoiselle Bouffard sat at her bedside hemming some towels and stopping her work from time to time to reread a letter written on dirty paper with a stylish picture of a dove holding a crimson heart in its beak. Suddenly she sighed:

"That funny Paplorey!" (He was a guard.) "He says such things, such obscenities! But what a good-looking guy! And all his hot talk is basically sweet. He's so *decin* and *senstive*."

This fat hussy was taking care of Irene!

But she slept, as oblivious to the dirty thoughts of her guardian as she was to the day that just saw her poor old mother imprisoned like her in the same hospital.

Can disembodied beings give a kiss? I think I can answer: yes, as grotesquely impossible as it might seem. Oh, I was drunk on the scent of all the flowers on her pale rose cheeks whose velvety smoothness I *felt*. I stayed there for a long, long time enjoying this touch that she could not imagine (would she even suspect it when awake?) and I forgot about my abandoned body and the dark spirit from a far-off constellation who had traveled through the dizzying paths of cold space.

Mademoiselle Bouffard went to bed with the light. I could not see my princess anymore but I breathed her, I inhaled her! And it was only in the early morning that an instinct stronger than my will and stronger than my passion, took hold of me and made me worry about Kmôhoûn and the other part of my *self*—the earthly rags that I had denied for hours on end… And yet I had to wrench myself away from Irene, who did not even know I was there.

I cannot explain anything that happened to me. Why did this driving force make me brush by the sleep of my princess' afflicted mother, and see that—calmed by a long rest in a comfortable bed that was undoubtedly much different from the pallet given to her by the diabolical greed of her cousin Frederic—her face relaxed, almost happy and hopeful—the old woman looked *cruelly* like my delicious Irene?

And especially, why at the moment when I was so moved by the smiling peacefulness of the old lunatic (a more touching scene than anything I had seen that day), did she seem like a prophetic warning? Yes, prophetic: I would see the chilling sight again, *almost* exactly the same, with my bodily eyes in another country far away:

Two men who looked like thuggish convicts, in a forest, chased a naked old woman whose long, dirty white hair slapped her back and shoulders; prickly twigs scratched the gray skin of the fugitive who jumped like a rangy, wretched goat—charging through spiky, clawed bushes, feeling no pain. And there was a clearing beyond the thickets. The woman ran faster and faster, but on the carpet of short grass, the hunters caught up. One of them reached out, touched the shoulder of his prey who turned around to bite him with her sharp, white teeth, strangely young in that face slashed with wrinkles. But his partner's close call enraged the other human dog and he hurled himself ahead, desperately, leaning forward, his two hands stretched out, grabbed the white hair, lost his balance and was thrown onto her by his wild momentum. He rolled over the body of the poor wretch and murdered her with his elbows, knees and huge bones. The two men who looked like convicts gloated. They dragged the bleeding body over the ground, then spread it out on its back and took turns defiling it hideously and, in case the victim still had the energy to scream, they martyred it with their fists and steel-toed boots. They took the human wreck and threw it into a wagon... The horse galloped away on the muddy road; the muck flew, splattered the sinister chariot with huge yellow stains and... everything disappeared.

III

Not thinking about anything, still scared by the hellish vision, I went back to my room where Leonard had fallen into a chair, his arms dangling, his eyes popping out of his head and staring in shock at a really hideous face—which was mine. The monster that looked like me was purple, black—in a frenzy, for sure. I understood Leonard's fright. Let's be honest, I had never been handsome. I was always ugly, plain and simple ugly—really *ugly*! You cannot deny me this. But never was my ugly face hideous. And yet, this head that rolled on my pillow could inspire nothing but disgust, hatred and fear; my tortured nose looked like a dented snout; my naughty eyes with normally yellow pupils (faded yellow) looked no better flashing these red flames—then green. A swollen tongue pushed out of my open, slobbering mouth. I was a horror!

What could the wicked Tkoukrian Kmôhoûn have done *in me*?

That's why I was not sure I wanted to rejoin my body.

The guard François was more used to apocalyptic faces than Leonard, but was still a little uncomfortable and sounded hoarser than usual when he spoke:

"He's been like this for more than ten hours. He was calm and sleepy most of the morning, but he wanted to say something when Bid'homme was here—he couldn't *espress hisself* and he got angry like you see 'im. Doctor Froin said he didn't *parlyze* his tongue, that it's a case like he's never *abserved* and so on. And there you go, their *medcine*! I don't believe in *sleepwarkers* or *shippers**! The *sargeon*, yeah! They'll show 'im! Cut out where's bad. Everyone can see what's outside! (or even a *trumor* inside—that can be *fected* by the *estruments*!) But the workings that is right on the inside, I can't believe that a doctor can *look at 'em* in the body.

---

* Shepherds

95

Wouldn't he need glasses? That might work with the *Rangain* rays [**] cept it's a damn joke!"

And thus the doctor was judged.

But Leonard was not listening to his dissertation. He wanted details about his patient.

"If only there was *sometin'* like it. If only he talked like a *phornograph*. It's too bad there ain't no *punited* damages for clumsy people who keep an eye on other people's patients!"

François was getting angry now. I could see what was going to happen and it was time that I stepped in if I wanted to stop a forever regrettable quarrel between these two eminent psychiatric aides.

I got over my horror and went to my body, suddenly afraid that I might not be able to reenter. But the Tkoukrian must have felt my presence: I was literally drunk in by my overly average organism that Kmôhoûn had not helped improve.

I felt him say to me: *"Aha! And none too soon! I couldn't talk! I didn't see any more writing—painting—whatever—in your damned brain: you took everything! I won't let you go away again until I have studied, learned and memorized whatever is necessary for earthly life—to paint them and write them for myself. I wanted to spout garbage at that agitated Bid'homme and that moron François… and nothing came out! Nothing but my thoughts and words of Tkoukra: I had a foggy memory of your language, but when I tried to use what I thought I'd understood—nothing—more nothing! I could use your larynx for nothing but angry moans… I was suffocating!"*

But I was not listening: I heard Leonard and François shouting names at each other; they were going to start fighting any minute now if I did not step in.

I said very loudly, coldly, with that flat voice that always freezes the most warlike champions for a second—especially when they are not expecting to be shouted at:

[**] No doubt Röntgen: X-Rays.

"Hey! What's going on? You're going to slug each other because the cat got my tongue! It was nothing! A simple nervous crisis that really upset me, it's true, but that is over with now. I hope, Leonard, that you'll calm down since no one caused this crisis—not François, nor anyone else. Give me something to eat; I'm starving. After that, you can go and do whatever you want; I want to be alone."

The two momentary enemies stared at me, dazed, *flattened*, as my guardian would say later. They moved away from each other, still threatening their fists so as not to seem to surrender too easily—mumbling meaningless insults and jerking their heads, chins stuck out, which perfectly illustrated their bitterness and daring and clearly warned their opponent to "never try it again" if they didn't want to "taste some of this!"

When we had finished lunch, the Tkoukrian and I, and Leonard had taken away his fading anger and heavy contempt that had crushed François, (when he was in the room and when he wasn't), the intruder inside me forced me to take pity on his hardships of the day:

"Ah! I had a hard time of it! I was hungry and thirsty—feelings I knew all too well on Tkoukra!—but I couldn't ask for anything. Plus, I was tortured by that awful puppet you call Bid'homme. He's the one who should be locked up! Compared to him, you seem more reasonable! Would you believe that he abused me, tortured me himself? I guess because I didn't answer him? I didn't understand what he was saying to me anymore, but I was almost sure that my silence was too much for him. François held me down and Bid'homme pried open my mouth and tried to grab my tongue, which slipped through his fingers—naturally!—but it still hurt a lot. I bit him, too, and as hard as I could! After that, he grabbed me by my hair and beard, tore at them like a Devil and knocked my jaws together! Seeing it was no good, he took me away to a big, empty, sad room and he ordered me to be thrown into an ice-cold bath. Then they shot a painful jet of water into my

mouth. My teeth are still shivering! Ah! The coward! We will get revenge! Do you want to?"

The poor Tkoukrian! They really tortured him well in *my* body! I felt the shooting pains in my head; my jaws were shaking and a bad fever burned and froze my blood in turn.

"Kmôhoûn, we will get our revenge sooner than you think. That scoundrel Bid'homme is done for!"

I'm sure the Tkoukrian gloated. He dropped the psychic tongue and said aloud in my voice, *"Bravo! The Enemy Force! The Enemy Force!"*

He, too, knew the Enemy Force, just like Mabire and myself? Of course! He had read—is it right, read?—the two words in my poor little brain, where my return just *rewrote* it in signs that were like letters, images, sounds... I cannot express myself anymore—everything I had ever seen, heard and thought in my life!

Kmôhoûn continued: *"Ah! I was very happy that you came back, Veuly! You are so useful to me that I feel—no kidding—a real friendship with you. I promise I will never drag you into anything that you'll regret; or if I do, it'll only be the result of my tainted past forcing me to."*

"I feel a lot better!"

"Don't worry ahead of time! I am thankful to you and I will hold myself back. I will tame myself!"

Oh! This was even scarier than the rest! From now on, I was going to be guilty of all the horrors that the past or present evil nature of Kmôhoûn the Tkoukrian might force him to commit! For a minute, I liked being a poor mental patient who was irresponsible for his actions! But this selfish joy of a coward and rascal did not last long. If the dangerous intruder whom I harbored was going to make me the *acting* witness of infamies that would hurt my loved ones—Irene—my people, my friends, (it's the same thing!)—those poor innocent devils who do not care about semi-nasty, not to say hateful beings—how desperate I was going to be!

I would put up a fight, ha! The fight of a lunatic who had crises!

I am going to live in a trance from now on! Ah! Kmôhoûn, I want nothing to do with your friendship if it cannot keep you—a Tkoukrian bandit, a primitive anthropoid? —the son of a worse star than this one—whatever you might say—from using me for your own ends!

Why didn't you try to incarnate in some tyrant? They are very weak despite the power that you think they have, and in spite of the abuses they commit. You could have chosen a headhunter from New Guinea or Mindanao, a Tuareg sheik, a Sioux chief, a Patagonian horseman, a bashi-bazouk, a warrior, anything! But that you came looking for me, specifically—me—a poor peon cobbler of verse, a failed bard like Sir Oswald-Norbert Nigeot (bing, bang, mechanics!), member of the Philosophers' Club and my fellow prisoner—me, the dried up fruit of so many jobs, famous good-for-nothing whose only fairly glorious merit is to be absolutely harmless—you have to admit that this is beyond all cosmic understanding, O Tkoukrian from the Aldebaran constellation!

"*I've already told you,*" Kmôhoûn answered, "*and I was speaking metaphorically—if you'd like—that I was bragging a little when I said that I had done long and patient research before subletting a small corner from you.*" Nice sublet and Kmôhoûn had found some wonderful expressions in my "eloquence shop." "*I was in a hurry and you were the first feeble soul I came across... so...*"

"But, poor wretch, did you stop to think that the body that you got into wasn't free, that it was locked up in Froin's institution? Now you have some idea of it after suffering Bid'homme's pranks and learning all kinds of things by reading my mind like a first edition. So, if I don't get out of here, the only part of this planet you'll study will be the inside of a mental hospital, and for the rest you'll have to trust my vision of things—my personal opinions!"

"*How could I have known this when I come from such a different world? And honestly, it was so grim there that the conditions of my present life seem soft in comparison...*"

"And Bid'homme's practices?"

"Hey! I don't suffer as much since we share the pains of our *nervous system. If you knew Tkoukra, you would learn to adapt, like me, to a lot of things! OK! We're friends now so I can tell you what life was like on that cursed star. Anyway, if I didn't, my memories would be carved into* our *head in spite of me and then you might end up becoming crazier than you are, totally confused by the grotesque images you see inside yourself and you would blame them on a more and more incurable madness..."*

In fact, since my return, I had glimpsed strange landscapes in my brain, hazy and muddled, which I was starting to worry about, scared of another attack of fever or dementia.

"I'll give you the gist of it," Kmôhoûn responded. *"After that, the rest won't bother you much when you see it. You'll have the basics that will keep you from being surprised by anything! And so I need to talk to you about my cruel past life..."*

"Good! Tell me something about your former planet..."

"It's a red star that I saw for the last time shining strong, but very tiny, just when the Earth was fat in space like a knurl on one of Bid'homme's spurs. This star is a chaos of blood-colored rocks. There are a few inhabitable valleys hollowed out between steep mountains; black-bottomed valleys with bloody walls under a charcoal sky, or copper depending on the time. The people there lead a life that would chill you to the bone. In those rocky deserts surrounded by the walls of impassable mountains are squeezed throngs of beings like I was, without homes, without shelter of any kind, under the long, abrasive, icy lashes of Northern winds..."

"Are they very different from the people of Earth?"

"No, not at all, they're a lot alike, but dreadfully ugly, disgusting monsters—I felt that today—with animal manes, skin the color of mud and blood, claws like curved swords, made to rip and tear, and bulging, bloodshot, haggard eyes, sometimes full of cowardly terror and other times full of merry cruelty.

"The inhabitable parts of the star are sometimes so crowded with living beings that all the bodies can't lie down in the narrow valleys; they can't stretch out. For days and nights on end, they stay standing up, cramped and pressed together. Their bones stab into the thin skin and lean flesh of each other. At a certain point, blood flows. Then, the Tkoukrians go crazy, start struggling, get their arms free and tear each other apart with their sword-like claws; thousands upon thousands of corpses fall to the ground and rot so fast that, after a few hours, they are liquefied and form a kind of mud. Less than a day after the carnage, crops of beings like them, but weaker, spring up from the organic silt. The horde of the strong who have survived run through this pasture and devour the still warm flesh. They get so drunk on blood that the star itself seems to scream in space. But many of the newcomers escape the massacre and grow unbelievably fast and everything starts over again! Born under such conditions, the inhabitants of Tkoukra are sexless. They do not know the comforts of love and they live only to murder each other. They know nothing but hatred and fear. The worst thing is that in other existences, obviously before degenerating (?), they knew the joys of love and tenderness that are impossible for them in their land of bloody pulp. And the vague memory of sweet, satisfied hopes tortures them to death. Have you heard enough?"

"Oh, yes! Yes... because now the cruelties of Tkoukra are etched into my brain all too clearly, as you said."

And I could not sleep that night, haunted as I was by the vision of the bloody mud star that I did not want to talk about, but that I knew about as if I myself was a Kmôhoûn with claws like curved swords, a Kmôhoûn with bulging, haggard eyes, shining with red and green fires.

IV

I spent six months down in the dumps, coming back to life only on the rare days when Kmôhoûn stayed quiet. A few times I hoped—no! I wanted to hope—that I had gotten rid of the Tkoukrian... or my madness, when the terrible intruder figured it was time to leave me to check for himself— psychically—some detail of earthly life. But after 24 hours, 48 at most, the hated friend came back, unnoticed by me.

I grew awfully skinny; I grew weaker and weaker. I could not stand this double persecution anymore! The insane asylum and the Tkoukrian were too much for a simple neurotic!

I could not get rid of Kmôhoûn, or at least I saw no way of getting rid of him.

So, I decided I would try to escape from Doctor Froin's institution. They had always treated me pretty well—I forgot about Bid'homme on purpose, but I would have to deal with him again soon—and I was relatively free. And I had known, for a very short time, an exquisite woman whose madness was charming to a sad patient like me. I was almost wealthy in my misery. But the bleak nights when the shrill, desperate voices of the women prisoners shrieked, and the painful scenes in the courtyards where the inmates stopped—sometimes—really— being men and turned into terrifying beasts, and Irene's leaving because of me—was it really my fault?—made me hate Vassetot.

So I studied countless escape plans of varying complexity and ended up with the simplest of all.

But before explaining all this, I have to backtrack a little, since I want—God knows why!—you'd think that sometimes I liked to make myself suffer—I want, I said, to tell about the visit from my cousin Roffieux, and the events leading up to the disappearance of my little princess, as well as the different avatars of Sir Bid'homme.

Elzear Roffieux, who was supposed to come see me on the Monday after I woke up in the mental hospital, did not show up at Vassetot until six weeks after I was "cast in the shadows."

He entered my room unannounced, which was pretty smart because. if I had known about his visit, I would have curled up in ball and ruffled myself up—in short, given him a welcome even worse than what he got.

I noticed right away that he was still worried about me. As always he was serious, energetically nice and friendly. I say *energetically* nice, not just nice with a natural, easy, over-flowing niceness. Elzear was above all else a "man of *diuty*" and a "man of character." You could not touch him. He was only nice or generous when he wanted to be. His good grace was calculated; he never gave it away for free. He brought it out when it was convenient, when it was his *diuty* to show it briefly. He paid for some things with this currency, but at their fair price and at the right time.

That day, he came up to me holding out his hand, with a tender—and yes I'll say it, serious—smile which bloated his brown moustache, and flowed into a beard that was a shade darker than it. His pale, respectable baldness clashed nicely with his pink, plump face. His dark blue eyes with their tiring sincerity shined like artificial flowers. His voice was deep and falt like a narrator:

"Well then, my poor Philippe, here you are! The place is no more cheerful than it should be, but your life is on the mend. I see they have noted a great improvement in your condition. As bad luck would have it, you only needed a lot of meditation. In a well-ordered society like our excellent modern world, where liberalism is balanced by unbending justice, everyone must pay his due, at least for a time, and buck up through the hard but helpful and necessary trials and tribulations. What do you think of this establishment where, I promise, you will only have to stay for the time that's necessary?"

"I think it's great, wonderful! I never want to leave!"

A faint glimmer of worry flashed in the eyes of the too sincere apostle. But I continued:

"As far as the anxiety you have seeing me here, I would like to reassure you… but it's you who acted so bravely when you stuck me here, sacrificing all feelings…"

"My dear friend, everything I did was for your own good, this time like the others."

"There was no other way of taking care of me?"

"No."

"I was a dangerous threat?"

"It's a principle of mine never to exaggerate. You were only dangerous to yourself."

He faltered a little saying this. He was hiding something from me—and it cannot be through sensitivity because I knew my Roffieux, I pretty much saw him for what he was—Oh, full of tact and scruples. His words proved this, but, but… Finally, he thought of something—and I have no idea what—that must have tortured him, because his eyes stopped bothering me for a second with that annoying sparkle of blinding sincerity. Now, they looked like the eyes of an old Klepht[29] battling with a reluctant tourist who has purposefully forgotten the name and address of his banker.

"You don't remember anything in particular about that last day in Dieppe—about the week before?" he insisted, reminding me of Bid'homme. "You don't remember anything you did that could have disturbed me and forced me to take such drastic measures to protect you against yourself?"

"I remember absolutely nothing, except a trivial argument with you, and—if I remember right—it was you who started it. We drank a lot of champagne at lunch and you, who are usually so sober, at least in public, were the one who insisted that we drink cocktails at the casino. I guess that's why you gave me the reputation of a boozer here."

He did not look happy with my rudeness; but you might say that he was relieved. So what was he scared of hearing me say? His eyes became supernaturally clear again and full of tender criticism:

"I gave you no such reputation. You yourself will take responsibility for this treatment…"

(In a mental hospital! And with a diet of diluted wine!)

"…I told you a hundred times that you drink too much and it would come back to bite you. But it's not about that. You don't remember the week before?"

Ah yes! I *racolleck*—as Frederic of Villiéville would say—that, a few days before I was committed, when my cousin and his wife were with me at the casino—always at the casino—an old lady who looked like a tired but wealthy harlot—a little gray, of course—anyway, she did not know or care about his legitimate spouse and she took Roffieux's hands and spoke to him, in her soaked voice, about the year 1892 and a certain house located at number 455 Moscow Street. Cousin Elzear was epic. He shoved the overripe hussy and not knowing what to say—him, the cool and brave—shouted at her:

"Aren't you ashamed of yourself, old creature, to bother a man whom… who… could be a father! In 1892, I was just about to get married! I do not know you! I have never known you! *And you promised me yourself…*"

He could not continue, realizing too late how absolutely stupid he was; and the old, luscious tart went away dignified and offended, but not before being a little revenged by pouring a bucket of spiteful names on the sorry Elzear. Out of respect for the casino, she had not vented her full reserve of utmost trash. But Roffieux was splattered and stained with names like "deadbeat," "womanizer" and "pimp," and he was pitiful and sad all evening long. But his wife, who was usually so prude, loved to see him so ashamed, and she kept making fun of his stormy youth and the hot and heavy weather on Moscow Street—Moscow! Ha! Ha! Ha!

She ended up putting me on the same wavelength with her moronic glee, calling out to me every other minute, forcing me to guffaw like an idiot, which I did not want to do at first—so, it was me and not her that Elzear, too infatuated with the dowry of that ignoramus, hounded with his bad mood and skewered with his seething eyes.

I started laughing while thinking about that ridiculous evening.

"What's wrong with you?" Roffieux almost shouted at me.

"Come on! Don't get angry! I was thinking about the old tramp at the casino."

"No! No!" Elzear scolded, "Think of something else to laugh about, especially at my expense, always at my expense, you bum!"

"Look! Now it's you who's going to have to be locked up! You're turning rabid! So, what's on your mind?"

Always at his expense! That's a good one. He was always richer than me, but I was always the one who lent a little, or a lot of, money to him, never to berepaid. I always "respected his goods" and, to speak like the exegetes of Scripture, it never entered my mind to covet his cattle, his donkey... not even, especially not, his wife. Oh! His wife! No way!...

It was strange that, at the very moment when I was picturing that unattractive, grotesquely carnavalesque and misshapen person, Elzear started talking to me about her—and in what a tone, good grief! You would have sworn that my nice cousin thought he was a prosecutor getting a confession out of a diabolical criminal:

"You might like to know," he lectured, "that my wife was very worried about your condition."

He would not stop staring at me. If I were writing a pulp novel, I would say that "his eyes drilled into me." I tried hard to feel guilty of some vile act—anything to make him happy—but my naughty conscience would not blame me for anything... Ha, that! But it was too much! Could Elzear imagine that I had evil designs on Mrs. Roffieux? Is that what my madness was about? Oh! Then the charming man considered me much sicker than I ever was! He should have gotten me a cage in the Agitated wing if he had such suspicions! Really, he was being generous! But no! I slander him: even he could not be as stupid as that. It was impossible! It would be the delusion to beat all delusions!

But yes! He thought I was upset and feeling guilty! His eyes flashed again and looked more and more vindictive. He could have borrowed them from a cheap paperback! I was in a fine situation!

He opened his big mouth and boomed melodramatically, "*She* is here!"

He did not add, "Tremble! I know everything!" But it was obvious that he was waiting for me to throw myself face down on the floor or, if I was too hardened, to say that lightning just struck two inches from my boots.

I was able to get over my initial surprise and muttered an "uhuh'" of such perfectly sincere apathy that his wrath turned into a kind of disappointed daze. Yes, disappointed, really. He was totally reassured—so be it! But his opinion did not last long!

For a little while, though, he was in doubt. He knew, maybe by experience, that all cowardly lechers are capable of hypocrisy. And even more melodramatically, he announced that he was going to get HER. He wanted HER to see me, for me to see HER! It was the confrontation scene!

The beast was much lewder than I could have dreamed and had never believed in the madness that I was forced to believe in, at least sometimes! He had brought me here only after thinking I was drunk, wasted on stupefying alcohol. He came to see me during my first days of isolation only because he knew I was in a coma after a violent fit that he thought was dangerous. In my lair, he was safe—unless he might seem perverted—and reassured by the idea that I could not budge an inch. He had not come back until now, when the news of my recovery sounded too good to be true. I had obviously gotten my strength back, and I could think of giving him a well-deserved, beastly thrashing. But jealousy had worked him over too much. Jealousy! He wanted to know—and that's why he had to come to Vassetot. Jealousy!! Really, he had a very low opinion of my tastes! In fact, Mrs. Roffieux, my cousin by marriage, was unusually nice to me for awhile. I was so ungrateful! I saw that only now, but I did not feel guilty about my crudeness.

Yes, jealousy had worked over the Othelloesque Elzear. My God! If his wife were infatuated with someone else, Roffieux would become the victim of dark designs that would end in divorce! If she were successful, however, and I became the legal owner of her sickening beauty as well as a pretty, very pretty collection of cash, bonds and other lovely papers—those things that you never forget once you have fondled them and whose loss plunges the heart of a common sense man into eternal sorrow! I would leave triumphantly from the house of Doctor Froin if I could take away from this lousy Elzear all earthly joy and leave him with nothing but his eyes to cry with and a pittance of 30,000 *livres* or so of income, the product of his flour mills and some cheap property! Ha! He would fight to the finish, to martyrdom, rather than be reduced to poverty! So, he was right to come and sound me out before confronting me with my accomplice? A few innocent kicks, a harmless meeting of my boot and his silverside, as a butcher friend of mine would say? And I would not have time to do much damage: he would have posted guards behind the door. (In fact, I'll use some slang I heard in the prison hallway—the door was simply *pushed up*.)

Elzear, who was always a man in control, an enemy of all outbursts, of all buffoonery, left waving his arms in the air.

Five minutes later, he came back, dragging a tall, skinny woman, young—but not so very pretty!—too blonde, a blonde between fresh butter and a towhead, pale blue eyes, skin like Paris milk on the face of a mannequin. It was obvious that she thought she was beautiful, distinguished and poetic, but her actual look of shocked innocence made her totally ugly and unlikeable.

Raoula Roffieux, née Fromage[30]—yes, Raoula! (Wouldn't some parents deserve the cangue[31], that wildly Chinese torture, when they saddle a child, who already has the most awful last name, with a first name as annoying as it is

108

unheard of!) Raoula! Raoula Roffieux, then, was the daughter of a fertilizer merchant, comfortably a millionaire, and a former actress of small town success. She had a very special upbringing. Born in the country, she attended, until the age of 19, the young ladies' classes in a big city in the North and took individual lessons in "urbanity" from elegant lady-instructors who had surely got their lovely manners from intimate relations with robot-podiatrists and their language from encyclopedias edited by American dentists or the inventors of snake oil who look at their reflections in the baldness of exotic diplomats. When her father was loaded enough with different metals, he decided to work on a wider stage and to abandon to other capitalists his Artificial Guano business whose motto, "On the winds of Las Chinchas," made him dream of the few Peruvian poets lost in Panthes (capital of the department of Seine-et-Scarpe). Raoula had just finished her studies in Paris with a Romanian princess (?), former laureate of the Conservatory of Vierzon who had been booed off many grand European stages and become directress of a model school. This school of perfecting where they taught young girls older than 16 "Salon Philosophy, Elite Manners, Conservative Respectability" and different *sciences* like that, finished transforming the already stiff Raoula into a first class mechanical doll. Every time you saw her—depending on your mood—you were either dumbstruck with admiration or you really wanted to slap her.

She left the Barbaresco Institute with an honor's prize for a dissertation on "Veiled Sincerity." a Certificate of Merit for the "Half-Haughty Walk," another prize for "Gestures to Keep at a Distance" and another Certificate of Merit for "Kindness to Inferiors."

With the Romanian princess (?), the only pronunciation allowed was that of the Conservatory of Vierzon because almost everyone knew that the French language developed, in the beginning, not around the center of the Seine Valley—as some illiterates believed—but rather between Romorantin and Aurillac.[32] (Some early playwrights did not forget this truth.)

In the Institute's brochure, there was a theory on vowels—front and back—that I will not try to explain here. Besides, I never really understood it. Raoula never excelled in the courses on "Rational pronunciation." She was not very musical, but really wanted an alluring and respectable voice. From the start, she was impervious to *mathematical euphony*. She cried a lot over this! She should have given up instead of shocking people properly by abusing the front—the frightfully front—vowels that are so common and vulgar, to pronounce all the vowels back, and even to change almost all of them into an open *a* followed—or not—by an aspirate *h*. She also set her *r*s to sea.

She said *bahrr* and *dahrr*[*] as they advise… somewhere. She even went so far as to whittle down Greek terms and ask for a *clyterr*[**] when she had stomach troubles.

So it is thanks to the lovely efforts of Princess Barbaresco that my cousin by marriage, prude and blushing a little under her pale yellow hair, spoke the following sentence that I am transcribing the best I can:

"Yah wahn't bahlieve, dahrr cahsahn, hahw sahrrrry Ah wahs to fahnd yah wahrre hahrr in thahs rrahnahwned baht ghahstly estahblishment ahf Dahctahrr Frrahn's!"

Since my phonetic spelling isn't clear, I have to translate: "You won't believe, dear cousin, how sorry I was to find you were here in this renowned but ghastly establishment of Doctor Froin's!"

Elzear glared at us and I knew what he was thinking. He still had not caught Raoula. The embarrassment and blushing of this huge doll could have been caused by the fact that she had not had time to prep herself from head to foot and she was sorry to have to show up like she did in a wrinkled dress, summer boots and a hat that did not match her accessories. But her voice did not tremble; she babbled her little speech

---

[*] Bear and dear
[**] Clyster, i.e. enema

taking her time, separating her syllables, stressing certain words: *sarrrry, rrahnahnwed, ghahstly*.

As for me, my indifference was almost offensive. I answered like I did not care in the least:

"Thank you for worrying about me, cousin, but this institution is not so bad. I like it here a lot. The place is full of wonderful people."

Was I really becoming a little crazy living here? That would be great for good old Elzear. But what if I were only faking it?

He wanted to know if his wife and I were in cahoots and he decided on a kind of naïve proof.

"Oh!" he said, "But aren't you cousins cold to each other! You haven't even shaken hands!"

There! Maybe he was going to nab us. We'd waited too long—or too short—to shake hands, or if we did it too strong or too weak, it would betray the guilty parties—if we were guilty. But the handshake proved absolutely nothing; it was completely cordial—a real handshake between cousins by marriage. But Roffieux did not look reassured. He was totally amazed, totally stupid.

And yet, a new source of energy lit up little flames in his eyes, which became distant and bleary. Seeing him camped in front of me with his hands in his pockets, his shoulders back, his head up in challenge, I figured that he was going to play his ace:

"My good man," he said to me, "you look so much better. Doctor Froin was right. You must want to leave here and I would not want to see you go moldy in such a place. But you need someone to take care of you. Whatever your problem might be, you have had a rough time of it and being alone so long has done you no good. So, I have come up with a way to get you out of here—well! Not right away, not right away! You'll have to pull yourself together! You want freedom and you need the protection of a strong and reliable affection. I have even spoken about my project with the person whose good will it hinges on. You know that Jeanne Stolz, who married Fernand Lacoste, has been a widow for more than a year now, and you know how strange and wonderful that kind woman is, pretty and rich, too!"

Elzear said this ceremoniously!

"You remember that she married Lacoste, who was not much better looking than a gorilla and acted like a bear, but it really wasn't because of the tremendous passion he had for her as much as a result of a friend's gossip. This Pylades told her that Fernand was terminally ill and that whoever agreed to marry him would be a pure and simple sick-nurse two thirds of the time. The pretty wife devoted herself to this lovely life and made Fernand Lacoste last five whole years, which seemed miraculous to everyone who knew him. She is much more than a sister of mercy. She is the Lover of Sufferers. She only feels romantic between a compress and a bottle of medicine. For you, she will change her program a little since you don't need a compress, but you will need, thank Heavens, to follow a diet and take a bunch of sedatives, and she loves that!"

God! How gallantly he said these things!

And Jeanne Lacoste, or rather Jeanne Stoltz, was an old flame of mine! Clever enough, dumb Roffieux! If there weren't my princess with her hyacinth pink complexion, it would be very tempting! Why not say yes for now to Sir Elzear and wait until later to explain myself to Jeanne, who is kindness itself. She would be perfectly able to help me free my poor Irene and cure her, too! And Roffieux, who had me locked up only because he was jealous, I saw now, would get me released right away, *right away*, no matter what he said— knowing that I would be busy with some woman who was not his—especially a rich and fair-minded woman ready to open her purse to the new cousin when he needed funds for some industrial or agricultural venture! See, Elzear was not only a giant flour miller known from the Valley of Orne to the Valley of Liane, but also a land owner and agriculturalist. And when he took a risk on an unsure affair—since he was born cautious and dealt carefully with Raoula's capital as well as his own—

he happily searched for willful backers who were easy to keep calm in case of bad luck.

I could soon be free, maybe tomorrow even! So I was quickly going to say that I agreed, that it was a done deal—using only a little well-deserved irony for Roffieux's questionable and somewhat offensive behavior. This desire for innocent revenge was poorly timed because just when I was about to fire off my harmless, goose feather arrow tipped with the "stamp of my stupidity," (as the grandiose Prud'homme would say): "Well now! All industries are open to you. You're going even farther than Madame de Foy. You're joining the pharmaceutical marriage with the money marriage!"

At that very moment, Leonard came in to announce the imminent arrival of Doctor Froin.

Roffieux stopped listening to me. He adjusted his cuffs, stroked his beard and took a comb from his pocket to fix himself up in front of the mirror with a stylish hairdo that any important agriculturalist should have.

Raoula took advantage of her husband's preoccupation to come up to me again and slip in very quietly, very quickly, but very clearly:

"Say no! There's blackmail in it. He threatened Madame Lacoste to force her to accept. He wants her money and knows you're weak… He knows something about her… I'll tell you later!"

My bubble burst right away. I was going to be a prisoner for a long time if I could not get out of the mental hospital, except by being Roffieux's partner in crime against a woman whom I had loved.

When Elzear finally turned back to us after a final stroke of his comb, and saw that we were at a respectable distance from each other, he came back to his idea of marriage and said to me triumphantly, but half-worriedly:

"Well then! What do you say to my project? Doesn't it sound great? You'll agree to it, won't you?"

I was truly sorry to hear myself forced to answer, "My dear Elzear, I do not want to get married, even to such a ravishing nurse!"

Roffieux caught Raoula looking at me. It was not the tender glance of a lover; no, it was much worse. In the young woman's pale pupil a dirty look *properly* sparkled, which I had never seen before. It was the look of an expert, lecherous dame. The husband turned pale and his nostrils flared. There were a few seconds of silence that seemed to last an hour. Then Roffieux pulled himself together and spoke like he was reciting a tragic poem:

"Put on your gloves, Raoula, put on your gloves, I tell you! We're leaving! It's late. We shall talk with Doctor Froin in his office. See you soon, Veuly! Shall we go? Are you coming, Raoula? Raoula, are you coming?"

My cousin was always formal with his wife, just like a Duc or the engineers of novels for "society people."

But the doctor came in just when Elzear was waving goodbye to me, which could have meant, "Goodbye, false friend!" or "We will meet again, villain!"

Old Froin always looked nice, simple, and kind of shy like all truly sincere people. He had none of that macho cockiness of nasty little brats like Elzear who just pretend to be sincere—no eyes twinkling with false loyalty, none of those hard, brutal manners that the jerks thought were "tough love." In Froin's eyes was unconditional kindness. And he looked a little sad, like good people do when they are irritated by the frustrating antics of human clowns.

I could see right away that he did not get along with Elzear. He nodded quickly to Raoula, very politely and not at all flattering. He was a free man who did not care about the noble jerks' anger or their hypocritical politeness—or their leprous urbanity.

"Well! Monsieur, you've had a chance to speak with your cousin," he said flatly and quietly to the loyal Elzear. "What do you think of him?"

I was very surprised to see the flour miller's radiant blue eyes darken and show signs of manly grief:

"A! I don't want to talk about it! I don't think he's well at all, Doctor, not at all!"

Raoula looked outraged by his shamelessness, but did not say a word.

"That's very surprising," said the Doctor. "This morning I thought he was calmer than ever, completely on the right track."

"Maybe so! But you weren't here while I was talking with him just now. I haven't seen him so disturbed in a long time. He needs constant attention…"

"You don't have to worry about that… But how can my presence alone make him better so quickly? I am not a magician or a hypnotist—too bad maybe."

And Doctor Froin examined Elzear like a curious painter amused by his model's character. Roffieux's whole face lit up with a bright, shining sincerity that the doctor seemed to dislike more and more.

"Well," Old Froin continued, talking to me now, "you were excitable and violent during your cousin's visit? But you seem very calm now."

I saw that he suddenly looked concerned. His eyebrows lowered together and one of his cheeks had a little tic:

"Tell me honestly. Have you been feeling those… morbid fears—you know, those fears that you haven't talked about for a long time, since my first visit—even though I asked you about them… You know what I mean?"

It was obvious that he was referring to that stupid "I'm inhabited like a wormy fruit!" but that he did not want to talk about it in front of Elzear—he did not want to supply arms to my cousin—the good man!

Luckily, Kmôhoûn kept himself quiet inside me and I could answer in total control of myself:

"No! Not in the least! And of course, you know that I'd had a terrible shock that day and I was talking a little off the cuff, without thinking!"

115

"Ah! That's better! And those are not the words of a neurotic!" cried the doctor, who had such a kind and happy smile that I was really sorry that I lied—but I had to!

"Anyway," Elzear insisted a little dryly, "I think you should look after him more than ever. I want him to get better!"

"Monsieur," the Doctor replied very calmly, "I have taken care of psychological problems for 35 years, and you can be sure that I am not careless with my patients. It does me no good to delay a cure—very much the opposite! And in this case, the patient is very close to being cured."

"Oh! My husband didn't for a minute doubt your *ahsperience* and your skill, *Dahctorr*," sopranoed Raoula when she realized Roffieux's blunder. She gave me another kind of dirty look since I could not wink at her. "He only wants to say that he is counting on you to finish healing our cousin who still seems so very, very tired!"

And both of them left after nodding to the Doctor and weakly shaking my hand. If Old Froin were not there, would I still have been given this priceless favor? They were forced into a semi-friendliness only to prove before a witness their noble and worthy affection for a relative who dishonored them.

After seeing them out, the Doctor came back into my room. At first, he said nothing. He shook his head, preoccupied, pouted, a little disgusted, and got lost in thought, then he asked me out of the black:

"Are Monsieur and Madame Roffieux your only living relatives?"

"No, I have a brother who lives in Paris… sometimes!"

"Ah! Very good! But why didn't you tell me that before? He's the one I should be talking to—not your cousins! Give me his address, I'm going to write to him—and keep your hopes up!"

Yes, I had my hopes up. Unfortunately, as I told the good doctor, my brother traveled a lot, with and without his wife…

in Egypt or India. Was he at home—in Esna—or in Mathura[33]? When would he get Old Froin's letter?

If it were not for Raoula's confession or lie (?), I would surely be on the verge of freedom!

I had a pretty gloomy evening, even if Leonard distracted me a little by telling me about the love affairs of a nurse who was very smitten by Bid'homme—that pretty heart!

But secretly, I was tortured by Kmôhoûn who was now pushing me to escape and as soon as possible—or he would *raise Hell!*

V

The following weeks, the rotten Kmôhoûn did not give me a minute of peace. The savage Tkoukrian perfected his art of persecution so well that, one fine night, I told him that I had had enough and I was going to do whatever he wanted. Too bad if *we* were caught, if the guards abused *us*, if *we* got what was coming to *us*! I did not want to hear that wicked voice anymore urging me to do all kinds of dangerous and violent things... to revolt—and even to commit rude and insane actions that would lead me straight to the Agitated Wing.

Didn't I dance one time—been forced to dance on my hands in front of Leonard who was caught between his friendship for me and his duty to report my deeds and then did not know what saint to pray to?

Another day, didn't I have to, despite myself, take advantage of a short absence of my guardian, who had left the door of my room open, to go prowling in the yard in the heart of the famous arbors? In one of these little arbors, I found a hideous nurse who was long and skinny like a Syrian nag. I had always hated that Olympia Chignoux, Bid'homme's ex-lover and the only female guard. (Ah! I'd forgotten Mademoiselle Celestine Bouffard!) I met her in all the dark corners where there was shadows and mystery. It was her poetic nature, I guess. Anyway, she was not completely young anymore and was totally cross-eyed with the shrewish face of a Salvation Army colonel. Well! The filthy Kmôhoûn injected me, little by little, with such a raging lust that I started playing the most obscene games with her. She was a little shocked—and the scene ended in the last outrage that she could put up with before losing her temper, but not all her decency, even for a beauty like her who was used to these kinds of compliments. Mercy! That old nymph must have had wooden legs! I had bruises!

And Kmôhoûn cried out, "*Ahh! What joy! This hasn't happened to me since I stayed in...*" such and such constellation!

Finally—and I will not talk about a whole series of the Tkoukrian's less vivid evil pranks—one day, I woke up around 2 p.m. with only my nightshirt on in a room where, luckily, I was all alone except for one person, the younger of the young Mortebranche girls (mentioned above)—a pretty woman around 30, protected by strict principles, to whom I testified—without knowing how the words got out of my mouth—like a sailor, calling (yes!) a spade a spade and certain acts by their true names, like that goon Boileau-Despreaux[34] advised us do—or pretty close. The worst thing was that my scanty clothing made me illustrate my words. Leonard saved the day. He frantically rushed in, threw himself at the damsel's knees and begged her not to ruin him by informing the Director about his neglectful surveillance and my disgusting speech spiced up with waving and shaking. He even ended up making her laugh and the good girl said that she would take pity on the poor patient.

But Kmôhoûn threatened to make me get it going with the girls all over again when Doctor Froin was around or at least some cruel devil who would tell the boss all about my dirty deeds. And I knew he would do it.

So, one night, around 1 a.m., when I finally could not stand some revolting scene that he was showing me as one of my own future escapades that I would accomplish within a week—I gave up:

"OK! That's enough; let's go! But you know, if they catch us, there'll be Hell to pay!"

"*Let's go,*" Kmôhoûn answered very calmly.

The Tkoukrian must have been a locksmith or a burglar in some other incarnation; and his despicable mind worked on my poor body with such force that I, who was so clumsy and hopeless at everything mechanical, took apart four huge locks and six *outside* bolts and a bunch of complicated security devices in ten minutes flat, without a sound, using only what tools were at hand.

There we were standing in the courtyard, in the murky, shimmering moonlight.

"*Don't shake like that,*" Kmôhoûn grumbled. "*The filthy people are all asleep!*"

Not all of them! I saw a fat human mass slip out of the shadows and come toward us; it looked familiar to me. Was it Mademoiselle Celestine Bouffard? It did not take long to find out:

"Is that you, Louĕdin?" sang the unforgettable Dieppe contralto of the Kallipygos[35] nurse. (Louĕdin was one of the guards of the Agitated Wing, an old clown who later became a monkey handler and then a prison guard in Montagne d'Argent in Guyana.) "Gosh, *hafta* wait fer you! I *ben* on the street fer 20 minutes, outside and no street even! Fer cryin' out loud! Course it's not *his* skin left out in the cold!" she yelled, grabbing me by my thin goatee. (Louĕdin had a foot-long and bushy beard!) "Hey, who's this dirty *burgle* who's out *warkin'* at *nigh* in the grounds? Aha! Ain't possible! It's Monsieur Veuly from the privates! 'Deed it is! Leonard ain't so stewed to let you wander round in the *nigh* at this hour!"

All of a sudden, she giggled. "Oh! Could it be that you have *sumthin'* in mind that you're *out in about* so late—or early? Cause it's mornin'! Who's you tailin'? You can tell me. I'm not one of them *pressies*!"

There I was, all embarrassed. I did not know what to say to this hefty dame. Kmôhoûn suggested to me, "*We have to amuse her for a while. Afterward, we will figure out how to get rid of her. Let me do it!*"

I wanted to say no because I was afraid of his Tkoukrian methods, but he did not give me time. I was totally amazed to hear myself speak without me—I was hard and rude and snickery—and before I realized I had opened my mouth…

"Tell me then, fat girl! Do you have any cognac in your room?"

"So it is you, Monsieur Veuly, who's *tarlkin'* to me at this hour, you so *proper* and a li'l proud sometimes? Oh, my word! I like you better like this! Fer sure I have some hooch in my nest. Well, not liters, but a tiny li'l what's left of the bottle fer... when that a patient needs to be a li'l revived. Come on!"

She took me by the hand to guide me—and whispered, "Ah! You li'l pig! So that's why you was lookin' at me funny t'other time with your eyes all *prickled*! I never would've guessed? *Such a decin' fella!*"

She held no illusions about herself—and modesty is always a virtue. Kmôhoûn was having fun now in my normal voice:

"I'm not made of stone—and neither are you!"

I was a puppet on the Tkoukrian strings and was soon playing freely with the vast rotundities of Mademoiselle Bouffard, which fully backed up my talk.

"If you're so cocky, you don't need *corgnac*," the Himalayan Infanta sighed. "Whatya gonna do after, huh?"

"I'll be tender and respectful. Let's still go see the little cognac—not to have a drink but at least to make a toast. Ho! A toast! Eh, Celestine?" Disgusting Kmôhoûn!

"Oh! But no! That's not fair! You really don't wanna! Ha! He's a torture! Lemme open the door."

We arrived. The little room that Mademoiselle Bouffard's imposing charms used as a nightly jewelry box looked like a hallway arrested in development. It was glowing with a pink and blonde light, just like the occupant, and was almost completely blocked up by a gigantic iron bed, sized to fit its precious cargo.

"Can't make a sound!" Celestine hissed quietly. "Hurry and take *orff* yer shoes!"

I did what she said, confused and surprised to be there, already regretting what I was sure to do. The plump nurse took hers off too. And since she did not want her long skirt and baggy sleeves to wake anyone up she took off her dress and blouse and stood there in her petticoat and corset. (One must respect one's neighbors' sleep.) The landscape I saw impressed me despite myself.

"There's only one chair. *Set* down, I'll *set* where I can... Hold it! On the bed!" Mademoiselle Bouffard continued, "*Than* it's not alright. Yer *mo'* close, so open the nightstand: that's my cellar!"

The "what's left of the bottle" was a healthy amount where my friendly hostess came from! More than a pint of "what's left!" We toasted very carefully, but often and fast. In ten minutes, the bottle had spoken its final word. In the meantime, Kmôhoûn kept me busy. One polish after another and the landscape grew and cast off its useless accessories. Just when the view was almost panoramic, my Tkoukrian, who seemed to know the sentimental Celestine better than I, whispered softly through my mouth, "Don't you have any more cognac? Say, for after?"

"Fer after... what? Ha! Dog! Yeah, there's another teardrop *somewheres*. I see what you mean with yer... after!"

Kmôhoûn was feeling good about his success and understood that where we were headed any new hesitation could be an insult. The last white mists dissipated under our careless attention and—onward into the panorama! A smooth and downy Sierra crowned with pink heights like the dawn—a bigger range, more lily white and smoother still—and maybe also forests—came into view.

"Oh! That's nice, *'cuz* I'm scared of you!" the lovely Celestine murmured. "Ah! My sweet!"

Of course I was only a little forced to explore and I started really enjoying my discoveries: I was ruined in their splendor—and what a wonderful catastrophe...

I'll never again say anything bad about people who are a little forceful.

It was unbelievable what Kmôhoûn did with me. I had been pretty depraved in my time, but, you know, I was no Turk, especially since my 30ies started mixing water with the wine—a relatively generous wine. And now I knew nothing anymore! Nana Sahib, Soulouque[36] and such characters of

122

"Humorous Stories" were children next to me. Oh! I was not proud. Instead I felt scared… Thankfully Mademoiselle Bouffard was not a girl to ask for mercy—on the contrary—and I shuddered to think of the trouble I would get in if I were back to my normal self!

But how did the psychic partnership of Kmôhoûn transform my physical organism so much? Yes, I was scared—and even angry and fed up: *it was anti-medical!* Unlike the guard François, I had an immeasurable respect for medicine, like all hypochondriacs.

Between attacks, the unflustered Celestine went to look for the teardrop of cognac. It was a teardrop, wept by a mammoth. She found the three fourths hidden under some laundry that she had to sweetly scent.

"Hey! I thought the cellar was in the night stand?"

"There's the cellar and there's the store." Subtle distinction.

A diabolical idea, worthy of Kmôhoûn, crossed my mind and I asked, "Well! And Louëdin?" But if I thought I could upset Celestine, I was terribly naïve.

"Louëdin?" she replied coldly, "It'll be for sh… Ya know, he can scratch his own belly fer now. When he doesn't see me in the courtyard, he'll know it's a no go.

But, in the long run, the alcohol and our feats of prowess got the better of the nurse's rich nature. Thanks to our cleverness, the strong young lady had drunk nearly a liter and a half of hooch while we (Kmôhoûn and I were sober as camels) had a little less than a quarter pint. Mademoiselle Bouffard fell into a heavy sleep, *lassata nec satiata*[37], since she was still sighing between hiccups, just before closing her eyes, "Ah! Dirty Dog! You should be famous! Let's meet up again—ya wanna?"

Kmôhoûn had reached his goal, *"Now, let's move out!"* he ordered.

It was lucky that the night watchmen were so inconsistent at Doctor Froin's! Without that wonderful neglect, they would have caught us 20 times over: we had left the door ajar!

Suddenly I shivered in fright—in horror! I could barely keep myself from screaming. I had just noticed a slot in the wall like the one in my room! I knew that Celestine guarded my princess, but—stupidly—I could not imagine that she slept as close to Irene as Leonard did to me. It was blasphemy! The pure sleep and blessed dreams of the Exquisite next to the drunken snoring and obscene nightmares of the erotic Bouffard!

Nothing but a thin wall between the beautiful Fay and the crude tart!

I had made myself famous in such a sorry way only a few feet away from Irene! Oh! If only I were wrong! If by some extraordinary and fateful arrangement the hooch drinker watched over my princess only during the day and slept somewhere far away during the night! If next door were just another nurse's room, I would feel all right! I knew that it was crazy but I wanted to see her with all my heart. I forgot about Kmôhoûn and I very quietly opened the slot...

Atrocity! Irene was there, too near! I was not a few feet but a few inches away from her! I became completely terrified in a different way when the overexcited Tkoukrian (appallingly!) groaned inside me:

"Oh! She's the one I want! And you too, you want her! That's your princess, whose picture I've seen in my head! She's so much more beautiful and more thrilling than her pale reflection tarnished by your dull and worthless soul! Let's go get her!"

I desperately held him back. Kmôhoûn threatened to make me scream so loudly that I would wake up all the guards. I did not want to—I would not surrender!

But something revolting happened. My body obeyed my sinister enemy more than me. And, despite my agony and my fury, it was obvious that the lousy machine also wanted to take me to Irene. And it was the machine that enslaved my soul, changed it as it pleased and made it a Tkoukrian soul!

My princess! I did not see her like before, radiant with the beauty of dreams. I imagined her in lewd positions—I caught myself thinking: *deliciously* lewd! And many other frightening words came to mind.

Desire took hold of me completely: take the key! We found it in the fatty's pocket after searching her roughly and thanklessly treating like a bulky package! We did not have to worry about waking her up; she was sleeping it off!

We forgot all about her once the door was closed again. We were in the dark. Quick, a match! The key was already turning in *the* lock. We had entered *the* room.

O Irene! She was beautiful, cursedly beautiful! Oh! Was it true? Lustfully beautiful!

I had to have her and... what? Grind her and rip her open! Ah! "I will have you!" I growled nasty words, filth that made me feel *painfully* good. I went to her; she was sleeping deeply.

The worst was done! Like the Spaniard in Richepin's story[38], I knew "sin with the eyes, crime with the eyes!"

She was naked! And I had uncovered her! Leaning over her, my eyes got drunk on her! I felt ashamed but delighted, especially since there was something wild, something animal, could I say *wonderfully hideous*, in this ideally beautiful body.

O, that smooth, blossoming chest, those firm, delicate mounds! Those soft, hollow bends! Then the lyre's curve! Those fine, fleshy lengths, those midnight blue shadows and those lightly coppered pinks!

But the smell of that maddening flesh enraged us, Kmôhoûn and me, and—suddenly—it was bestial and marvelous, a wildly exquisite rape. Could I have done it without Kmôhoûn?

She woke up, struggled and then submitted. She shook with a spasm, and then suddenly, too late—I was going to say: fortunately too late—her whole body revolted, her whole being, which was stronger than me. I rolled onto the floor and sobered up for a minute. But Kmôhoûn—maybe it was only Kmôhoûn—spurred me on again. I did not think that my fall made too much noise, so I threw myself upon Irene again. She pushed me back... She had recognized me! She looked sad and so angry that she was speechless; you would have thought that she had totally come back to her senses.

"Oh!" she cried out, "It's you! Filthy coward! You, a coward? You!"

Tired of it all, but goaded on by Kmôhoûn, I became very worried about what she might say! I twisted her arm and crushed her. I was going to tame her again!

She screamed in anger and pain...

For a few seconds, I could faintly hear quick footsteps in the long, endless hallway, but I did not care much. I was going to triumph again, I was triumphing again... when my neck was clamped by some kind of vise. Then I was lifted up like a wisp of straw, shaken out, planted on my feet and shaken again...

I wanted to fight but it was a lost cause!

The head guard, Dornemain, ex-military, a giant with a flat nose, a Neanderthal with a gorilla's jaw, held me with only one arm as if I were a three-year old child. My angry struggle amused him—that was all.

Madame Robinet, the head nurse, (how impressive these titles were under such circumstances!) watched the scene self-satisfied and dour.

"Ha! My little rat!" Dornemain shouted. "Ha! My little bastard! Ha! My dirty little dirtying dirtball! Snot the first time for this son of a toad! He's the one who made that super work for me in D ward. For a larksmith with a vice, there ain't just one! I couldn't really *sespected*, I couldn't even *esamined* the door of his sty! He's a pet of the administration! Can't bother Monsieur Veuly, says this one, gots to give him everthing he wants, says that one. And he's got better, they're telling us, gonna leave soon, they warn us! Course he is! I'm gonna go see Doctor Froin with his most calm inmate, his inoffensive, his specialized case that's... a belly like an ass! We caught you in position, as they say..." (I guessed by his strange voice that Dornemain was citing his authors.) "Bid'homme is a jerk like they say? Mebbe, but he knows his work. He *brieved* me: Veuly! Nuthin' but a *prack*, a swine, a *bover*! What he needs

126

is a kick in the ass, the coat of conduct, the jet in the mouth and a good soaking. He knows these *unnerneaths*, Bid'homme does, nuthin' more to say!"

The head guard stressed his words by shaking me enough to bring down the mast.

Madame Robinet broke in for me: "Now, Monsieur Dornemain, I know you're very *ortraged* but don't *ferget* that he's a patient. It's not a vice, it's an *abration*. He din't choose it. It could've been the *archeduchess* of the *morganartic* palatines or me myself..." Madame Robinet puffed out her chest. In spite of her apparent learning and her respectability as a mature lady, she imagined herself—hypothetically—attacked by such flattering frenzy. "...or *me myself* and it would've been the same old story. Can't brutalize him, you understand!"

"OK! OK!" Dornemain groaned. "But I can still put this li'l one in his cell for the night... And *tomorra*, *wartch* out for the *warter*!"

We went back across the courtyard, Kmôhoûn and I, much more quickly than we came. When I lost my breath or tried to slow down a little, Dornemain kneed me in my lower back and I miraculously sped up. And how to explain this: I was both outraged, swollen with rage and soft as a kidskin glove—desperate and sorry beyond all possible measures—and I also started laughing hysterically?

Maybe Kmôhoûn was making fun of me by humiliating me at the worst possible moment and he figured my defeat and my anger were too funny. There was no doubt about it; but that was not all. I thought that Madame Robinet's *lingo* was meant for my personal amusement.

We went through the door where I had come out and stopped in front of a real fortress gate. Huge iron bars and armor-plated double doors screamed in the night. We entered a low vaulted corridor at the end of which more metal doors glowed behind a small gnome-faced guard swing a lamp.

Soon Dornemain opened one of the cells and launched me in with his boot. After that, he closed it up. The locks made sinister music. My executioner's steps faded away and the dull clang of the double doors told me that the moral avenger was again in the open air! And the iron prison slept.

I groped around in the dark. My cell was tiny: I stretched out my arms and touched the door with one hand and the padded wall with the other and then found that my room was as long as it was wide. Bending over, I felt a kind of bed with webbing but no mattress.

I sat down and waited for the day, which took centuries to come. Alone, in the dark, my awful glee and my rage died down and I was soon plunged into abject misery.

What had I done?! O Kmôhoûn, you did not make me feel crazy, you made me feel cruel! It was your fault, your ugly, shameful fault, you filthy savage from a star of puss and blood. Now Irene was lost to me forever! Irene! Irene!

"*Well, don't be as stupid as you usually are!*" the Tkoukrian answered. "*Your lover boy cries won't echo in here: it's a padded cell! So, you didn't see, did you, since you were all gaga over her, that thanks to your cowardly crime—what a good joke!—thanks to the turmoil that her fear and, if you'd like, her wrath caused, your princess with pig's milk skin was cured of her insanity. You are—or rather I am—her benefactor.*"

"Shut up, you revolting elemental pest!"

"*I am not a pest or an elemental, to use the language of your ignorant sub-occultists; and you know that perfectly well. I am a man like you, from another planet—that's the only difference—and from a planet better than yours, even though the life they lead there is more miserable.*"

"From a planet of asexual cannibals who know only hatred and fear!"

"*If I were asexual, I guess I made up for it tonight. You don't even thank me for the reputation of a warrior that you owe entirely to me. You seduced Celestine Bouffard and didn't you see that the venerable Madame Robinet, the witness of your prowess, thinks you are a very nice creep and that you would only have had to give the sign and... What! That dignified beauty! You weren't tempted?*"

"Be quiet, pig!"

"*I'm going to be quiet for now. But think about it. Am I such a monster after all? I'm a good friend! I'm not ashamed of you like you are of me. I'm your brother!*"

"Well then, let me forget about you for awhile."

"*OK! I'm going to take a trip for a week or two. Aren't I nice? I'm going to go back to your famous Paris where I recently spent a few very nice days and nights. I'll leave you to Vassetot and the courtesy of adorable Bid'homme. (I didn't tell you that?) I love your Paris, especially the Maubert quarter and even more the Théâtre de l'Ambigu. Now there's a theater! I feel at home there! And when you leave, ha ha, you can misbehave, even when you're just an astral body. Unseen, unknown! Known, yes, however! (Or at least suspected!) I gave out some dreams there that were kind of... vivid and a little sad to a few beautiful, romantic ladies who were totally available, strangely enough. And the middle class! I tried them out too, but it's not so good!*

"*If I didn't feel like I was in school inside you, I would skedaddle out of Doctor Froin's and go party in Paris without even kissing a body! But I haven't finished my lessons. When I've learned what I need to know from you, good old grouchy mental patient, and then possessed one or two emperors, a half dozen kings and a few Presidents of the Republic in order to be totally in the know, I've decided to disturb no one anymore and to be the happiest ghost that ever haunted people at night (you know what I mean!)—the beauties of the night and, sometimes, for a change, the wildest ringleaders, girls or women!*

"*But I'll miss you. I like you a lot in spite of your gloomy thanklessness and your rudeness to a pal. I'll come visit you sometimes, at least to keep up your reputation of tough gladiator that I've just earned for you. And so, good night. I've no taste for violins. I do hope that they will have freed you by the time I get back.*"

Although I was cooped up in the worst padded cell I could possibly imagine, I soon felt wonderfully free and alone. Kmôhoûn had left: happy hunting!

But my satisfaction did not last long. I waited impatiently for the day, and in fear, too! What was going to happen to me? If only Bid'homme was not told before Doctor Froin! And what would the Doctor say to me? Would his kindness and generosity keep him from looking on me as a wretch or the most degenerate of crazy brutes? I was flooded with shame and disgust! Maybe in the end it would be better to be tortured by Bid'homme than to suffer good old Froin's scolding.

Who knows, maybe, if the dwarf inflicted his evil treatments like he was sure to do if he came first, the good Director would take pity on me?

He might think I was punished enough and spare me the harsh language I deserved...

There was a steel blue glow in the cell from a small window. Slowly, slowly it whitened. I thought about absurd and confused things: about La Place de la Roquette, about Russian penal colonies, about pontoons anchored in polar harbors, about the guillotine, about people who came into a cell around this time in the cold early morning: "your appeal has been denied!" about hapless men forgotten in a mine after a cave in and who see the light of day only through a faraway crack, about igloos buried under the snow, about melancholy brass music in the courtyard of barracks, about the rattling of arms, about the dull thunder of crosses shaking the ground, about a parade of soldiers, about a demotion in rank. The horrible voice of an alcoholic roughneck stuttered stupid, angry words...

But what I heard was the alarming clang of armor-plated doors, the cry of iron bars, and Bid'homme's guttural, booming baritone coming closer.

"Where is he, the barbalot, the flastergast, the grustymuck, he's going to dance this time, the salampuff, the vandabond, the dammastledspijingloomer!"

(And Bid'homme was from Doubs! You'd have thought he was from Saint-Flour!^{39})

Ah! I could tell that I would not see the dwarf this morning playing the young, thoughtful doctor for the pictures, his favorite role of late! It was the Bid'homme in the holy water font who was going to buck me! He was already kicking the door and must have snatched the keys from a guard because an epileptic grip forced open the lock and the iron door was—definitely—thrown against the wall.

The friendly psychiatrist jumped on me like a tiger cat and nailed his huge hairy fingers into my neck while his boots hammered my shins. He bellowed, "Blankard! Blastard!" at least ten times in a row. I could not resist dealing him two phenomenal blows to his skull and I was sweetly satisfied to hear him hoot in rage. He let go of me and sat down hard on the tile floor.

The thrill of triumph did not last long. Bid'homme sprung back on his feet, pushed two oversized guards in front of him and ordered them to grab me by my back and my ankles. Thus I was carried away, head down, without dreaming of any resistance for the moment, just like the day before under similar circumstances.

What surprised me was that, despite my hatred for the quack and the terrible grudge I held against him, I knew, at the time, in some way, he was right to punish me as if I was a slave or an animal and he was my master or trainer. My little revolt in the cell was enough for me and yet I still felt guilty. This alone proved that my mental state was not improving.

Of course, all these feelings were vague.

Bid'homme let out an Apache war cry and tried to kick me with his spurs. My *porters* had to get between us! One of them even grumbled aloud, "I won't let go of the patient fer nuthin' and f... the doc in the shower. I'm gonna tell the Director. *Ben* long nuff that I wanted to do it!"

The other agreed, "Sure nuff can't let'im go on. It'd be crooked!"

131

At the same time, without thinking, they planted me back on my feet and held me gently by my arms.

Bid'homme heard nothing and saw nothing. He gloated and sang:

"*We're gonna sh... ower his ugly crown,*
Way aye blow the man down!"

We got to the bathhouse, which was in a kind of hall that was new to me and the assistant doctor handed me over to two other guards who I had never seen before— two brownish, stocky gnomes who looked like brothers and were obviously new employees of the institution.

"Go on," he barked at the two big guys. "I don't need you anymore. I have *my men* here!"

The door closed on my would-be defenders.

Now Bid'homme played nice, the good boy with his mates. He joked; he was having fun:

"We're going to have ourselves a few laughs. We're going to put out the dangerous fires. Strip the satyr naked for me and after that—to the big tub!"

Even with me, he was cheerful. "Yeah! My loafalot, you're going to have fun! There's plenty of room in the fish bucket. You can use your fins. You can do whatever you want: dive and bathe at the same time! And then, you know, these two here!" (pointing out the gnomes) "they're first-rate practitioners. I trained them in the good old days in the model hospital of Baume-les-Dames! Don't worry, they're from my own family—Bid'hommes! And they'll stop at nothing to satisfy a friend of the family. Go on, cousins! Let the games begin!"

The hideous monster stumps were strong as street thugs and quickly tore off my clothes—along with a little skin—and at Bid'homme's command, "Into the juice! To the toadling!" they brutally folded my in three, knees to chin and toenails touching the tops of my thighs. And then they threw me head first into a huge, deep pool. My head hit the bottom, but I managed to get back into a relatively vertical position. Standing up I had water almost up to my mouth, but at least I was able to breathe. It was the very thing my torturers were waiting for.

Two jets of water that felt like torrential rains struck me: one full in the face and the other in the back of my head. I was blinded; I choked. I felt like my brain box was going to shatter and my face became mush. Like the famous Gribouille,[40] I dove, but after 15 seconds—maybe—I had to raise my head and—quick! —with all my force, take a breath of air. But I barely had time to do this when the two spears zeroed in on me. It felt like two masses of icy lead were breaking my neck and crushing my face. And what a terrible noise in my head! Oh! It was awful! I was going to die... I couldn't take any more! I couldn't stand it! Air... Help!... Air! O the shocks!... O the suffocation!

It lasted a long time! How could I have put up with it? Maybe I had the instinct to wait to poke my head out until the torrent let up, for a second of calm. Then I probably sucked in air and sunk down again like a cannonball. I know that when I hit bottom, I still heard the mass of water thundering on the surface of the tank.

It was a kind of tragic bobbing for apples.

I soon become more and more savvy and breathed better and better. My will power came back to me; I was going to get out of the pool the first chance I got! Ah-ha! I jumped higher the next time and grabbed the edge of the huge basin. It was made of rough and thankfully strong stone, and I had it in my grasp... Victory! I got two jets of water on my back! But my lungs were free for more than 30 seconds and more and more! Still more! A new resurrection and I had my feet on the ground. I could see clearly! My eyes still hurt badly but I could open them wide. No time to lose! I had to run—run! I did not dream of escaping the bathhouse, but only of staying alive for as long as I could. Now I had the force to fight for half an hour—in half an hour, anything could happen, even the death of Bid'homme!

The buffalo's cousins missed their target now. I was too nimble for them when I was on solid ground. Their torrents missed me nine times out of ten or only nicked me.

Bid'homme ran all around the tank chasing me. It was very funny!

Ouch! They broke my shin! They must have let go of their showerheads and started throwing chairs at me! I fell down. The quack picked me up and gave me back to his two lackeys.

"Into the water! To the toadling! But you have to let him get out sometimes! The half-drowning, then the chase! That's the game!"

The three gnomes convulsed with laughter.

Their awful game did not last even one minute this time. Before I was hit with the first heavy burst, before I even disappeared into the icy tank, I saw that the door was open and Doctor Froin was watching and listening!

It was over! The three gnomes let me go in peace.

I could not recognize the Director's voice. It shattered and clamored:

"Ah! Bandits! Scoundrels! Murderers! Murderers! I caught you this time! Ha! You've reinstated torture in my establishment! I should have sent you to prison! Monsieur Bid'homme, you are nothing now in this hospital! Pack your bags! If you need a reference, I myself will write it up! Get out of here right now, you hear me! I don't want you here, no matter what. Get a move on or I'll call the police! And what are these executioner's henchmen doing in my place? Didn't I throw them out last year? Out of here, you bums, or... here's a bat, and let's see!"

The three artists slouched out of the room.

I got dressed again as quickly as I could. I had a long cut on my right leg. An overturned stool had blood all over it.

Doctor Froin paid no attention to me. He was now so appalled and upset that he was monologuing:

"Everything that happened is my fault! When you're suffering, you can't be responsible for a hospital like this... And I was already warned about Bid'homme... And I didn't want to believe them! Only once! And I didn't even put him under observation! But he was reformed or—at least—I thought so!

But one doesn't have the right to *think so* with a responsibility like this! One have to observe everything, supervise everything oneself! In fact, if the poor man is crazy, it'd be better to lock him up here, right away. I'll know this soon enough! Ah! I'm growing old—losing my health! Only taking care of some of my obligations—and not very well! I have to retire and put another doctor—a younger doctor—in charge!"

Just then, he saw that I was uncomfortable and I did not know what to do with myself: should I stay there or, on the other hand, should I run away fast? Despite my pitiful state of mind, I still had a glimmer of common sense, or rather of self-interested, selfish cunning. If I explained right away, it would sound less wild than later when the Doctor would have got over the shock.

So, he saw me and walked straight up to me.

"Monsieur Veuly, your behavior was reprehensible. I'd like to believe that it was not entirely your fault, because you'd gotten drunk with that hateful girl Bouffard—Yes, the scene was very easy to reconstruct!—and acted like a Turk. But this is not the time to treat you as you probably deserve. You are sicker than ever and badly affected by the savage tortures of those bandits. And I am guiltier than you in all this. There's no more supervision here! If I stay here at Vassetot, this mental hospital will soon become like *The System of Doctor Tarr and Professor Fether*. Do you know that story by Edgar Allan Poe?"

He softened up while talking to me and, little by little, I saw again my good old Froin, the gentleman idler who enjoyed his reading. And this despite the fact that he was, maybe, being threatened with a scandalous reputation, a smearing press campaign and the tag of senile indecency!

He continued, totally calm, "You don't know, my poor boy, how unlucky you are! It was only a little while ago that I got a letter from your brother before you carried out those horrors! In the letter, Monsieur Julien Veuly is begging me to free you when he comes tomorrow, or the day after at the latest, guaranteeing me that it will be no problem for him to take

135

care of you at his house. I had to telegraph him to postpone his trip because you'd had a serious relapse. And maybe I will have to write to him to tell him the details the incident. What I say will surely change his mind—I didn't want to tell your cousin! In the meantime, I'm not going to enjoy having to deal with you. I won't let them put you back in your cell. In the infirmary, there is a comfortable room where you cannot come and go as you please. We're going to put you there and I dare you to break even one of the locks; your fist is only human! Now, thanks to you, all the rooms and dormitories of Vassetot will soon be fitted with the same locks. Plus you will have *two* guards to stay inside your room. I'll leave you Leonard because you are used to him, but I am assigning you a kind of giant. You will weigh less than a matchstick to him…"

But the Doctor stopped talking. He had just noticed that the ground under me was turning red. And he saw the bloody stool and understood everything:

"Oh! The degenerate fiends! And here I am talking to you about a clampdown without seeing that you were injured by those Fuegians! I'll get you patched up and to bed. My dear Veuly, you're a nasty person, but I'm upset for you, too. If I can get at the two bandits who did this to you, I promise that they'll go back to the big house. Let's get out of here…"

My leg hurt so much that I could barely stand up.

"…out of here and get you to bed. After that, I will see to your wound; then I will file a complaint…"

It was useless for me to tell him that I approved of no police and no court, that I could very well take my revenge alone when I was free—old Froin was not listening anymore; he was already running as fast as his rheumatism let him.

Fifteen minutes later I was lying on my mattress in my old room—for the time being there was no talk of the mouse-trap-room or of titan-guards. An antiseptic bandage relieved the pain in my wounded leg a little and the Director, sitting in an armchair, gently scolded Leonard, whose weepy moustache drooped.

"I should have chucked you out," Doctor Froin concluded, "but since I've always been pretty satisfied with you and since the patients can't deal too well with changing nurses, I'm doing you a favor this time. But listen to me, if you make the slightest mistake from now on, your goose is cooked! You won't get off with a pure and simple dismissal!"

What did the boss mean by this? He managed to look very intimidating, which seemed—was I wrong?—to make Leonard feel better.

When old Froin had left us, my guardian came up to my bed and commiserated with me. He had a priceless look of shame, guilt and innocent mischief:

"He's a good man that Doctor Froin but *lissen* up, Monsieur Veuly, I'm hum*or*liated..." (Lovely mistake of *spoken* spelling) "...and you know, when these Spahi[41] ideas get a hold of you, before you go escaping my virgilance to go *saturate* your bad vices, it'd be more simple for you stab a *lethalizing* knife in the *religion* of my heart as they say in *anastomy*..." He looked wonderfully pretentious and self-satisfied.

He liked showing off his learning so much that he forgot about his remorse.

VI

Fifteen days later, there was nothing on my leg but an almost painless scar. I went out for the first time, together with Leonard and monitored by an air brigade. My guardian walked next to me, two attendants trailed behind at a short distance, two others eyeballed me at the bend of a path and Auzoux, the ex-arsonist, popped up in front of us every once in awhile. I was passing in front of the window of... *she* whom I did not see anymore, when I almost ran into Doctor Froin who was coming out of the Women's Building.

"What are you looking for over here?" he asked me a little sharply.

He made a sign and the guards turned away, Leonard went off and Auzoux vanished like a shadow.

"...I think I can speak to you like I'm going to," the Doctor continued, "because, truthfully, I often think you're totally reasonable despite your relapses. You are one of those neurotics, more common than you might think, who are present at their own stunts and hate them, even though they can't control themselves. Their fits of perversity and their stupid crimes scare them because they were watching themselves the whole time. They witness themselves playing their insane roles while they are tyrannized by a kind of parasitic will that wipes out their free will for a few hours. They are totally conscious of what they are doing and are the worse off for it. More often than not, I think they're smart enough that we can cure them without worrying about talking to them about their... mistakes, working hard to bring them back to their senses, which were only temporarily damaged..."

And I heard him mumble, "Yes! The injury! But that doesn't explain everything!"

"Well," he continued out loud, "you know that you won't find what you're looking for here. The lady whom you mistakingly wanted to... win over?—what do I know?—is no longer in the establishment.

138

"Maybe I'll be doing you a favor by telling you what happened; at the very least, it will be food for thought. The scandal that I was afraid of after your assault did not break out. They obviously wanted the profits of a clever blackmail more than the glory of supplying copy to the journalists of Dieppe—and besides, Monsieur Bid'homme's cousins just had to go and find Monsieur Letellier. He turned out to be less stupid than he looked—and very influential. He was very careful not to cause the least embarrassment. And he was sly enough to know whom to talk to. So, a few days after the… incident—the parties concerned—the eternal Parties concerned—sent me a polite note, but written in no uncertain terms, urging me to leave this establishment, which was run in a 'too unorthodox' manner, at the earliest convenience. And I am negotiating with various parties… The change of management will only take a few days… I will almost be happy to leave because if the transfer of Vassetot under such circumstances produces financial results, which I have never been blessed with, I will feel like I haven't been completely useless for the last 35 years of my life. I might even congratulate myself for retiring when the lazy management and the ineffective supervision, both resulting from my weak state of health, put the reputation of the hospital in jeopardy…

"Anyway, just as I was digesting the chilled bitterness of the pushy letter, Monsieur Letellier showed up in my office with two young, properly authorized psychiatrists. I spent the worst hour of my life with these practitioners and their client. I was cut to the core by their ironic politeness, their meticulous interrogation and their harsh assessment of the situation, which was not made easier by their insincere respect to a 'very tired old man.' I wish they would have just slapped me around and kicked me in public. When we were in the patient's room, the poor, innocent cause of so much… so many tragic events, I felt like I was a cowardly executioner and that my three visitors were the strong, noble heroes of a melodrama—maybe even avenging angels—but they were a little too fidgety and clean-cut for that.

"So the two very young doctors talked with the patient for 20 minutes, asking her questions that insulted me in the most hypocritical way. Finally, the more serious one, who wore gold, Chinese-shaped glasses and was prematurely graying, swung around to me and fired off, 'But, Monsieur, this lady is completely reasonable now. Twenty years of close friendship couldn't convince me more than this calm and natural conversation I've just had with her. How is it, Monsieur, that you haven't, *at the very least*, had some doubts? And she just didn't get better yesterday! I certainly wouldn't accuse you of carelessness, but this is a matter of conscience, Monsieur, a *matter of conscience*! Why didn't you tell Monsieur Letellier about the lady's improvement that you should, *at the very least*, have noticed? Otherwise what should we think? Excuse me for being so *frank* with you. I know that I should respect your long, long career and the tiring years of overwork that it must have cost you, but have you thought about your responsibility? A psychiatrist should not lose *any* touch with *any* of his inmates. Oh, I would never think of criticizing you! I am just observing and sorry to have done so!'

"Monsieur Letellier turned white with anger. 'Doctor, how is it that my wife got better and I knew nothing about it?' he asked.

"Then he became sarcastic again: 'This here's a special establishment: everything's good in the end. Accidents that might cause the worst damage anywhere else, cause the most positive reactions here. I know what you're going to tell me, Doctor Froin: you were expecting a positive result from this accident, from this experience, I should say, because it is an *experience*, isn't it?'

"I tried to make the gentleman see that he wasn't keeping up his appearance of politeness and that he was insulting me. But I'd had enough troubles for one day. Then he calmed down a little and harassed me with elegant obscenities that even my two young colleagues had never heard before.

"The patient—for I believe you can have a fit of clear-headedness, but not a fit of recovery—finally spoke up and said that she didn't want to stay in the mental hospital, but knowing how much Monsieur Letellier hated noise, she had decided to wait, without saying a word, for her husband's monthly visit. She didn't even then say what had happened, not wanting to hurt me, and in any case, she felt sure that she should be released. Wasn't she completely over whatever mental problems had forced her to be committed?

"In spite of my doubts, which I refused to share with my two colleagues, who had seen her for less than half an hour total, I was forced to sign the release right there and then. That's it."

I tried to express all the guilt that I felt for the evil I had done unwillingly, but the good man told me to be quiet and said that he was glad to be getting rid of a burden that was too heavy on him.

He looked so relieved and peaceful that I was *almost* fooled.

Anyway, I knew that if I pressed too hard, it would be cruel. And this time the damage was done for good. How would I manage later to *delicately* make the Doctor accept an even more difficult compensation?

Then a new anxiety attacked me: not only was I desperate because Irene had left—and it was my fault!—a result of my *crime* (I would almost say!)—, but I was also terrified at what might happen to her now under the thumb of Monsieur Letellier! And I abused old Froin's kindness by asking him this question:

"But, Doctor, this poor woman might suffer a lot—and all because of me! Isn't it true that her husband is a pretty awful person?"

"It's an exaggeratation. He's very popular in the district. In fact, he's so popular that for the first time he's running in the next local elections unopposed! That's the only reason he doesn't want to make a fuss. That was what he said: no fuss! And even though he was not very nice to me, I don't think he was mean. For sure, he has good reason to hold it against me. I know how to put myself in other people's shoes!"

Popular in the district! Naïve old Froin, that's not the whole story! He's obviously a crook!

Doctor Froin was going to leave me and, even though I was still haunted by the sad, tired vision of an already feeble and consumptive Irene, tyrannized and controlled by the awful Letellier whom I pictured totally repulsive—a *nice* politician!—I could not help thinking about another question that had nothing to do with this obsession. You would have thought that Kmôhoûn had come back! I was completely surprised to hear myself ask:

"And the new assistant doctor hasn't arrived yet? What will happen to his predecessor since you have... dismissed him?"

The Director became worried. He looked at me for a minute without saying anything, and then he seemed to surrender to an irresistible force. He shrugged his shoulders and he let slip out:

"Monsieur Bid'homme! Well! He will stay here longer than me, but it's not good news for him... You want to see him?"

My first reaction was to say no, but I thought better of it... Bid'homme still at Vassetot? But then he was... committed—sick?

"Yes, certainly, I would like to see him, just a quick look!"

Was I low enough to feel avenged?

"Well, come on!"

But Doctor Froin still seemed unsure. It was like a thought suddenly came to him from somewhere else... or someone else. From the *Enemy Force*? And he said almost unconsciously:

"After all, since you were one of the patients he liked the least..." (this, of course, meant that he hated me the most!) "maybe the sight of you will make him angry enough to wake him up from his... present troubles. Maybe it will produce a healthy effect on him?"

Let's go! Always the contradictions! The *egzitation*—as Leonard would say—which is dangerous for me, will be helpful to Bid'homme, whom the Doctor has finally seen as an arch-lunatic! And basically, this pandered to my theory of individual cases. I couldn't stand doctors like Bid'homme—precisely!—who accepted only one way to cure any given illness—the disciplinary cure at that!—without taking into account the individual character of the subject!

We went back now to my building, but down a hallway, farther away from my stairs and up one floor. The Director called out, "Macheburg!"

And one of the heavyweights who had shown pity on me the other day came out of a cubby-hole like the one where Leonard used to sleep and he opened the door of a large room whose shining woodwork above the usual upholstery dazzled me.

A heroic-comic spectacle was in store for us. Monsieur Bid'homme, with his boots on and wearing fake leather spurs cut into stars, with a riding crop in hand, was straddling a narrow table fitted with string stirrups.

Doctor Froin went up to him and congratulated him on looking well—he was blue-green!—then he asked if everything was alright.

"My God! Everything would be better if my occupation as horse doctor wasn't so grueling."

"Are you eating enough?"

"My horse eats everything, but the result is the same. A horse is omnivorous and expensive. I'm going to try an automobile."

"Good! But aren't you bored? Wouldn't you like to read something, perhaps?"

"I don't have time. The practice of my art *devours* all my spare time. With a nag like this, and patients to drug, purge and whip, I don't have any time to myself. Every minute on the road and then there's some broad asking me for a consultation. I give it from my horse, instead of dismounting. Broads, they're always having problems in a bunch of disgusting places. It ends up disgusting me, as good and human as I am."

"Would you like to see an old acquaintance of yours?"

"That depends... a patient?"

"Yes."

"Well then, bring him in. I have a batch of mugwort here that I don't know what to do with. Will he have to be carved up too? I love that sport because I know nothing about it. I'm not a surgeon! I'll probably maim the bastard patient—what a race! Bring him forward!"

"Here he is."

"Hold on! I didn't see his hideous face; I thought he was a guard. But that's it, that's really it! A patient's mug! That's the real deal! But wait—it's Grustypot, the young literary pirate, or his other name Nigeot, bing bang mechanics!"

"Not exactly. It's Monsieur Veuly."

"Ah! The camel! Charming boy, to boot! Stick out your tongue, my friend. That's three francs! We're going to have us a purge, my dear child, with a sublime corrosive of vitriol and dog crap."

He stared at me, searching for something that he could not find. His eyes looked angry and then confused.

"Veuly! Veuly—or rather Agénor Biscaillou! You don't know what it's like to be a doctor! I didn't want to be a doctor! What I got, paddlings when I was a kid, wallops to crush my skull! My father had his own ideas: he loved drugs! He wanted to make me fill people full of them—a philanthropist, I tell you—a f...lippin philanthropist! How did I get my degree? A mystery! I learned nothing at all. An old imbecile named Froin—not you, Doctor Peskyass! Not you! No! A lousy psychiatrist, that idiot Froin, paid for my school to look the other... to be generous! Ah! The stupid oaf! My father loved it— not me! And I was so bored in Paris, in that f...lippin Latin Quarter where you can't give people a good thrashing without going to the clink!

"I started liking medicine only when I found out that a Doctor had the right to f... mess with his patients, to push them to the edge, even to poison them a little without a sound from anyone—not the half-dead or their stupid relatives—and this swine Froin who always paid—this gave him gloves, for the fattening!—and who forced me to be with the lunatics, the goddamn lunatics! They don't consume enough poisonous chemical products—the freaks! Too bad! I still gave a lot of eleven o'clock broths to those brain cripples, those human wrecks, those degenerates turning back into animals! And I did it ever so subtly; no one ever suspected a thing, Froin least of all, the smiling, meek, hydrocephalic hypocrite!"

The Director did not bat an eyelid. He whispered to me:

"You see, he's completely gone! The boy was so close and affectionate to me when he still had some common sense!"

Maybe I was crazy, but I *saw*, yes, I saw more clearly than old Froin. Sad to say, but there are good men whose kindness deserves to be punished—a good beating! And they get it, sometimes, without even knowing.

The Director was distracted by his sad speculations, so Bid'homme motioned to me to come closer—and I obeyed automatically, not seeing what an idiot I was until it was too late. (It made sense that I criticized Doctor Froin who, at least, had the excuse of overblown kindness!) Too late because Bid'homme had already grabbed my wrist and held me with a force multiplied tenfold by insanity. He breathed into my ear:

"Veuly! Dirtbag! Bunglebrain! He thinks I don't recognize you, the big idiot! Hold on! Do I recognize you?"

He slapped me hard on my back—violent and painful. The pain sent a strange energy through me, too. I pulled myself away and kicked him to the floor. Four irons in the air and Bid'homme grunting like a pig. All this happened so quickly that Doctor Froin did not have time to get between us.

The demented psychiatrist was already back on his feet, swinging a huge rusty nail around. The rust of the nail and the thickness of my jacket saved me from a nasty scratch. Macheburg ran up and had a hard time holding back the gnome who threw away his nail but wanted to fight with the guard. He grabbed him around the waist and tried to lift him for the fall. When Bid'homme saw that he could not get the upper hand, he let go, slipped away from Macheburg and started rolling around on the floor. He bit the legs of the overturned table that he had used for his mount, kicked at nothing in the air and rolled around some more yelling like a wild Indian.

Macheburg ended up getting hold of him again and with the help of another guard who was waiting in the hallway slipped the crazy thing into a pretty little straitjacket.

Two days later, when I went to the bathhouse—in the new room—I was surprised to meet up with my Bid'homme again, calm and noble this time and dressed simply in ox-blood shorts. He was ordering around some nurses who were watering him carefully and gently:

"A little jet like for a baby! I have delicate *scapulae*," he said. Then, he called them a "bunch of buggerats"—there were two of them—and said, "You're taking the skin off my ribs! Watch out! I'm turning around; take care of my loins as well. Now, the other side! Not too hard on the kidneys. There, there! Pigspickers! I told you not to aim for the coccyx and especially not to unscrew it!"

(O, the anatomist!)

"I don't have a spare. Now take the Devil by the horns— a little summer rain on the skull. A little rain, cannonizers! I didn't ask you for a flood!"

(The water was barely harder than a spray).

They did not shower the menacing dwarf! The guards were still scared of him. The ex-psychiatrist did the hydrotherapy himself; it was as simple as that.

"Enough! Now give the patient two liters of good Bourgogne wine, a whole leg of lamb, very rare, and a dozen fish; after that coffee and an after dinner. It's little Bid'homme, my favorite loon, a delightful nut whom I will cure in six weeks. I have to take care of him—and gently—or I'll f…lick you into the water! To the toadling!"

He patted himself on the head carefully and lovingly. I was touched by his tender affection for himself and the nurses did not dare laugh...

Suddenly, a door opened. A person entered who was not young or old, maybe around 40, tall, thin and pale, who looked like a parish clerk or an old-fashioned high school principal, clean shaven, the nose of a duck, the eye of a hypocrite and a snooper, a nose like an upside-down hook. He carried a huge tome under his left arm and a ring of heavy keys in his right hand. His suit was entirely black from his tie to the drab gaiters that highlighted the hypnotizing, waxy shine of his large, flat, long, long shoes.

It was the new assistant doctor who had arrived that morning. Two hours after setting up, he knew everything about the insitution: the patients, guards, horses, grounds and dependencies, and his puckered lips showed that he had also formed his opinion about everything—very unfavorable. He spent just over than a minute examining me—I should prove an interesting case!—and addressed me very quickly: "Too much liberty! I know many things about your case. Too much liberty! Bad system; we shall change it."

After that, his shifty eyes took a kind of photograph of me and when he was completely sure that he knew me by heart, from the scar on my left eyebrow to the bump that deformed my right boot, he turned around and ordered Leonard, who was present at the scene, to come with him for a minute.

In the hallway, he spoke quietly to my guardian who came back preoccupied. For the first time, I saw distrust and almost disgust in him.

The new assistant doctor, more and more the school principal, shook his formidable ring of keys while walking. I guessed he was making a second round—the afternoon tour. Oh, the assistant was active! If you could honestly say that an institution like this had known a happy period, then you could also say that the good old days of Vassetot were gone.

The man with black gaiters went straight up to the nurses and in an icy voice that froze me with fear—yes, fear!—in me,

147

wretched reasonable madman that I was, but sensitive like a little boy:

"Are the patients giving the orders around here? Well! That will have to change! Do you know what I mean, guards! If you are servile toward any inmate at all, I shall have you run out of here without references. Shower the patient!"

"But Doctor..."

"*Shower the patient*! Not that! Put him under the new nozzle! No sprinkles! Take away this watering can; the column of water! Quickly!"

There was a short battle between the guards and Bid'homme.

"Attach him to the iron posts: tie him up, tie him up! Don't be scared!" the assistant doctor ordered.

I got out of seeing or hearing the ill-fated Bid'homme. He had a sort of glimmer of understanding in his eye and started trembling up and down his poor naked body—then actually bellowed.

Doctor Froin left the following week. I had no friend in the institution, except for Leonard since I could hardly count on Magne, Nigeot and the other members of the Philosophers' Club. They were prisoners like me, beings under watch, souls in Limbo; they had fine thoughts just like other men, but they were too much like me. Everything about them was ambiguous. One day, you'd find them full of wisdom and think they were Greek sages; the next day, they would look more serious than ever, but be warped by the most childish obsessions. Since I almost never left my room anymore, I saw them less and less... They made me sad and I am sure that I made them sad, too.

Leonard was often lectured by Doctor Barrouge, the assistant doctor, and became a kind of cartoon jailor, not so aggressive, but he spied on me sometimes as if he was waiting for me to pull some dirty trick.

Everything was against me: the new Director, Doctor Le Lancier, obeyed Barrouge hand and foot. He was a fat, yellow man with a ferocious face. He was angry, a real screamer. You would swear that he was going to smash everything up, but he was afraid of his assistant like fire and knew who was the head honcho, the prophet of Allah, head of staff... or worse...

Leonard, on one of his good days—you could count them now—told me that terror reigned everywhere in the establishment, not the Red Terror, but the *Barrouge* Terror. Six guards and four nurses had been fired: Among them was Mademoiselle Bouffard, caught by the assistant doctor exactly when she was talking about going to down a shot. Poor Celestine! Why *talk about it* when it was so simple just to *do it*?

The day after, Leonard asked me again if I wanted to have some exercise, since I had not "shaken the dust off my *joints*' since *Wansday*." He added that if he wanted to take a stroll, it was because the thing'was strictly forbidden. But, he concluded, I was in full *esurection* and "Black Stockings" and "The Dragon"—our two tyrants—were busy investigating the women's building about some *arcles* of clothing that had disappeared. They would be there for at least two hours and in an hour and a half we could already have got some air. "How'd ya like that?"

I gladly accepted and we were soon on the grounds admiring the work of a group of farmers who looked like morons of Valais relieved of their goiters.[42]

"Should we go see the Agitated?" my guardian asked.

"For what?"

"There's sometin new: it's *decrated*!"

"Let's go!"

When we got to the gloomy building, I did not notice any change and said so to my guardian.

"But yeah it's much better than before," he answered, "it's *decrated* with an owl *orment*."

I opened my eyes as wide as nature allowed. There were only the two dancers I saw six months before.

They were practically calm today and their gamboling did not make me dizzy. One of them was banging the bars of his gate with his knee, which did not keep him from dancing a

149

frenzied little jig at the same time; the other seemed to be sa-
botaging a bourrée folk dance; he chuckled a little sarcastical-
ly; both drooled lightly.

"Looky to the left!" said Leonard, fed up. "You're gonna
like what's *decrating* the place'"

A third gated cave gradually revealed its hidden mysteries to me.

At first, I could only make out an obscure form: a little
man was squatting on the floor. After a little while, I saw a
jockey's helmet, boots and tattered pants.

Then the pygmy got up and took two or three steps toward us, suspecting that we were watching. He carried a pail
that he put between his feet and squatted again, this time in the
full light. Armed with a little ash shovel, he took out of the
pail—feces.

I was forced to back up, but I could still see him. The
pseudo-jockey dropped his shovel and, with his hairy hands,
made little cakes like the ones the middle-class kids in sailor
suits make with sand on sophisticated beaches. Then he bowed
down before his works and worshipped them devotedly. O
Pygmalion!

Leonard and I made the mistake of talking to each other.
The jockey-artist threw himself at the bars—in a single
bound—like a monkey at the zoo trying to grab hold of his
visitors. After that, he hung by his knees from a crossbeam of
the gate, fell down without hurting himself, then tried, with all
his force, to stick his head through the bars of his cage. He
huffed, hissed and spluttered like a cussing cat: Oh! That scrub
brush moustache, those mean and laughing eyes! It was
Bid'homme!

Ah! I quickly turned tail! I really hated the dwarf, but
what I had just seen was too much... How did I have the awful
courage or the rotten cruelty to turn back? To turn back and
look at the hideous, pitiful captive who leapt around like a
tiger and shouted: "Cannonizer! Schnitzlicker!"—his eyes all
bloodshot, his face swollen, his hair on end. Suddenly, he

leapt forward and knocked his... muzzle against the bars, hard enough to break his teeth. I ran away with all my force.

Yes, how could I have turned back? Ah! Kmôhoûn had come back to me and was laughing horribly... to hurt me!

It's finished! I would escape from there the first chance I got: tomorrow, when I would be a little less sick with fear! I knew how to do it; it would be very simple. For the moment I had to hide myself somewhere, under the furniture or under the covers; I had to be in the dark and see nothing! Even as a child, I knew no terror like this!

With the extraordinary resilience of the sick, I woke up the next day ready, happy and full of energy. Bid'homme's crisis and Kmôhoûn's return were like fate telling me what I should do: I had to escape this nest of Despair and Fear, fast and quick, and start searching for Irene who personified light, happiness and Joie-de-vivre! I did not care much about the politician Letellier! You could tremble before a madman like Bid'homme, who had something infernal about him, who was a kind of distorted Kmôhoûn, but to fear a future merchant of amendments, a cur who brought along two Doctor Diafoirus[43] to confront a good old boy like Froin when it was so simple just to climb on the roof, drop down through the chimney and fall upon the enemy without a single guard being aware of what was happening... to fear a Letellier! Ha! No, of course not!

I would escape very calmly this evening at nightfall— and even ask the gatekeeper for the cord!

But my heart was suddenly racked with a strange re-gret—my heart that wanted to love only Irene! I figured out that I had a kind of grotesque and pretty deep affection (what kind? Obviously it would be difficult to explain; it was un-clean but almost tender—tender? Yes, to a certain point), a real affection for... Madame Robinet!

I guess this feeling stemmed from the real courage she showed for awhile. The extraordinary woman had an unfor-givable crush on my naughty, ridiculous and poorly built body. She might have been scared of the ogres Barrouge and Le Lancier like dragons, afraid enough to turn ashen gray whenever one of these Syracusian tyrants raised his voice, even far away from her—afraid of even thinking of violating one of their orders to the point of being forced to sit wherever, on whatever, on the ground if necessary, if she were found guilty; she had risked everything to prove to me her sinful passion. It was stronger than her!

At the worst possible moments, at times when it was dangerous to be anywhere near me, with the two evil devils prowling around, she came to my room, sweating with excitement, usually with only a few minutes to spare. She came up with the most outrageous and ingenious excuses to send my guards away—I had two now, Leonard and François—, and she bombarded me with her crazy declarations of love—and the appropriate demonstrations—for if I suffered from not being with the adored Irene in body and mind, I was not stone and I admired heroines like her, even when their jowls were starting to droop. Plus, her emotion and her passing weakness, her paleness and her need for protection, her soft voice that was kind of sweetened by fear, all this gave her a born-again youthful grace, which women who are truly women only lose very late in life. And really Madame Robinet—Aricia!—was not that old! Kmôhoûn slandered her by calling her "venerable." She was not old at all, barely mature. I did not want to know her age! And what if I did know it? Big deal! Age is a convention: many young women of 45 would find a thousand things to envy in her. She was a brunette, a beautiful brown—a good color. One did not often see eyes that were so blue, dark and sparkling, or white skin that was so delicate and satiny, and curves that were so delightful. Aricia was a little strong, very, very plump, but firm, wonderfully firm—much more than Mademoiselle Bouffard. She had kept her powerful lines and her robust form that would have turned on many a younger man than me—and others older and more experienced. And if there was only one truly splendid carnation in the world—that pink and dark-haired Irene—I could also accept whiteness as a mark of lesser beauty—a warm whiteness, as opposed to those glistening blacks and somber pinks, lily white. Could I forget that there were radiant blondes? No, but...

Aricia was fastidious about her clothes. She could take them all off in an incredibly short time. No half measures with her; no bulky fabrics, and one couldn't really be scared of being caught with a woman who got undressed and dressed again so skillfully. It was astonishing! A real talent—and rare! And I bet that, in case of danger, she could have disappeared gracefully, hidden away in the first corner she saw, despite her size—very reasonable, after all was said and done.

Let's admit that this wonderful passion was not ignited at the beginning from the purest fires of love. When I interested her for the first time, she saw a side of me that would never make her guilty of having gone through a period of platonic passion. But then, what woman could ever have become passionate about me for sentimental reasons? It would have been an aberration. I could not imagine an Elvira[44] innocently sighing in front of the monkey house at the City Zoo where a few of my peers were showing off their athletic dexterity. And besides, they had four hands—which would be an excuse if necessary. Anyway, she never wanted to impose on me or to take me for an idealist dreamer. She'd be ashamed of such an imposture. It would lower her in her own eyes.

My guards were used to her little visits and—not without reason—trusted her real strength. So, one day, they asked her to watch me for an hour—time enough to pay their respects to two of their cousins just arrived by car from Dieppe. She and I had the chance to chat calmly for a while between two outbursts of affection that proved to me, as usual, that she possessed a kind of special poetry.

Barrouge and Le Lancier were busy again with one of their stupid but fortunate investigations. Someone had stolen a hernial bandage in the women's wing—always in the women's wing!—and four guards on whom suspicion fell were holed up with the inquisitive directors. We were in no hurry:

Aricia told me a few little secrets and then started—I do not know why—talking about Bid'homme. That's when she confessed so adorably:

"That dirty little oaf! He must've ben joking when he asked me if it was me, Madame Robinet, who'd wrote a book 'titled *The Country House*, saying I was country enough for it! Write a book! Me! I was only four months in school when I was li'l. I never wrote nuthin' 'cept on the walls on the street and you know it wasn't *Long Live the Emperor* or church songs!"

O smiling, tender childhood of Aricia! I would love to photograph one of those walls!

Finally she "took off the gloves."

During that lovemaking—I use the term reluctantly—I did not have Kmôhoûn's help. He was vacationing in some meadow blooming with the curs and cutthroats of melodrama and, without Kmôhoûn, I did not fully trust my powers of... continuous seduction. But since my organism was still a little under the Tkoukrian influence, Aricia had little to complain about. Had I achieved the ideal that I made her imagine? I do not know, but if she was disappointed, she apparently took responsibility herself in all modesty, blaming the failure of her physical charms, because she did not breath a word about any possible disappointment and looked totally satisfied.

Kmôhoûn followed the train of my thoughts and told me very delicately, which was not like him—he must have learned it from some young women who were sad with love's craving:

"*You know, she deserves a reward; and don't thank me for helping you give it to her. What I've learned makes me really feel for her and I made a promise to myself. So, I'll gladly prove how much you appreciate her.*"

We became fast friends, the Tkoukrian and I, when he was so thoughtful and generous.

So we were in complete agreement. We were going to pay off today what we owed to an excellent woman whose behavior we could not praise enough. After that, well! We

154

would leave her, but not forever. Kmôhoûn promised that he would visit her for me; from time to time, he would make my astral body come back like a loving ghost, conscious of its duties, to offer the deserving Aricia a demonstration of my very honorable respect during the night.

And Aricia came today at the perfect time, when my guards luckily had a hell of a thirst. Thanks to Kmôhoûn, the dear woman was transported to Seventh Heaven. She cried and babbled, "Never... ne... never... I've never... loved like that!"

Around 8 p.m., we sent Leonard, who was none too happy about it, to get some tobacco in the store. Then, we tied up and gagged François with a cord that we stole from the deep pockets of his uniform. The rope was probably meant to paralyze us for a short time in case of insubordination, since the straitjacket was not always in reach of our tamers. Therefore, our rough treatment was only fair.

We stuck our victim under the bed after taking his keys. I put 200 francs in his vest: "For you and Leonard to share." We double-timed it out of there after putting on a poncho with a huge double collar—and a dented felt hat; there I was, looking exactly like the guard Patoulet, stooped and skinny, with a poor, pointy goatee, messy and deformed most of the time. I worked the locks of my door without too much noise, slipped down the hallway, gingerly went down the stairs, found the door to the yard open, as I expected, and legged it to the path that led to the caretaker's, to the road, to freedom! The twilight was very dark. Without much ado, I passed Leonard coming back from the store by a route that was as unexpected as it was out of the way—and when he called out to me, "Come 'ere, old beggar, my smoke went out gain and I *fergot* to *git* my *martches*."

I answered perfectly calm, "*Martches*? I ain't got *nun* fer ya ugly mug, ya big *galoof*."

I have to say that even when I was not thinking much about playing cottage Casanova, I studied the dialect of my double, whose speech was easy to copy thanks to his exaggerated country accent. I spoke "Patoulet" like my native tongue and my words were particularly well chosen because they reinforced once again the reputation of a superhuman goon that the pseudo-guard had earned.

Leonard went his way unsurprised and I walked faster and faster to the exit. Let's go. Good! Ah! Old lady Grollon, the caretaker, is at her door. Lucky for us, after all. No light to fear, no mistake to make by lowering my hat too much or too little over my nose:

"Who's dat, Missah Patoulet?" the skirted sentinel shouted at me. "I've a good mind not to pull this string to leave ya go out. Ya 'nother party to run to at this hour?! It's the li'l maid *agin* in Lenient who *warks* up yer blood?"

"Don' say nuthin', Madame Grollon. Dere's good grog in Lenient. I'm gonna hunt up a li'l jug fer ya and a good stogie fer ya man."

"'Oly Jeepers, get goin' then!" exclaimed the woman with the cord.

And I was on the road; and it was that easy! It was only then that I got scared!

I did not want to run. High step it, but not too fast, that was best... I avoided the town—and also the woods where they would look for me first. There was a road less taken in the evening over behind the cemetery. The ground was muddy and full of deep ruts all year round. Too bad! It led the other way, toward Vercheville where a train for Paris came at 10:45 p.m. That was less stupid than getting on a car bound for Mesnil-Mauconduit, which was closer, but the station was watched. For a normal walker at a good pace, it took three hours to get to Vercheville from Vassetot; but I had a compass! No one would think me smart enough—you would pronounce that: stupid enough—to run so far. I would arrive on time; I only had to *stretch it out...*

It got darker and darker. All bode well. I took a leisurely dump behind the cemetery; but I was moving forward, I was moving forward!

156

Aye!... I had never followed the path to the end. At a bend in the road there was a house lit up—two houses—three houses! Dogs were barking... I was going to get off the road, climb over those bushes and go behind that bunch of trees. But they saw me. A man carrying a light shouted:

"Hey! Night *warlker*! Whartcha doin' in dat bush?"

I got over, but could not untangle myself from the brambles that were gripping my pants.

The man was on me. He let go of his light and grabbed me by my pants, not caring about getting pricked. With the help of Kmôhoûn, I would have been stronger than him if I were on my feet, but my I was compromised by my position. Caught around the waist I was badly situated for battle.

And then the peasant called out, "Yo! Zidore! Bailhache! C'mere! Dere's a damn pitchfork robber in the bush!"

Ten seconds later, I was gathered up like a nut. I could not even think of fighting back; three pairs of vice grips crushed my arms, ribs and shins.

Without knowing how it happened, I ended up in full light, lying on a kitchen table, still held down by force—and angrily biting the brim of my hat, which had fallen down over my face.

"Ah! Ya! Dis is too much!" said the light-man. "I'm not such a d...unce! I done fished me up a guard from Varstow. Ain't dis ya, Missah *Patolay*? Fer *shore* it's 'im—'cuz it's his hat and cape!"

A fat redhead called Bailhache ripped off my hat causing all the teeth in my jaw to dance.

"'Oly son of a tow! It ain't 'im!"

"Whozzit den?"

"I'll tell ya," Zidore grinned; he was a tall, bony lout dressed like a polecat. "Iit's a dam' pig loony runnin' 'way from Varstow!"

"We *cain* take 'im back dere *tanight*!"

"Mebbe dat be not good fer now. Dat be too soon. Dere be some dough in it when dey 'ave a 'ard night of it and start missin' der loony!"

Despite my sorry situation, this fantastic psychology made me want to laugh out loud. I imagined the *grief* of Le Lancier and Barrouge?

"So, Pupin, ya think we otta give 'im a li'l sumthin' to chaw on?"

"He cain chaw his hand in da room. It's too much spendin' fer us. We ain't got da *raward* yit!"

"Ho! Iz not like with ol' Froin! Da new ones promised to pay fer the captures!"

"Meantimes, we gonna bed 'im in the *hayshark*. Wait fer day *tamarra*!"

It was just like Leonard had told me. The brand new director and his worthy acolyte were going to train the country folk to be Cuban watchdogs. And they would feed their enthusiasm.

They threw me into a fetid night. The first thing that happened was I almost got sick. Luckily, I found some long candle matches in my pocket, contraband bought from the Vassetot store. Each of them could stay lit for almost two minutes. I lit one and looked around.

The *hayshark* where they plunged me was a shack full of garbage, wet straw, broken furniture, busted old pots and pans, rabbit pelts and foul smelling rags.

I sat down on a pile of empty sacks, grubby but nearly dry. The door was solid. You could see that they had recently fixed it like new. Was this the result of Vassetot promises? The roof was not so good. Some crossbeams were rotted and, in a few places, I saw the slates. But before thinking of making the least effort to break the bars of my stinking cage, I decided it would be best for me to wait, to wait a long time. The natives of the bush were going to go to bed early, but the three manhunters would probably be in good cheer tonight. It was a nice windfall to capture one of the precious exhibits of the neighboring menagerie. I bet that they were toasting to my health and calculating the next day's bonus that would give them some extra cash. They would not be sleeping for a long time. Patience! I also heard the dogs snorting sometimes. I only had to give them time to calm down. Later, when they would be half asleep, a noise coming from the house would not seem so suspicious to them, at first—and I could undoubtedly gain some ground before they were on my heels.

I smoked a few cigarettes to make the air breathable. Soon, I had the chance to congratulate myself for being so cautious. Footsteps came up to the shack; a bar of light flashed under the door; I quickly put out my cigarette and lied down, curled up in a ball on my dirty sacks. The door creaked. A ray of light shined on me full in the face. I had the feeling that my reddened eyelids, red like a seashell, were becoming transparent. The voice of Pupin, the boss, who had tracked me down, baritoned cavernously:

"He's sleepin like a '*air* in its *ferm*!"

(This proved to me that my enemy, the human watchdog, had no really exact idea about the customs of *hares*. This would redeem him in the eyes of environmentalist sportsmen: they could lower themselves to a manhunt, but not to poaching).

I waned in the dark. Hours passed. I continued to smoke. I was not sleepy at all, but numb, with no force to think. At best it was like I saw confused images passing through a fog: Irene, old Froin, Bid'homme, the two new directors, François tied up, Paris that I was, maybe, probably, going to see again—then a certain hallway in Vassetot, cold and white, which suddenly made me a little scared. The dogs were not budging. I lit one of my little candles again and looked at my watch: 1:30 a.m.

Kmôhoûn, who had not made a noise since we had left the mental hospital, suggested to me:

"It won't take much force. You only have to take off five or six slates at the very bottom of the roof, on the right, exactly in the only part that you looked at without seeing."

I lit up another match. In fact, on that side, all the wood was rotted. Pupin and his cohorts must have been totally preoccupied with the state of their door not to have noticed this.

I got—or *we* got—to work. It was harder than Kmôhoûn the observant had imagined. Firstly it was impossible to get enough light on us. We had only *two* arms and I had my hands full, holding a match between my teeth and trying to light another one every minute or so, in spite of the fact that those Victoria Matches were extraordinarily long—because when the flame burned halfway down the little stick, I had to spit it out to avoid burning my nose. Plus, the wood of the cross-beams was wet, but not as spongy as I imagined. Kmôhoûn *electrified* my nervous system with all his savage energy, but it was only with great effort, and little by little, that I was able to take apart the joists and beams. I had to keep scratching matches to know where I was and to be very sure that nothing was going to fall on my head. Then I got on with my termite job. And I had to be as quiet as possible: so I progressed slowly and worked hard for a good two hours before I could easily lift half a dozen slates.

The moonlight enshrouded the *shark*'s trash in greenish blue... Now I needed all my meager dexterity. I jumped onto a crossbeam that was still solid and then I was on the roof, which creaked less than I thought it would.

But watch out until the end! No fast moves! The dogs growled. I stood still for maybe ten minutes. Then I jumped, as noiselessly as a cat that just looted a pantry. Fear gave me stunning agility—velvet feet—real tomcat paws. I tiptoed away and took off before the dogs completely woke up.

Oh! Then there was a racket to terrify the devils. The atrocious beasts bounded after me, howling. I had just enough time to climb a tree. Shutters banged, doors screeched and voices shrieked. Soon there was the craziest parade of people who—in a veritable flood of lights—ran to the foot of the tree where the dogs were jumping. (You could see almost as clearly as in a red, fantastic sunset.)

Five or six men crowned with cotton caps, half naked children looking like tadpoles and a few dried or fatty female monkeys dressed in potato sacks scampered around and hooted. Among these graceful visions a tall woman with flabby, gelatinous flesh, endless and skinny pale salmon colored legs and a huge bouncing butt—grotesquely indecent thanks to a torn shirt, her only veil, which was far too short—stamped her foot furiously and then wiggled around like she was doing a hula dance. She cried and barked:

"Where's dat pig at who *warnts* to rape us? Where's he at so I cain murder 'im? Let im just try to *farce* hisself on me! I'll show 'im!"

And it went on like that until she ran out of breath.

One of the men—I recognized Zidore—got up in a baker's shirt and knickers that looked like tar paper, came up to my perch, scratched his head, winked an eye and said profoundly:

"Thar he is: we gotta fetch a ladder!"

The whole Boeotian group rushed to the houses and the stupid dogs, against all canine customs under such circumstances, followed their human comrades yapping, jumping around like ladies' lapdogs, wagging their tails and generally being good dogs who were proud of their noble watch.

There was no time to lose. Beneath me, a little to the left, very close by, there was a roof that was really too steep, but I could not worry about the slope: I let go of the branch, fell onto it and slid. I could not grab hold of anything and dropped down like lead, rolling into the void. Next thing I knew, I was on a pile of straw, not too stunned. I got up, kicked up my heels and legged it across the field…

The route led me—I do not know how—to Vercheville at the break of blue day.

Still sick with stress, I hid in a half demolished limekiln close to the station. I cleaned myself up as best I could, scrubbing myself with a handful of well-dried hay that luckily padded the disused kiln. My clothes were not too ripped up. How had I managed not to lose my hat? I inspected myself again. My outfit was not too bad to look at; dirt was pretty much everywhere, with no big splotches. I looked like a sloppy country bumpkin, but normal.

At 7 a.m., I left my shelter and entered the station on the off chance... I had all the luck. The ticket booth was open and a train was leaving for Paris at 7:30. I asked for a *thard clarss* with a perfectly raw accent. In first or second class, I would have drawn attention to myself.

And in the beautiful, floral blue morning I sat down on a luxurious bench waxed like parquet, amidst the rattling and pulsing of a monstrous train whose raging asthma shook the entire car. I lay my head in the corner of two comfortable wooden partitions softened by the old filth and various pomades and I slept.

I did not wake up until I was in Saint Lazare station.

PART THREE

I

"Is it really you?" my brother asked. "I was going to leave this evening for Vassetot since I haven't received any answers to my latest letters to Doctor Froin..."

A chambermaid, visibly taken aback by my strange and careless appearance, but even more disturbed when she learned that I was the brother of "Monsieur," had just brought me into a little Japanese salon, or was it Turco-Arabic... No! It was Hindu, but it had everything there, kakemonos, lacquers, mosque chandeliers, low tables for *caoua*, furniture from Travancore, *pankahs*, a rug from Amritsar, weapons from Hyderabad, vetiver tatti screens for the windows, and so many other things! All the familiar odds and ends were crammed into the crowded room. You had to be careful of your knees and if you wanted to stretch your legs, it was better to go outside.

My brother had been sitting and writing at a little teak table inlayed with ivory and nacre. He got up, called out, took me by the shoulders and kissed me. A different guy than me, my brother—lucky for him! He was over six feet two inches tall, had a face with large features framed by a black, graying beard that fell in shining waves on his vest, and shoulders so broad that he was a constant danger to the sconces and bookshelves. He looked gigantic in the low-ceilinged drawing room.

He cried out again, "My poor Philippe! Caging you up like that, the rats! But look here: you're nothing like what they said! As far as I can tell, you had a touch of melancholy! And this Froin who called me and then told me something different and then after that, played dead! I was really upset. I really didn't want to go butting into your affairs again, but this time, too bad! I was going to show up at your Froin's and play his bones like castanets."

As open as he was, Julien wasn't telling me everything. He was furiously—that's the word—kind and devoted, ready to give his blood for his own, or even for a simple friend. He was courageous like people are only in the most deceitful novels for young girls; he was afraid of nothing in the world, absolutely nothing—except his wife! If my sister in-law decided that it was right for me to be in a mental hospital, and that it was wrong for her husband to interfere in my business, Julien would have fought with all his strength to make her change her mind, but he would never have entered on even the first step until she agreed.

I told him as quickly as possible what happened in the institution that was livened up lately by Bid'homme's riding and was now turned into a branch of the Police Department. I was careful not to mention the squatting of the warlike Kmôhoûn in my poor brain, but I told him about the *attack* on Irene, blaming my savage brutality on a fit of lover's madness—I had not yet been cured at the time, etc. It was only when I was sure I had come back to my senses that I wanted to escape the hospital, which was haunted by bleak memories for me.

My brother listened to me and tried not to lose control. I thought that if Monsieur Bid'homme had had him as an inmate instead of me, the dirty little psychiatrist would not have waited for the last week to give up horse riding. He would never have found a saddle soft enough for his sore rump.

When I had finished my short speech, Julien sat there like he was torn between confusion and anger. He stroked his beard, then made a fist and then, unfortunately, opened his fingers. I say "unfortunately" because his fingers closed again at that very instant on a very fragile chair back that he reduced to splinters.

A little calmed by this modest use of force, he grabbed me by the ear and started laughing a little nervously:

"Naughty boy! Rascal, come on! You know I'm not prude, but you have your ways! But really, it's none of my business and I don't like virtuous people much. The main point is that you're here. I'm going to write to this Le Lancier and tell him that I have you, that I'm keeping you and that I'm sweetening you up. He won't send the police to get you, will he? I won't let you go back to Vassetot, even if you ask on bended knees—and weeping to boot!"

"Hey! Calm down!"

"Come on! You're too nice. Let's have breakfast. You must be starving."

I asked to wash up, change my clothes and brush my hair. In ten minutes, it was done.

I was all cheered-up: the hallway was decorated like the drawing room with fabrics and exotic objects, another bric-a-brac; it looked beautiful to me, like a gallery in an Indian palace.

In the bright dining room, the crystal smiled. I reveled in my freedom, sheltered with one of my own, to whom I was not some kind of outcast only interesting from a medical point of view. Here, I was loved and pampered. The Le Lanciers and Barrouges would get a fine welcome if they talked to me in this house like they did over there!

But my sunny good cheer was clouded over: sitting at the table with her whole face held in check, tightened into a cruel grimace that could only have been translated as: "I'm waiting and I'm annoyed," I saw Adrienne, my sister in-law, the classic example of a strong woman—and not very forgiving. She was, should I say it, rough?—and her energy was too manly. She was a little like cousin Raoula, whom she respected a great deal. Like the wife Roffieux, she had never been wrong once in her life; she was perfect in her relations with her entire entourage—O the astonishing, dreadful species of those perfect people!—but her perfection was depressing and you'd wish she had some lovable, little flaw.

I do not know why—and it was very bad on my part—but she made me think all the time of that steamer called *The*

165

Refrigerator, specially designed to transport meat from La Plata and whose holds were kept at zero temperature, even on the Equator. When she looked at me, even during a heat wave, I always thought I was going to cough. How did my poor brother not become consumptive around her? When I had the chance to admire her gray eyes, like the gray skies of Lapland, her vaguely Junonian profile, her whole beautiful body, full without being fat, tall but not too, harmonious in its way, I suddenly became a very young child again, and was sorry for all the lowdown tricks that she knew about even before I had done them and that she thought were typical of me.

I can also say that she considered herself simple and a good person, completely refined, without too much grandeur, full of airs—and that no one seemed to "spruce up" enough for her or "blossom" enough when she was around. She constantly criticized people for being stuffy, tight-lipped, closed up "like a tomb." Didn't she pull out all her charm to please them? In a good mood, she had a proud little strong voice, friendly but superior, that dried up the slick words of every lawyer-politician. I knew men full of self-composure whom she had tried to put at ease and who, many years later, still had a kind of mental soreness from her.

She stared at her husband, who was in front of me, and said to him with no comforting kindness in her heart: "I hate to criticize you, but you knew that I had a stomachache this morning!"

My brother's back stooped under the weight of massive guilt; his shoulders sagged maybe even more and gave him a look of infinite sorrow: "I wouldn't apologize for being late if I didn't have good news to tell you that you will be really glad to hear. Guess who's with me—who's going to have breakfast with us?"

You could almost see Adrienne's face light up a little. My sister in-law loved having guests, even if it was just to show off her talents as the lady of the house who was unappreciated by my frivolous brother. She was pretty nearsighted, so with no unnecessary shyness she placed squarely on her nose—which had a purity of design that was fully Greek—heavy glasses whose lens looked like little crystal goblets.

In spite of myself, I stepped to the side and stood directly behind my brother.

"Let's see, Julien!" Adrienne cried a little impatiently, "Stop playing around! You know very well that you are big enough to hide a stable of horses if you wanted to stand in front of them!"

My brother stepped aside and I was visible to his wife's disappointed eyes. The glasses fell and Adrienne's entire face was saturated with boredom. Nevertheless, always the respectable woman, she managed a little welcome smile that was so forced that I was almost sorry not to have gone off to South America like I had intended, for a short time. Then she shook my hand so coldly that I suffered the premature pains of rheumatism. I was frozen stiff from it.

"Ah! You have left… the countryside? I am delighted"—(her mouth pinched)—"delighted to see you in good health. Pauline, a place setting!"

She called for the place setting as if she were ordering the chambermaid to give me the knout, a good whipping, and she looked at me with more and more obvious disapproval.

"So sit down! It's… charming that you gave us this… nice surprise. But why haven't you written to us?"

Whatever she felt, she sounded stern. I felt like she was examining me with a kind of disgust, like she was sorry she did not know I was coming. A short trip to her country house in Ville d'Avray would have saved her from the obligation of having to eat next to a lunatic who was *maybe* not cured. My brother knew that she would not get over it until I had left, so he had to get rid of me as soon as possible! Besides, I knew that was his usual tactic when she dreaded seeing people who were, in her eyes, damaged, unpresentable walking disasters, poor relatives.

I lost the cheerful confidence I had had with my brother whose affectionate welcome had raised my self-esteem.

167

Sitting between Julien and Adrienne, I was stuck in the hot seat—guilty—or, at least, accused of something unknown but dishonorable. I tried not to even move much and when I did, it was wooden. As always when I was intimidated, I suffered a thousand little physical irritations. My forehead and back and all my limbs itched. I was tortured by a chronic cold that gets up to its tricks whenever I want to behave myself; tortured—because suddenly—O paralyzing catastrophe!—I realized that I did not know how to blow my nose anymore! If I tried to do it, I was going to be disgusting and hateful; I was going to smear my whole face and make my sister in-law sick to her stomach. They did not want to criticize my country manners, but the four eyes that were leveled at me broadcast terrible things; I would sit there covered in shame and sorry enough to cry, like a little boy! I heard myself breathing noisily. But I did not want them to notice my stuffy nose, which had already, so many times before, angered my whole family, and had already, too often, made so many friends and acquaintances form a very poor opinion of me. Because it's like that! We others, the poor disagreeable characters, are often judged on some little physical problem that is considered—God knows why!—a revelation of a moral defect, of a certain baseness of character. I was sure that Adrienne and even my brother, as good and devoted to me as he was, were right then thinking or wanted to think: "If this boy doesn't blow his nose, it's because he knows perfectly well that his sniffling annoys us. He doesn't want to offend us out in the open, so the wicked little brat is doing his best to be disgusting without risking anything. He's always devious like that! I wonder why he came here! He's out of place everywhere."

But I couldn't say to them that my cold would get better when I was out of sight of my sister in-law!

The breakfast seemed very long despite Julien's good mood. He told me about his last trip to southern India, between Trivandrum and Cape Comorin, his discussion with a Thasildar idiot who refused to rent him elephants, explaining that the Europeans implanted far too subversive ideas in the huge, intelligent masses... He was still dazzled thinking about the green splendor of the forests there, the short sunsets of ruby and topaz, the fading twilights of garnet and amethyst and the beautiful, calm nights of dark sapphire. He had to leave his wife at Mahé and she got bored, but she found some faint traces of French life. You would think that she traveled only for that: to discover in the wildest countries the household interiors and people's manners that reminded her of the faraway life and customs of the plain of Colombes or the plateaus and valleys of Seine-et-Oise[45]. Adrienne let him talk and when he had finished, she very coldly explained her aesthetic:

"In the first place, I should say that I was done with traveling. And for ten years, since his first expedition, I hadn't traveled with my husband and I don't know why I was so foolish last year when he left again. If Julien keeps up this obsession to explore the Middle and Far East, let him have it! I'll wait for him at Ville d'Avray or here. From the start of his wanderings, I hated the too blue skies, the blinding light, the awful jumble of plants and trees and those tribes afflicted with *unnatural* colors. If that's what they call 'beautiful' and 'picturesque,' it's too beautiful and too picturesque for me. We were born in a reasonable, temperate country where the Sun is discrete and the trees are modest. There is no true 'beautiful' without moderation, without a certain mediocrity, as Julien would say. Oh well then, long live 'mediocrity!' It's not normal, it's almost indecent for a levelheaded, well-raised woman to enjoy these exhibitions of extravagant and barbaric pomp... And I will say everything I think, even if you make fun of me: those countries are not like they *should be*!"

I wanted to burst out laughing and it was torturing me, cutting off my breath, shaking my sides for many a long, long second. (O Kmôhoûn!) Julien was floored by his wife's stupidity, by that dressed up mental retardation that you would never imagine was so dense, massive and monumental! Somehow, I managed to control myself, but not before I was found out by the stupid but arrogant Adrienne. And that's the woman who passes for superior! These superiorities are made up of self-confidence, gab and an instinctive knowledge of the stupidity level of their conversational partners. This last quality is often called tact. But tact is not infallible, as I just saw.

I felt even more uncomfortable after Adrienne's display. I wanted to be 500 miles from the dining room where she spouted out and where everything except Julien was turning against me. Even the room's furniture disapproved of me. Gentrified by my sister in-law, it asked me what I was doing there, I who had not paid for it, I who did not have the right to use it (I barely had the right to *admire* it). The most insignificant objects made heinous jokes about me. O how right Katherine Kent-Child-Walker was to speak about the "depravity of inanimate things"[46]! (inanimate?) The salt spoon fell onto my plate and a little fireworks of sauce shot up and stained the tablecloth. A cork found its way—how?—into my pocket and when I finally decided to answer the call of my cold, the cursed little cork showed up in my handkerchief like a tiny, hideous doll in wine-stained swaddling clothes. And I was not calm and cool enough to—quick!—hide it; I stared at it for a long time, sad and stunned. My silverware stand rolled under the table; I made the huge mistake of remembering an annoying lecture about accidents like this, and the even huger mistake of quoting it while forcing myself to laugh like an idiot.

With one glance at my brother, I understood that he was painfully surprised at my condition. Adrienne shrugged—barely!—her shoulders and looked scornful. I was lost, drowned! It was impossible for me to answer when they talked to me, or I babbled incoherent nonsense. I looked at the grandfather clock and asked, "Does it make a sound?" just to say something, anything... Was it also that this new absurdity might wipe out the memory of the other ones and start a conversation that might point their minds and eyes to a point in space other than the one I occupied? My plan did not work. The four eyes—sometimes six when the glasses were brought into play—were leveled at me more and more firmly. I understood that I had a stupidly childish expression on my face, then another look that was despicably pretentious. I was hateful and revolting!

Kmôhoûn was grumpy and kept saying to me every five minutes, *"These people know that you're not cured—that you're crazy, crazy, crazy!"*

What a relief when Adrienne slipped away after coffee to let my brother and me smoke at ease! But I was soon put back on the grill.

My brother looked worried. He examined me slyly. He did not know what to say, so he made small talk, but kept cutting himself off. According to an old wives' expression, he "didn't have a head" for what he was talking about. Soon he got tired of pretending:

"My dear Philippe, I'm not going to beat around the bush like this for two hours. I think you're totally... better, if you ever were what the folks at Vassetot and those creeps of Roffieux said you were. But something has happened to you between the minute you came into my office and the end of breakfast. Did you drink before coming here and the alcohol didn't take effect until a while after having one or maybe a few poisonous aperitifs, as sometimes happens? When you first got here, you seemed under control, but at the table, you turned into that little 12 year old boy who didn't want to go to cousin Pigeon's house for dinner because the venerable, gloomy relative always stuck him between two weird, irritating monks whom he was deathly afraid of. When they dragged him by the collar to the pathetic old lady, that Philippe was dotty during the whole meal. They couldn't get a word out of him that didn't sound ridiculous, and his behavior was disgraceful. One time, they caught him washing his fingers in the coffee cup a few minutes after flatly refusing the finger bowl that they'd offered him, as was the custom in those gothic times—yes!—, and what was worse, after pushing back the little balsamic dish against the plate of Father Gigoudas, who was sitting next to him, and mumbling politely, 'Thanks, Father, much obliged, but I never touch the stuff!'

171

"Despite your graying moustache, I thought you were just now suddenly rejuvenated to 22! You were only missing the black crown, white fangs and razor sharp look of Father Bougniassou, outraged at what he took as an offense to his Superior. Tell me the truth, did you go to a bar before you came here?"

"I arrived too completely sober!"

"Then what is it? What's wrong with you?"

"I'll give it to you straight. I know that I annoy Adrienne and her self-righteous, stern face makes me sick."

"And I was planning to keep you with us and then take you to India next year!"

"Since your wife doesn't travel anymore, I'll be glad to go to India with you; but as far as staying here, it's beyond my force. I'll try to see you every day, but I have to stay somewhere else, in a place where the proper ladies have no access!"

And Kmôhoûn, taking advantage of the fact that I was not thinking about him, forced me to add, "Ha! But when you're a widower!"

Julien was not angry. He looked at me for a minute without saying a word, and I saw that his eyes, which never looked hard despite the imposing eyebrows and thick eyelashes that made them blaze with a pretty wild sparkle, became very gentle—a gentleness that hurt me:

"My poor boy!" he cried. "It's not you anymore! Hey! I'm not saying that those idiots at Vassetot and that scoundrel Roffieux were right when they said there was something wrong with your brain; but there's something strange, something unnerving, going on with you. I want to take care of you here—right here. No mental hospitals, no annoying treatments! I know people who will understand that it's simply a problem of nerves and who will pull you through with nothing but a little mental discipline, laying out a nice, calm program for you with a few distractions and outings…"

Kmôhoûn kept me from hearing the rest of the sentence. I thought my head was going to explode. The Tkoukrian howled and stormed, but for me alone. Only I could hear his

172

awful racket and his abominable explosion of rage made me panic. I was about to say something stupid again—after so many other things—but I could not talk reasonably anymore. It was a *psychic racket* that no one would be scared of, except me—but I was stunned by it. I did not miss a single word that Kmôhoûn yelled, even though he did not articulate any of them. But I do not have the least desire to repeat them all here; it tumbled out like a torrent of trash. I would be forced to write pages and pages on which the most terrifying curses and the most revolting obscenities would be repeated again and again. This whole flood of filth, moreover, could be boiled down pretty much to this: *"You lunatic, moron, agitated idiot! Don't you see your crook brother's scam? Ha! I knew it! They're not doing it to me! Let's f...ly the coop—and quick! They're going to have some fun in this... this... whorehouse! And you will have your rotten... whoremonger of a sister in-law to stir up the foul... pimp guards that they'll give us. Your brother is a crap-stained pig, walking dung,"* etc, etc. And I'm softening up many of Kmôhoûn's terms! Pretty, yes, pretty, my expression *psychic racket*. Charming soul, that Kmôhoûn!

I calmed the Tkoukrian by promising, very sincerely, that we would not stay long in this apartment that was decorated with the body of the delightful and indulgent Adrienne. I too was afraid of the intelligent doctors whom my brother spoke about. If these superior men were going to discover the Tkoukrian soul in me and torture me for a long time and to no use to get rid of it? Come on, I was becoming crazy again and crazier than before! But too bad! I did not want to stay there! I would rather be ungrateful to my brother; I would escape that very day…

Julien continued without noticing my distress and terror:

"…You'll be treated like a prince. You don't want to deal with Adrienne? OK, we'll arrange it so you'll never see her. I'm sure that in less than three months you'll be completely back on your feet and able to take care of yourself. So, instead of holding you back, I will insist that you get some air, travel and go wait for me in India, if necessary, where I can't go back before a year…"

I agreed with everything he proposed, like I was won over by his generosity (what a vile hypocrite I was!), but my decision was made… and how. I would be sorry to run out on the best friend I had, but his projects were too dangerous for me.

To Julien's great surprise, I started talking about Vassetot again. Kmôhoûn pushed me and I eagerly obeyed. Since I had not mentioned the name of the dear little woman who was treated so horribly by me, and since I was sure that old Froin, no matter what he said, would not have spoken of the attack in his last letter, I pretended to remember all of a sudden that, "of course! Indeed!" my brother also knew about the country where I was imprisoned… More sociable than me, he probably, "isn't that right, Julien?", knew many more people. The Roffieuxs, too, saw quite a few people. Those wicked folk generally loved society, like everyone who needs to escape from themselves.

"…It looks like I'm saying something bad about you, but you understand me, and you know that I understand you: your sociability is all about supporting the boors, not searching them out…"

"Oh! Don't talk to me about the Roffieuxs!" Julien roared. "They're scum! The rotten beasts knew when I was coming back. They wrote to me and never said a word about what happened to you. I'm very angry with them. Adrienne feels the opposite, but it's too late to go over again what I said in that letter of garbage I sent to them. Hold on! I'll tell you what happened instead. It was full of ploys. The Roffieuxs, I know now, didn't trust Doctor Froin and wrote to my wife to not fill me in on the tricks that were playing out at Vassetot. I lied just now when I told you about my letters to the director of the mental hospital. It was Adrienne who wrote in my name, without consulting me. She did it for the best. They said I shouldn't see you, that it was terribly dangerous for you in your condition. So, I knew of your committal only a very short time ago…"

(OK, so that explained the letter in which *Julien* demanded that I be released on his arrival? Crap! Adrienne's cunning to make old Froin wait it out and show him the good intentions of the family.)

"…How did I learn about it? After an argument with your sister in-law, the first we'd ever had together and that I'd rather not talk about, you understand! I'll tell you only one thing that's true—miserable old liar that I am!—you have to understand that I was leaving this evening for Vassetot and that I was going to demolish Froin. I didn't know about the new management of Le Lancier and the problems of the poor gentleman whom I was very innocently slandering. Will you forgive me?"

Would I forgive him? Good question! I recognized here my old Julien. He could rival the most generous people in the world, be prepared to break the bones of a tribe of ogres, real or imaginary, but would never admit that his wife—the atrocious tramp!—could be as royally sickening in her stupid and unjustifiable hatred as Roffieux in his ridiculous jealousy, maybe topped off with greed.

Try as Kmôhoûn might to harass me, repeating 20 times in a row, *"You'll see! Your brother is just like the others!"*, he finally had to accept that my mind was made up and he was wasting his time. He soon got back to his original idea: *"So, don't let yourself be distracted from your project by these revelations of beautiful family sentiments and hurry up and get the info on where you can find your princess."*

I was already trembling from being so foolish. Could I wait for the Tkoukrian to leave to find out about what was so close to my heart? My brother was not the only one who could guide me in my search and Kmôhoûn would not always keep track of *all* my thoughts. Anyway, he was only updated on my findings by inspecting my cerebral picture gallery when his wild transports were almost tolerable! O poor self-complacency! I was mad at myself.

But the small victory over my tormenter, by forcing him to keep his accusations against my brother to himself, intoxicated me with a kind of courage. This would calm him down, the Kmôhoûn!

"*Good! It's agreed! I'll be quiet,*" the man from Tkoukra gave in. "*But get busy with our business.*"

It was too late to go back. The damage was done. So I said to my brother, "Forgive you? Don't make me laugh! You're too much! Let's talk about something else."

And as if I was asking for business information (with Roffieux I had been able to study the diction of the most eminent industrialists and merchants of Caux), I dropped the question, out of the blue, like it was nothing:

"By the way, you probably remember meeting once at Elzear's a certain Letellier. He was just about to be named representative of the ninth district of Dieppe in a by-election. I need to see him. Oh, it's nothing serious! A matter of a tobacco bill that's left over from my incarceration. What's he like?"

"An animal! I haven't seen him for years and it wasn't at Elzear's that I met him. Roffieux and he don't see each other. I was told that he got married and made his wife pretty unhappy. But when you say that he was *just about* to be elected representative, your calendar is off; it was over six months ago that he scaled the gallery of the Chamber and exasperated the Government that he claims to support. He's an obstructionist of the first order and awful about the colonies. They're already saying that the Minister is trying to get rid of him, so he's going to make him governor of some faraway possession. I'm sure his address is in the telephone directory."

My brother went to get the fat volume and then leafed through it. "Here! 750 Boulevard des Invalides. I'll go with you if you want."

Ah! No, really! Julien had already offered to go for a walk with me. It was perfect. I would take advantage of his excellent idea to disappear at the corner of the street into traffic or a crowd. Later, I would go alone to the Boulevard des

Invalides, and at some impossible hour, at some time when my brother would not think of finding me there!

But what was going on in my head? Everything was mixed up now. Weeks for me were lasting centuries and months were passing by like days. I was off by six months in my calculation! And what else had I learned? Irene was unhappy, just as I feared. What should I do? Ah! I was going to steal her away, for sure! There was no other solution.

Julien got up, lit a cigar, grabbed his hat, gloves and cane and took me to a big store where I dressed myself up again half-civilized. Then we strolled for an hour or two with a Swede, a Japanese and finally a Bulgarian who were, it seemed, the only true Parisians whom we could meet that day between the suburb of Montmartre and the roundabout of the Champs-Elysées.

I began to think I would never escape. There was no crowd. Not the smallest traffic jam. The streets were pretty much deserted.

Around 5 p.m., Julien told me that it was too late to go to the Left Bank—that we would go tomorrow—and that he had to go get news of a sick friend, Rue de la Boëtie; we would only stay for a minute.

When we got to the house of the so-called dying man, a servant told us that Monsieur had been able to get out of bed. My brother was radiant, did an about-face and asked to see his friend. We were led into a kind of library where we found the convalescent and too many of his family. There was a lady with a leonine mug (the wife), a son who looked like a lion cub, totally red-haired, totally tanned and totally curly, a thin brown girl sculpted in solid wood and as shapeless as the famous Jeanneton doll[47] and an old maid with a nose like a candle snuffer. The thin faced, disdainful and nosy ex-invalid welcomed Julien unenthusiastically and measured me up with obvious malice. I knew this Monsieur Jagre in the old days. His family, however, I had not known—seen but not known—and I had never tried to bond with him, being preserved in vinegar as he was seemed rather nasty to me. I was always surprised that my brother liked him so much.

When Julien reminded him that he had already met me, Monsieur Jagre seemed almost ready to shake my hand—with much reluctance. He struggled, stretched out his fingers, which folded back like the petals of a sensitive plant, and then after thinking about it, just when I was going to grasp those reluctant phalanges as gently as possible, he firmly took his hand back and hid it inside his buttoned up, elegant frock coat, which was as skimpy as its owner.

My brother was obviously too attached to the precious patient to hide a family problem from him and had notified Monsieur Jagre of my holiday in Vassetot. The other members of the tribe, likewise informed of my dishonorable accident, looked at me through thinning eyes, more scornful than pitying, then stared at their chief and, finally, faced with his scolding attitude, resigned themselves—no guilt involved—to ignore my existence. They would try to pretend I was not there even though, I'm sure, my presence annoyed and disgusted them. My brother, who had not followed this dramatization, sat in an armchair and began chatting away and congratulating the cordial Monsieur Jagre on his speedy recovery. They kept ignoring me. But, when I was about to sit down without being authorized, the lady with the leonine mug pointed out a seat for me. Then she turned her head away in horror.

Everything about this family was falsely pretentious, petty bourgeois. They were good enough impersonators to appear well mannered, which might impress a bear like me, but they were too stupid to hide the vices of their upbringing, which had only made them arrogant, vain and cruelly scornful of "inferior" people. They were sick with the "right" kind like my sister in-law was sick with the "proper."

Julien must have broken a primordial law of etiquette recognized by these puppets when he brought me into their sacrosanct den, because Monsieur Jagre's little face was pocked with disgruntled twitches. His shiny skin was stretched out on his jutting jaws; the curve of his upper lip became convex; his cheekbones looked like two walnuts; his thin, rounded nose pointed at his mouth. The sociable sufferer nibbled his frayed moustache angrily and answered my brother's gush of sentiments with little alarm-like grunts. The lady with the leonine mug, whom nature had given a deep voice exactly like a big cat, once in awhile bellowed short phrases to show Julien that she did not like him anymore.

This woman, who was obviously energetic and an enemy of hypocrisy, hated being too subtle or obscure. When my brother had reiterated his pleasant surprise, Madame Jagre did not mind cutting him short:

"Surprises of this kind are wonderful of course, but there are others that are in bad taste to come across."

She glanced over in my direction and then stared at poor Julien who knew what she meant and blushed as much as I turned pale. He looked a little angry at the dear woman, but his good nature immediately got the upper hand. I was sure that he said, "Madame Jagre is as natural and frank as anyone could wish: she's an original—but maybe I shouldn't have brought Philippe here."

He did not want to leave his friend's wife without having eased her resentment. His friend held a grudge, but he was going to try to appease the mother:

"How pretty Adele has become!" he said brazenly. "She looks charming today. And what a nice girl, so sweet and well raised!"

The rectilinear young girl was flattered and smiled, but the matron was not disarmed:

"You're too kind, but she is still far from perfect. Well! In this day and age a young woman sometimes has to be in strange surroundings! Even at home she is forced to meet all kinds of people!"

You had to see the scandalized and disgusted looks of the lion cub, young Jagre, whose crumpled face just then looked exactly like the muzzle of a sickly, scornful tomcat— and the old maid with a nose like a candle snuffer!

The eyes of the whole clan converged on me, ordering me to leave, to disappear. Because of my feelings for my brother, who was already getting ready to stand up, maybe even make a scene and mess things up with a family he liked—he had depraved tastes!—I was cowardly enough to try to get into the good graces of this enemy race, or at least to calm their anxieties about what they must have called "my gross mental illness." So, taking the bull by the horns, I babbled and fumbled through this outrageous remark that I thought, at the time, was a kind of clumsy but friendly joke:

"Oh, Madame, it would have to be a very thin varnish to flake off at a simple contact. I am sure that thanks to a mother like you, the young lady, your daughter, has... a thick and solid coating..."

I felt myself turn pale... Ah! The atrocious Kmôhoûn must have collaborated in this lovely sentence! And, in fact, the wretch was laughing inside me with all his force. He was glad that I was the only one to feel his laughter. I saw all the Jagre faces become hateful and vicious. The father was going to hypnotize me. His pupils had turned phosphorescent. Then he lifted his little, almost invisible chin and flared his nostrils with contempt. He turned back toward my brother and said to him, as if to prove that I was not there and my last words were null and void:

"As you were saying, Monsieur Veuly..."

And the conversation went on for maybe five minutes, very cold and very formal.

Julien started to get up but Madame Jagre did not want him to be able to brag about leaving of his own free will. Her mug hung straight down with deep wrinkles and her voice rang out cavernously:

"There are too many of us in the room. We are making my husband tired: I will leave for awhile with the children... Goodbye, Monsieur Veuly..."

Everybody was already standing except for the convalescent tomcat.

O these people sick with the "proper!"

My brother was on his feet before the others. He made a sign to say goodbye and the five Jagres gave a little nod of their stiff, automaton heads. There was no question of handshakes or words of affections.

On the street, Julien gave me a friendly pat on the back and started laughing: "I didn't know your teeth were so hard: a *coating*! And thick and solid! That's a bit too much! Oh well, you had every right to put that old Bogey Monster in her place. I'm glad the husband's on the road to recovery. That will save me from going back to that lair of felines. And when I think that Jagre was a good kid! But that was a long time ago!"

My brother thought that I cheered myself up at the expense of this family of big cats! Why not admit to him the awful truth? But I know what he expected from me. From now on, I would not be able to be with friends or acquaintances without thinking that they are watching me, scared and hostile and on the lookout for a crisis...

Julien went into a tobacco shop to buy some cigars. He was busy making a careful choice of his fake Havanas. He was not paying attention to me. Here was the opportunity I was waiting for! I tiptoed out of there, skipped down the street, turned a corner, hailed a cab and, 45 minutes later, I was sitting in a little restaurant at the Place du Panthéon, next to the Hotel du Périgord where I had decided to stay for a night or two. My brother would not come looking for me there and, tomorrow or the next day at the latest, after stealing away Irene, willingly or by force—absolutely!—after a visit to the bank and the necessary round of shopping in the stores on the Left Bank, I would say goodbye to Paris, to its pomp and its products, and catch any train whatsoever that would take us away to... a still undetermined country.

II

If I meant to isolate myself before accomplishing the heroic deeds that were to exemplify my short stay in my hometown, I have to say that I did not have a chance. I left the restaurant and had just sat down at the Darcourt to have a liberating coffee when a friend came up who recognized me right away. It was an old, old partner to whom I was thoroughly indebted—who had 20 times over done the impossible to get me out of the most boring and complicated matters, and I was never able to pay him back.

Of course, I was glad to see him even though I knew that in my present state of mind I was, for sure, going to do something stupid that would make him like me less. And I did. He had the nice, but very unfortunate, idea to invite me to breakfast the next day.

Ah! I could just see myself there, haunted by the constant obsession of beings, true or imaginary, who would study me and watch me to catch me red-handed in madness; while I was sitting at the table in a house where the family was so big— husband, wife, mother in-law, three kids, two cousins and an old uncle!

Nothing else for me to do but eat—at my slightest action—movement even, that I would not make but that I would be *about to* make, one of the hosts would be able to guess everything! I couldn't accept! I couldn't! No! No! What could I say? What excuse could I come up with? I was no longer myself!

I answered a little sharply, "Tomorrow! No, thank you! Impossible!"

"Then another day?"

I saw that my excuse really stunned him: "There's nothing I can do! I'd be in a bad mood!"

And my friend piled on the arguments to prove to me that I had no reason to shy away like that, that I was being rude; but he could only get out of me that eternal refrain: "I'd be in a bad mood! I'd be in a bad mood!"

He left, not very charmed by my good graces. For a long while I sat there kind of overwhelmed—with a heavy weight on my heart.

But the Darcourt, which I had chosen because I thought it was not very popular with my old buddies, had become the meeting place of everyone I knew in my school days!

There was a Haitian, Remilius Saint Val Antenaz, whom I thought forever hunkered down in Port-au-Prince and who had shown up in the Latin Quarter six weeks ago: anyway, he had his return ticket to Saint Thomas and Puerto Rico in his pocket. A good, jolly guy like most of his countrymen, he tried to make me laugh and got as an answer to his jokes only my new refrain, a little changed: "I'm in a bad mood!"

Surprised and feeling sorry for me, he got so worried that he started speaking Creole, him the purest of purists—and said that his "dar breda at sore" (translation: dear brother has been bewitched)—and soon he went away. He was dreaming, I'm sure, of the *ouanga*[48] and dark, evil spells, but he was shining from head to toe, shining from his silk hat to his polished boots, shining from his black agate eyes, from his snow enameled teeth, from his dark golden face, from his black, satin-like suit, from his shirt like a white firmament among the twinkling stars, from his ring-fingered hands...

There was Dubousquet the doctor, Graindorge the lawyer, Galusky the Ohnetian[49] engineer, the poets Mauvel and Bonancourt, the painters Croy, Luz and Brillac, the musician Brice, the incomparable Sâr Assourbanipal Dupont, competitor and enemy of Péladan[50]—less talented, for sure! There was even Judge Persil and the ex-student of the Ecole Normale Supérieure Le Birgrier, deserter from the Rue d'Ulm, entered into holy orders and turned into the fashionable preacher. A preacher at the Darcourt? I must have been dreaming! There he was, though, but disguised as a Roman Monsignor, which astonished me.

183

There were hundreds, now, squeezed into the café, but a space was left free in the center of the room.

Suddenly, they closed the doors and lowered the thundering metal blinds. The owner of the café waved his hand and Irene fell from the ceiling—Who? Yes, she! Irene!—who began dancing totally naked on the square of white board surrounded by dark costumes among which the Monsignor's cassock burst out like a tuft of violets amidst scabiosa. Irene danced naked, bent down, stood up, arched her back, seemed to offer herself completely with a frantic lewdness that depressed me and carried me away... and someone grabbed me by the arm and shook me. I recognized the poet Nelix. Thanks to him they had published many of my poems in the *Revue Rouge*, the only Parisian periodical where I had the pleasure of seeing my name in print. The Darcourt had returned to normal and this time I was no longer dreaming:

"Well!" cried Nelix. "What's this then? I caught you sleeping with your eyes open like some wide-awake sleepwalker, smiling so very sadly at a bottle of cognac on the counter. You didn't start smoking opium, did you?!"

I told him my story—the short version so I would not tire him out—and did not hold anything back.

"That's all very nice," he told me when I had finished! my little narration, "but you're not going to stay here till 2 a.m. In the lovely spirits I find you, you'll probably get drunk like a member of the temperance society and, once loaded, think the pier on Boulevard St. Michel, or even the mouth of a sewer, was your bed in the Hotel du Périgord. Let's spend a couple of hours at my house. I live really close, remember. You can get your balance back among levelheaded folks and I will take you back to your caravanserai later."

I resisted for a minute, more afraid than ever of my friends' families. But Nelix pretty much forced me by dragging me along without listening to me telling him off, and soon I was at the Panthéon, and then on the stairs, and finally, without knowing how I got there, in a large, bright room where unknown but pleasant faces looked at me cheerfully. A hitch: Nelix's mother had a terrible migraine. I promised myself to escape as soon as possible and said out loud, rather clumsily as I usually do, that I would not stay long to bother her.

Unfortunately, my friend told me about one of my old poems (?) that he had been wrong to think was acceptable. I was dazed with a heady whiff of vanity; I heated up; I talked; I sparkled with stupidity. They served tea; I rambled on, more and more satisfied with my ridiculous self despite the traces of bewilderment on the still friendly but maybe embarrassed faces. I finally figured that I had tired my audience enough and that a swift retreat was called for. I was going to save myself; I even prepared my farewell speech when—O fatality!—the doorbell rang out loud and clear. Right away a gentleman came in whom I figured was some visitor.

And me, for my part, the poorly brought up bear, full of fairly reasonable contempt for books about "puerile and honest civility," I was just about to remember—very inaccurately—one of those pseudo-sophisticated authors! I forgot about Madame Nelix's migraine… What does Madame Augusta du Pont-aux-Choux in her immortal and no less astonishing book, *Politeness*, say about not playful but bourgeois suave?...

I cannot quote her exactly, but the gist of it was something like: "When a sufficient number of persons come together in a room and a new visitor is announced, the person who came first should take leave without pretense, but with stoicism." It's very well thought out: it's a clever little law against clutter. But, unfortunately, as I had my head upside down, I translated it thus: "When an escaped patient from a mental hospital finds himself among friends and sees an unexpected gentleman arrive among these friends, the said mental patient will not take the trouble to budge, but appear to say like Madame Jagre: 'We have enough boors like that!' and will not forget that the *last* person to show up has the strict duty to get out first. Otherwise, the mental patient will make it understood that the intrusion of the gentleman annoys him deeply."

So I stayed, I stayed, rooted there—lavishing the most god-awful examples of my charming stupidity on them with Asian magnanimity. It was even worse because the new guest was witty and nice... But why didn't he leave? I could not look like I wanted to teach him a lesson! It lasted such a long time that I finally remembered Madame Nelix's cephalalgic pains and—through pity—was going to act impolitely by giving up my seat, against all my good principles, when the stubborn visitor got out of his chair and said to me, after looking at the clock:

"Monsieur, please excuse me but it's getting late. My mother, as you see, is not feeling well... and I have to say that I too am completely beat and..."

Horror! He was Nelix's brother and HE WAS LIVING THERE!

I wanted to drop through all the floors in one fell swoop and crash into the refreshing darkness of the second catacomb of cellars! Just then, the real text of Madame Augusta du Pont-aux-Choux came back to me, put back in place. Ah! It was complete! (Too much!) What a filthy clod I must have looked like! I made fun of the strict lady's civilizing prose, but for me, to be so obnoxious was too cruel, by middle-classism—middle-classism! Me! In fact, what did it matter that I did the opposite of what was accepted by socialite snobs, if I had no respect—in my way—and ended up with this lovely result!

Certainly, Nelix's brother was being generous and I deserved to be kicked out, but I was covered in shame.

I do not know how I managed my exit... Ah! Ah! What a situation. I was suffocating! I guess that when I got on the street I high-tailed it out of there. I would never again go over to anybody's house—ever!

I had made great use of my first day of freedom! Would I know how to behave from now on decently enough that they would not throw me in the first Charenton[51] asylum available? And I was the one who wanted to steal away Irene! No, it was impossible! I was going to hide... far, far away!

III

Dead tired, I slept like a log almost all night long. Early in the morning, however, I woke up from a nasty nightmare. Monsieur Jagre, more tomcat than ever, his eyes like green candles—O Alfred Jarry![52]—or at the very least like green flames, chased after Irene while meowing, snarling and swearing. He caught her and bit one of her ears, then her neck and he sacrificed the body of my poor little princess in the most erotic fantasies. Madame Robinet was undressing herself like a flirt—a riding jacket and nothing else—with her... hips so overblown that her huge calves and sturdy ankles seemed skinny in comparison. She sat on my head to keep me from running to help the Exquisite. Nelix, with the voice and accent of the Haitian Saint Val, read some of my poems in which I celebrated these abominations, and the whole family, which my sister in-law Adrienne was suddenly made a part of, chased me with clubs onto the deck of a large black steamer setting sail for the Antilles. Why for the Antilles? I had the feeling that I would find out that day.

The disturbing dream evaporated at the dull sounds of the first strokes of the propeller and I cracked open my heavy, irritated eyelids. I recognized the room of the Hotel du Périgord.

The weather was dark and red, a bad omen. It looked like clouds of soot were brushing against the chimneys. But despite being tired and kind of down in the dumps, I washed myself up with unusual energy, decked myself out in the luxurious binding of brown cloth bought yesterday with my brother and made myself beautiful, I would say, if my appalling mug did not object to such a flattering expression. I had a quick breakfast and dashed into the street.

My old Paris looked completely different to me. I might say it was sulking—or warning me? Of what? Of bad luck? Of a simple problem? Its sooty houses were making faces at me. I felt lost, like a stranger among passers-by who were slower and more bored than those I bumped into on the Right Bank yesterday.

Here was a calmer Paris, less annoying for the country folk I had become, but also colder, and maybe more disturbing. I knew very well that it was an absurd impression, but I felt it was floating like a kind of dreary fatality over these districts in contrast to where the wide, brand new streets disemboweled the masses of great black anthills... On the Boulevard des Invalides, I looked for number 750 and found it at the end, near the Rue de Sèvres.

It was a big residential house, too modern in style, with ridiculous cupolas that made it a sort of uglier Bon Marché[53].

What was I going to do here? What approach should I take?

I interrogated the doorman, a bureaucrat in a blue coat sparkling with spotless buttons. This important and dignified administrator gave me enough information to support, to a certain point, the warning of Paris' Sinister Bank:

"Madame Letellier? She left 12 days ago with Monsieur who was named Governor of *Gobaloupe*..."

Aha! The Sinister Bank! If I understood the lodge's dignitary officer correctly, Irene, whose husband had been catapulted to Governor of *Guadeloupe* and its dependencies (official denomination), because he had harassed the ministers too much with his more or less colonial heckling, had boarded the liner for the Lesser Antilles on the 10th at Saint Nazaire in the company of Monsieur Letellier, who was "attaining" his post. What should I do?

I ran, or rather a horse and carriage ran for me, to the office of the Transatlantic Company—on the other, even more dangerous Bank.

A steamer was leaving from Pauillac on the 25th for the Antilles, Venezuela and Colombia. If they did not take me by force back to Julien's home, this was the boat that was going to carry me to my princess. It was the 22nd. If I left that evening, I would make it to Bordeaux with two days to spare. I would be perfectly safe in that city where no one would ever think of tracking me down.

My impatience was feverish; it was so childish that I thought I could not wait to board the express (at 7:55 p.m.) anywhere else except around the Orléans station. The cab brought me near the wine market to a restaurant that I had heard of awhile back. I needed all my force for another sleepless night—in a train, this time—and I crammed my conscience, very ignorant, with the same kind of nourishment that I stuffed my belly with, which was obedient, luckily.

But how was I going to kill the time that separated me from the blessed hour when I would finally begin to move a little closer to Irene?

It was not yet noon. I swallowed my coffee and wore down a dozen toothpicks—that's a sport I do not recommend. I smoked cigarettes and had a little glass of cognac, purely on a whim. Out of despair, I was about to make little pots out of the menu and wine list taken out of their fake, red morocco frames when two gentlemen—I knew them well—came in to put on an act for me. Very serious, very dignified, looking very profound they entered the restaurant with tiny, cautious steps, as if the floor here and there were booby-trapped with nails.

They did not see me. The dining hall was pretty well stocked with enthusiasts of green salmon sauce and Bordeaux rib steak.

The two gentlemen sat very close to me—at a table that faced mine: as a screen between us, we had only the leaves of a plant that looked like an upright beet.

They took off their things, one his enormous top hat, the other his fedora that reminded me of Finistère[54], which I glimpsed once. After ordering their lunch from the waiter, with a great profusion of somewhat ecclesiastical gestures and a litany of recommendations mumbled under their breath, they began talking together, still *sotto voce*, but the acoustics of the room were favorable to me and I did not miss a word:

"Hey! Leaving together! We were lucky, but the Club members must be out of sorts without us!"

"The most... absolutely beautiful thing, absolutely, yes! is to... bing bang!... have shaken off at the same time our... mechanics!... our pawns—bing bang!—of mutual relatives!"

"We're going to establish a republic for the two of us... of truly free people of whom we, the two of us, will be the presidents and the administrators!"

"But what came over Le Lancier to... mechanics!... to... to write to our families to tell them that we would be—bing bang!—cured?"

"Oh! We were in the boarding school for three years, we were the last two serial numbers called a luxury—O strange luxury! Before leaving, Old Froin asked them not to increase our monthly pension. Le Lancier found a loophole to keep his word without keeping it. He didn't ask for one penny more from our dear blood or uterine relations, but he spent all the painful deposit on giving us a good thrashing, after, of course, making sure that two other colonists would occupy the room and pay triple what we dished up in the establishment."

"Well thought out; and all the better for us! So we... mechanics!... to Chile?"

"That country was pointed out to me by the fluidic advice of Mage Oïrl who navigated on the sailing ships of the Bordes Company."

"And once... absolutely there?"

"We find a Chilean businessman who, through the French Consul, will trim our excellent cousins or uncles of some of our money that they were kind enough to keep to themselves. Since we are no longer mental patients—the Faculty represented by Le Lancier has signed our diploma of mental health—, we have a right to it."

"Do you feel as... absolutely, yes! as perfectly cured as you say?"

"Hey! Hey!... we'll watch out for each other—huh?— And then when we fix up a mental hospital over there, they won't focus on our little eccentricities. We'll have foils! It'll

190

be sublime! We will hire as guards only very nasty people complete with police records and we will tell them that their first duty will be to accept, no questions asked, all the thrashings that the inmates want to give them!"

"Oh! Wonderful!" cried out a little too enthusiastically Monsieur Oswald-Norbert Nigeot, my colleague in Apollo and ex-co-inmate.

He cut himself short, worried, and looked around to see if his excitement had drawn anyone's attention.

Then he noticed me—grew purple, wine red and then green under a lining of amaranthine broken veins. He quickly whispered to his companion, Doctor Magne, whose lovely face of a Greek Sage fell apart and scowled. He, too, had seen me now—out of the corner of his eye—and my two philosophers got up almost at the same times, turned their backs on me and got ready to change tables.

(Meeting up with an old partner in misfortune made them ghastly afraid).

"Don't you find that there's a dreadful draft here?" asked Magne.

"Yes, we would be—bing bang!—better over there, behind the... mechanics, the... screen."

They sat back down far away from me only to get up again and find another place. The screen did not hide them! They repeated their little game twice more, always peering in my direction with terror. I said out loud in a low and barely understandable voice:

"Those people are not cured! I'm saner than they are!"

"*Twiddledeedee!*" Kmôhoûn hummed. "*There's no one reasonable here but me—in you!*"

But the new Hanlon-Lee[55] had finally found a geographical position to their liking. The counter and the fat lady sitting behind the monument loaded with oil and vinegar bottles and mineral water sheltered them from all prying eyes.

I lit another cigarette, paid my bill, and got ready to leave in order to make the two accomplices feel better and let them have their breakfast in peace. But Kmôhoûn had other plans.

191

While I was trying to make my way to the exit, the Tkoukrian suddenly *dragged* me and headed for the counter. Unaware, I was going straight toward the two philosophers whose faces had the most touching look of agony.

I still wanted to pretend not to see them, but Kmôhoûn absolutely insisted on making them suffer to punish them for trying to escape from us.

I was terrified when an awful voice—that of the so recently dreaded Bid'homme—came out of *my* throat and pronounced these words:

"Aha! Grusterloins! Mandypaps! Buggerats! Eat well and digest better, because in exactly three hours we're going to stick you in the tub—to the toadling!—and under a lovely torrent to boot!"

A few customers looked scandalized, but quickly went back to contemplating their dishes.

The eyes of Nigeot and Magne were like billiard balls; you would have thought that their ocular globes were going to jump out of their orbits. The poor companions already looked like lobsters who were a little less nearsighted than average. It was a picture without any beauty.

Magne, who had more natural dignity than his partner, soon reacted against his fear, put on a friendly face and, coming to terms with the situation, pretty coolly shook my hand:

"Oh! Monsieur Veuly! What a pleasure to see you again! Sit down with us, but by God, don't imitate that infamous Bid'homme! It gives me the creeps!"

Nigeot was colder. I had scared him and he held it against me. His hands were red—like raw meat, as he himself said—and were still shaking; his ugly crimson-yellow nose, which would make the Spanish flag pale beside it, still quivered a little:

"Always the filthy dog!" he grumbled. "Vassetot should never have released such a wretched—bing bang—poet. A dishonor to the Art. You'll publish… what do you call it, chapbooks, filthy… mechanics!"

His narrow Mongol eyes had a malicious *varnish*—I would never say a *sparkle* when speaking about those tiny little ugly stains of glossy brown. But he got carried away:

"I myself will never publish… machinery at 3.50 francs or less. Trash! Make poems for myself alone, or, if necessary, for Magne—and also for two barmaids at the Folies Bergère[56]. The only three intelligent people I know! Oh, beautiful and exquisite poems! Rhymes? Soothing echoes; no good-for-nothing rich Parnassian rhymes. Rich rhymes! Oh! It gives me the feeling of a—bing! bang!—of a… kick in the ass. No mystery, no tricks, no machinery, all those… mechanics. Rich rhymes, like Baudelaire (?!), who had the right—but didn't abuse it!—to rhyme richly because he was HIM! Oh! Subtle rhymes, not too many, but distant, strange, striking, sad, blue, sweet, exquisite reminders! Perfectly, yes! No mechanics, no bing bang, absolutely not!"

I could not help thinking that this habitually maniacal idiot was right 100 times over with his obscure but understandable poetic theory. It was one of the few times that I heard something sensible said about it. And he loved Baudelaire! Ah! All the worse for the superhuman poet, but all the better for the lousy stooge Nigeot! This impassioned admiration might, perhaps, in time, make the stench of his cretinism bearable. I also knew that at Vassetot the senile Oswald-Norbert was already obsessed with the godlike author of *Les Fleurs du Mal*, and this was the only reason I liked the Chinese with raspberry jelly.

But Kmôhoûn badgered me. I had to—*absolutely yes!*—persecute the two ex-inmates, cured or claimed as such:

"I heard," I said to the Manchu bard, "that you're going to Chile…"

"H…heard, h…how?" mumbled Nigeot. "You heard us talking about it!"

His entire face was furrowed with little red and yellow ravines.

"Oh! Trash!" he cried. "Words, it's the mechanics again! It's tiring at first to speak—and then it's caught by the *Others*,

193

the savage *Others*! The poor *Me*—and Magne is a *Me* whereas you are a pig, a miscreant *Other*—the poor *Me*—there're maybe 500 of us total on this foul earthly globe!—why can't they communicate together without straining their larynx!"

Nigeot agreed with Kmôhoûn.

"And then everything's...mechanics, effort, on this dung pile of a planet! You have to get dressed and undressed. You can never stay *in a state*, you always have to *change states*! Idiots, pigs that we are! You're comfortable in bed, aren't you? Oh well, crack! You have to get up! You're okay when you're up? Oh well! Bang, bing, bang! You have to go to bed! Get dressed, get undressed! Trash! Mechanics! We lost our fur, our hair, rubbing against it and scraping it with these damn costumes! Look at the monkeys! A lot prettier than us; they look better and have no mechanics to wear. Mechanics, you know, is everything that is against thinking and good old lassitude: movement, stupid moving of arms, arduous stupidity of being a well raised human, no revolt against the stupidities tolerated by the cowardly mob, who's happy to tyrannize itself when it's already pestered by the *padishahs*. Yes, look at the monkeys, the pretty monkeys! No mechanics to wear, lucky devils, good old monkeys! Nothing to do but chuck water on themselves whenever they feel like it!... And when they're ready! Oh! Real world! Pile of crap where you have to work, even just to button up your shirt! Oh! When will we be in a higher world where they won't have these appalling paws? Nothing but little things to fly in the warm blue—warm! You know? Little... mechanics... oh! bing! bang! No mechanics— infamy!—little feathery things like the little... things that chuck turds on our heads from up in the trees and after cry out tweet! tweet! in the air, the... what do you call them, the... birds, totally, yes!"

And this Mongol who spouted his Polynesian or Gabonese opinions was originally from Saint Etienne[57], a city that was so busy it was like industrial epilepsy! But, in fact, it was very simple! He was "tired from birth," as one of my friends used to say who felt the same way, but had nothing to do with Saint Etienne.

All things considered, Nigeot was honest, more honest than me who did not dare confess so bluntly my love and veneration, however sincere, for wonderful Laziness!

But doctor Magne interrupted him:

"Nigeot, my son, you're losing your marbles. We're going to Chile not to dress up like monkeys or birds, but really in order to set up a great establishment... We will talk about it again... Monsieur Veuly, we have also decided to convert the population of Chile, which is far too Catholic, but gentle and manageable after all, to the worship of the great malicious goddess who in reality reigns over this calamitous world: I mean Madame August or, if you prefer, Widow August, that... fertilizing deity whom the mages Oïrl and Shnoumah worship, that strange ex-wife of an herbalist Brahma, who, by imitating those birds perched in the branches that Nigeot was just talking about, by cluttering our poor human existence with filth, will end up, despite everything, bringing us luck in this world or in another. Nigeot is extremely revolutionary and used to have Morovash as his god for a long time, the enemy of city sergeants, cops or agents; but I have brought him back to healthier ideas. He has dethroned his false immortal and runs now to the raised altars of Madame August."

We had really provided an opening for poor Doctor Magne and his mythology tired us. Kmôhoûn, who, just before, wanted to force me to threaten to go with the two philosophers to Chile—only for a laugh, to see their faces—now thought of nothing but leaving.

The future mental patient-missionaries were deeply gratified that I, or *we*, were leaving. They had resigned themselves to put up with me, but I was not a'wanted man, not the least in the world. Since they had left Vassetot together, they did not bother each other at all; their destinies were the same. But I, whom they were not expecting to see, was a kind of ghostly reminder of the sadness back there. And then, if they felt free, even cured, or at least adapted to reasonable people thanks to

195

the signed release of two certified doctors, any old co-inmate who suddenly showed up made them feel like wretched lunatics on the run.

So, I had to keep a safe distance from now on—if Kmôhoûn let me—from anyone who knew me because to all of them, crazy or sane, I brought pain and suffering.

How would I deal with Irene? Was I also going to frighten and humiliate her? She had more reason than any other human being to fear my presence! But a sweet, conceited foolishness took hold of me again: Irene was Irene. She was not like the *Others*. She would forgive me. Wasn't I coming to take her away from the abuse of that monster Letellier, the *evil magician*?

A doubt still ate away at my heart, but I got rid of it quickly enough. It was like I snatched from it—from this doubt—its claws, or rather talons—and it was turned into a big, black, mutilated bird—silly and pathetic. This strange materialization of a doubt scared me again. I was surely becoming crazier and crazier: but as long as I was not attacked by wild madness before I saw *Her* again, nothing but to see *Her* again... Oh! Irene! Your burning black, caressing eyes are going to cure me! You love me, you have to love me, as absurdly ugly and stupid as I am! You must have forgiven my hateful brutality. The passion that I experienced for you— before and after the crime—was always or almost always so pure, yes, so purely tender that there were moments when the Invisible World forgave me, when space existed no longer except for me and when I felt your heart, your adorable heart, beat against mine!

My euphoria did not last long: I suddenly remembered that I still had a terrible chore to do. It was absolutely necessary that I find Messieurs Cash and Nothingelse, bankers, and ask them for everything of mine they had—money and valuables. I wanted to walk with my princess across the entire Earth until she found a kingdom of a few hectares to her liking in some madly blue country.

Cash and Nothingelse had their offices on the Right Bank—luckily not too far from the bridges. I showed up at the office of those movers of Franco-Yankee metals—metals and people—gave my first and last names, turned in some documentation for proof and asked for everything that the bank held in my account. A typically Irish gentleman, but with an unusual nasal accent, the most anti-musical Kentucky *twang*, consulted some records, took a very small piece of paper, scratched out a smaller addition, opened a drawer, extracted a few blue bills, some silver and even some pennies—and put under my nose the sum of *312 francs and 45 centimes*!

My silent fury, then my bewilderment, did not impress the transatlantic junior banker. He explained to me in all seriousness that what he had just done would be very irregular if "my *laygal* avisor, Messiah Roffiah" had not said that I could have this sum (he said: "this thing" and pronounced: "thas thang")—that "Messah Roffiah" had put all the rest "in his packet" and placed my sesterces "alsewhare"—he didn't know where:

"So, I have a legal advisor and it's Monsieur Roffieux! I am very surprised that my cousin forgot about this little 'thang.' There is no amount too petty for him..."

My Celto-Yankee made an excuse for Elzear by telling me that the amount was not entered into the account when Raoula's husband came and my scrupulous relative "baliefed it ha'nt come." So he said I could "git" it and so I "gat" it.

The excellent Kentuckian closed his window and I could do nothing but leave—to go brood over my amazement on the street.

I paid off the cab. My means no longer let me move around in these gliding cages; even the bus would not take long to drive me to ruin. There were still the wagons and carts, but the cart drivers had taken the annoying habit of unloading their passengers with whiplashes—and then I could not find one. Anyway, it was totally useless for me to go back to the Left Bank, I had enough to get to Bordeaux—but afterward? Supposing that I could buy myself a third class seat on a transatlantic, I would arrive in the Antilles without a penny. I could still work for my passage, but the steamer Companies accepted this combination less and less. The sailing ships would be better for me. I would find one at Nantes, but the trip to take me on the lower Loire was much more expensive than from Paris to Le Havre—and there I would have my choice of ships.

I knew perfectly well that Roffieux was stuck in Le Havre on business at that very moment and that it would be beastly of me to say all the stupid things to him that he deserved if I met him. But too bad! I was not going to worry about such a crook. If his pride was flayed, he could patch it up with a cash bandage because I was not going to sue him! I recognize no kind of court.

So, I got back on the train at Saint Lazare station and, a few hours later, the Havreans hanging out on the quay of Orleans saw me strolling along, sad but full of hope, watching the ships about to sail. It was too late for me to join up with a ship owner or a captain, but tomorrow there would still be salty blue or green water and the great big wooden toys.

IV

It was 11 a.m. when I left the office of Monsieur One-sime Bourdon, owner of the West Indian Clippers line.

This notable businessman directed me to Captain Le Coatmabergastmelen, commander of the three-master *Augustine Bourdon*, which was leaving in two days for Pointe-à-Pitre (Guadeloupe).

Just as I was turning onto Rue du Chilou to reach the quay, I noticed two silhouettes on Boulevard de Strasbourg who were very much not unfamiliar to me. In spite of myself I slowed down. My silhouettes stopped in front of the Post Office and then started walking again, moving closer to me, very slowly... I could tell that Elzear and Raoula were not expecting such a surprise... that I had not gone over easy on them.

Kmôhoûn jumped for joy. *"Give them both a soaking!"* he giggled. For a second I was just about to follow his advice because Elzear was so glowing with kindness, his face was so handsome with hard, male sincerity and his shining eyes said so clearly: "I am the severe but blessed upholder of the law," that he was asking for wallops like iron attracts lightning.

The unspeakable Raoula also had a disgusting look on her face. You would easily figure that she felt like an "ahrrah-proachable and ahdmahrably grahcious wahmahn and thahnked heavahn to hahve only sentimahnts that were ahttrahctive, ahlahgant, discraht and wahnderfully dahli-cious..." Well, yes! I was heading for them, with my cane raised!

When they recognized me, they both, briefly—but very decidedly—stepped back: if they were not so respectable, I think they would have turned tail and ran like cottontail rabbits. But their instinct of what was "proper" gave them fake courage and they smiled at me so nicely that I was the one who lost my composure. I was frightfully embarrassed by my cane held up like Guignol's club[58].

Not knowing what to do, I struck the sidewalk hard a few times so that I would not surrender completely. Words came to my lips and wanted to get out. Kmôhoûn also tortured me. He drilled me to say what I had to say, but instead I said almost like I was teasing, certainly not like I was threatening them:

"Creeps! Bums! Con artists! Oh, I've got you now, crooks! Pirates! Miscreants! Thieves!..."

They figured they could pretend that I was taking it all as a joke:

"You're getting carried away!" Elzear said ironically. "Why not say calmly that you wish we had come to see you again in Vassetot? But we've been so busy! If it weren't for that we would not have let you wither away..."

"And I don't lahke thaht lahnguage. It spoils mah plea-sahre to see you agahn!" Raoula hummed.

"I was so glad to hear," Roffieux continued, "that doctor Le Lancier gave you your release... on my request..."

And he moved as if to block a slap that he thought I was going to give him for having so much nerve. You would have thought that he was used to this kind of reaction... but I was not offended. I was confused!

Yet, I insisted on telling him what I thought about his behavior—and bluntly:

"You know nothing about what happened in Vassetot, little brat! And tell me, you cheat, what did you do at Cash and Nothingelse's in Paris?"

"Something that you will thank me for from the bottom of your heart, later," my cousin preached. "I risked everything, your anger—and maybe worse than that: your contempt!—to defend you against yourself. I will put up with your abuse if you want to dish it out. I will bear anything at all. I'm only happy to have done you a brotherly service."

"Ahnd we expect no thahnks!" the tragic Raoula grum-bled. "Our ahffection was only in your intahrest. You cahn villahfy us. Fahrgive him, Ahlzear!"

My arms fell to my sides! (They forgave me!) And I could barely get over it to mumble, "These people are too much for me! It's too hard! I'm done for—sick—finished! Oh! You know, it's not nerve that you're don't have!"

I threw my cane in the water and turned away. A few feet away from my cousins I heard Elzear, who lost his head for the first time in his life, cry out to two policemen showing up—too far away thankfully:

"Grab him! He's an escaped lunatic!"

But I was the one who chased him. He had time to take refuge in the Post Office. If I made a scandal in a public building, they would throw me in the slammer for sure. So I left, casting a worried glance at the public security guards who had heard nothing: they had just pounced on a cart driver for an infraction—shoved him around and cuffed him. I could get back to Rue du Chilou and head to the Canal. Elzear would not chase me now. I hurried anyway, looking over my shoulder from time to time. There was nothing in sight. But I only felt safe from all interference—police, psychiatric or fraternal—when I crossed the plank that joined the *Augustine Bourdon* to the dock and went down the stairs to the back room.

Smell of tar, tallow, alcohol and tobacco—for our hardship that was ignored by the French State-supported company.

In the white paneled room hung with yellow nets, in the greenish light pouring in through the gunports, portholes and two kinds of hatchways, Captain Le Coatmabergastmelen drew some strength from a glass of very strong smelling, very dark grog. He was a man in his 50s, tanned and with a formidable tawny beard where the autumn daisies had not yet blossomed. Heady blue fumes rose from the *puro* that he smoked, which was not quite as fat as a banana. The Captain looked at me kind of bitterly and without much gentleness in his voice asked:

"Who authorized you to damage my stairs and ruin the floor of the room?"

"I have come from Monsieur Bourdon."

"Ah! Now that's a name! That's different. Do you like it spicy?"

"Who? What?"

"The grog, of course!..."

And Monsieur Le Coatmabergastmelen passed me a banana of tobacco that, once lit, made me imagine what the warm breezes of Earthly Paradise could be like...

"I like it rather strong... with very little sugar."

"Great! I'm going to send you this that they call raging. Plant your butt on a seat. Take off your hat. There's no hooks here. Tell me the purpose of yo'gracious visit, my dear sir."

The Captain became sweeter than the most sugary grog.

"Captain, Monsieur Bourdon assured me that you would take me aboard as an apprentice pilot."

"Ah! Son of a bitch! And aren't you ashamed, at your age?"

The Captain unsweetened immediately. He sent me my glass of grog with a gesture that meant: *it's poured, you hafta drink it!*

"But, Captain, Monsieur de Fialligny was a pilot's apprentice at 40 and I'm not even 35."

"Yes, he's a legend in the merchant marines, and he stuck us here with some damned precedents. I saw it the minute I was about to be forced to board the Shah of Persia and the King Denis of Gabon. What are you going to do on board? You know f..."

"I learn quickly and I have strong arms."

"OK! That will come in handy to haul up. What did Monsieur Bourdon offer you a month?"

"200 francs because of my ripe old age. He gets the young ones at half price."

(Well, yes! I would land in Pointe-à-Pitre with less than five *louis*.)

"200 francs! Done! You know that in loading a pilot's apprentice, the ship owner doesn't settle on monthly payments; it saves the cost of a *real* man who he'd pay without this boarding of an infirm. This is going to mess up my whole team. I thought, maybe, this time I'd escape the blow of an apprentice because we leave the day after tomorrow and I have my people complete. Now I hafta send a *real* man walk-

202

ing who I signed up eight days ago. It's... f... a bitch! Well, it's too bad for you! You don't know anything and you'll hafta pretend like you do... otherwise I'll f...loor you in chains! You want another grog? You see how I am! Demanding, very demanding—and you realize that, my boy!—but a good boy— glass in hand. Tell me, you want again a grog?"

"No, thank you."

"Oh well! Get the Hell out of here, but come back tomorrow morning at 7 a.m. You'll buy your duck boots, your so'wester, polish, heavy flannel shirts and a blanket for your cabin*. You'll bring all that and you'll present yourself dressed in blues: that's the uniform on my ship. You'll give a hand to board *the bucket*."

---

* Cabin: a berth in ship lingo.

V

I will say nothing about Pointe-à-Pitre. I was sick the whole time during the unloading...

We raised up for Martinique where we arrived in the morning. I learned that Madame Letellier, the wife of the Governor of Guadeloupe, was also suffering—my poor little princess—and had gone to set up in Saint Pierre. That's why I was still on board the *Augustine Bourdon*.

I had five francs to buy my goods in Martinique because I had paid ten louis to the Captain for the month. It took us exactly 30 days to get there from Le Havre. I counted: 22 days from the cape of La Hève to the harbor of Pointe-à-Pitre—an extraordinarily fast crossing—six days to unload, a day to ballast and 24 hours to sail with free wind from one colony to another.

It was apparently not the custom to pay on the boat; you had to arrange things on the return with the ship owner. But I told Le Coatmabergastmelen that I was frivolous and would do something stupid on land, so he agreed to lighten me of my load of dangerous metal. Like that, I would not rip off the Company of West Indian Clippers—because you must already know that I would never have set foot on board a three-master again if I could have gone alone along the smiling shore that curved down there in a green crescent.

Not that they treated me badly on the blessed *Augustine Bourdon*. The Captain was obviously a good man, sometimes hot-headed, but generally lenient, whatever his wild yelling and screaming might say.

Unfortunately, the other sailors had already raided the colony's harvest and it was not going to load up with logwood in Haiti or anywhere else that would give me the least chance of satisfying my little princess and earning the money that I absolutely needed if I wanted to steal her away correctly.

And while Le Coatmabergastmelen was getting a little impatient, for no good reason, with the doctor hired by two cursed cod-fish boats carrying—in addition to their reeking cargo—a contagious flu and pneumonia from Newfoundland, I went over my memories of the strange crossing, totally entranced, *along with Kmôhoûn*, by the incredible beauty of the Caribbean landscape—green with all the greens in the diaphanous blue, trembling all over with thick vegetation, feathered with the high, shiny palms of coconut trees—and by the charm of the long, multi-colored town casually laid out along the last ripples of the doleful, warm, clear, dark emerald.

Yes, it was a strange voyage! I loaded vegetables and coal for the cook, I polished the brass of the *roufs* and the room, I learned to scour a deck in the morning with the seamen, and during the day to clear off the pinkish white boards of all traces of… dog crap (the Captain's dogs). I cleaned the chicken cages and the head—charming sports! I had to work aloft, perched on the rope ladders of the yards when I already had a hard enough time just hanging on. It was difficult for me to get used to the aerial tasks and my chicken-heartedness often made my more hardened mates laugh. But really, the first time was the scariest. Under heavy weather, in the wild ballet of waves, the ratlines seemed, at times, like rubber bands about to snap and at other times like razor sharp blades because I had to climb the rigging barefoot like my comrades. The black sky and the mad flight and shrill, mournful cries of gulls increased my terror. I caught myself thinking sometimes that I was one of the damned in a freezing, dark Hell with brutal torrents of water instead of flames.

I acquired a few talents. I learned how to coil the *halyards* and the *down hauls*, to resin the masts, to make the tow with old lines and especially to scour *without sand*, a thing which I am rather proud of. But, as satisfied as I was with myself, I never could impress the Captain with my nautical skills. Sometimes when I dared to show off after finishing a task that I thought was utterly remarkable—and maybe superhuman— he shrugged his shoulders and not to be mean, but kind a belittling me in a friendly way he said:

"Yes, you're a good little *old young man*, but old, old for all that and chicken and lagging. You could never even command a Marie-Salope (one of those dredgers that take away sludge from the ports); I won't put you on the tiller anymore, even in open water—you do nothing but yaw—and in the landings, I'd commit a crime if I let you at the helm: it'd be like I was trying to murder my crew and myself too."

He was right, of course, but I was offended all the same, especially since he refused to teach me to take bearings, telling me that I was too much of an idiot to even wipe my own ass.

We also spent a few nasty nights before catching sight of the Azores. The black hours were never much fun in mid-Ocean, as long as we stayed in the so-called temperate zone. The impenetrable darkness, without the flickering light of the smallest star, the disturbing and almost hostile cold, the sweeping, sad noises of the sea that seemed to spew out threats, the squinting glow of the signal lights in the fog of Erebus, the baleful cries of the man at the anchor lost afore, leaning over the dark chasm, the depressing chimes hour after hour—all this called up death and the abyss. And if a strong gust of wind joined in, life became intolerable. And those times when we were completely exhausted, barely warm under our blankets and we would be woken up with a start by the alarming cry, "All hands on deck!" I felt the soul of a murderer. I could have strangled the Captain, the Second Mate and the Crew Chief to top it all off. We jumped out of our cabins half-dressed in pants and vest, without even dreaming of putting our boots back on, and we gushed out—literally—from the sailors' quarters. We staggered onto the bridge swept with icy blades, we rolled on top of one another, we got up and turned into a chaos of bumping, tumbling and epileptic leaps on the slippery, viscous and flooded boards; a madness of orders and counter-orders, a gymnastic dementia of climbing and falling in the shrouds, on the tops, on the ladders of the mainsail, of the lower and the upper, the topgallant and the royal, then again on the rope of the low mast, on the tops, on the dancing ratlines, which were more solid when climbing

206

down, and then on the bridge showered like one of Bid'homme's patients… And you would be climbing some-where else in the dark and the storm and the blowblasts, the shattering bundles of sea. Our fingers gave up and slipped off the tarred hemp, grabbed at it again frantically; too bad for the nails that were torn off!

In the morning, they would say that a longboat had dis-appeared or that a *rouf* had been half demolished and in the beautiful blue and cheerful weather, we set the sails back up and thrust off with free wind or a tailwind on the sea of lapis lazuli that rolled again like little watery hills that were still dangerous in spite of their smiling cerulean sparkle.

Anyway, I would not have shined as a sailor. The Cap-tain was revolted by my awful clumsiness and stupor and he tried twice to "open my mind" by putting me in irons after some monumental, boundless stupidity. But he had to abandon all hope of making me a tolerable topman and be content with loading me with the filthiest and most revolting chores. Since he was not, I repeat, a bad man, in spite of the stercoraceous names that he called me day and night, and since he had easy grog and was in a good enough mood during the days with a good breeze, I will keep a fond memory of him with nothing dreadful about it.

And Kmôhoûn? That ex-eater of raw Tkoukrians played dead; he completely deserted me. It was only on the night be-fore we got to Pointe-à-Pitre, on a calm sea and under a sky that was cheerfully shining with the laughter of stars, that he woke up again to criticize me like any dishonest Aldebarian would do:

"Your hideous fear is so brutal that it ended up affecting me, me the bravest of the brave of Tkoukra!"

It was despicable and ridiculous. He had been absolutely wasted by fear and he did not even have the courage to save himself and go to Paris, far from the storms, to see what was happening at his dear Ambigu!

But I escaped him for a few hours, quite involuntarily too, during our last night at sea between Guadeloupe and Martinique.

I did not think it was possible that what I saw was only dream. We had just got up to replace the starboarders. It was midnight, but the *nocturnal azure* was so clear that I thought, at a certain point, that I was living in the center of a huge sapphire, dark but wonderfully transparent. I was awake like it was noon, dealing with the stunts on the rack of the mainsail; I could even see the flaws in the rope, bumps and fraying, and clearly made out two little spots of coal tar on the halyard of the topgallant. Suddenly, I felt like I was getting bigger, like I was rising in the air, then I knew, no question about it, that I was no longer in my body. I saw my body from above making the same movements as what my instinctive will usually told it to do. Then it got smaller and disappeared... There I was floating, vague and ephemeral, in a bluer and bluer atmosphere. I crossed the luminous zones where long rays quivered, blue, green, silver, pale gold and bleached opal. It was glorious, but despite my immaterial state, I was still too close to earthly life not to experience the horror of the abyss and the feeling that I was lost in the unknown sublime of the Infinite. Who would find me in this immensity, who would take pity on me? A voice reassured me: was it the voice of Jeanne Stoltz, the former lover whom the generous Elzear had destined for me? No, and yet... My average intelligence barely understood what she was saying (too sublime); I had only a very inexact, very incomplete and very remote idea of it, no doubt obscured by crude misunderstandings, but I sensed that certain human souls are, as an exception, too graciously beautiful to exist only shut up in their sad prison of flesh; that each of them has a double like the most sparkling stars in dazzling constellations that are invisible to the earthly world... and that... I floated toward the stellar reflection of Irene. Very quickly, I crossed vast spaces in a more and more adorably troubling light. The night of emptiness existed no more for me between the archipelagos of Worlds: here were solar systems that the astronomers of our planet never dreamed of, myriad stars that seemed made of ideal gems (and how petty is this comparison!)... Then, in the blinding abyss, a star grew and grew and seemed to rise up to meet me, to surround me and imprison me in its dazzling horizons. It was like I was captured by a huge sphere of rose gold that was rising up around me and was going to absorb me. It seemed like I was rolling—a spirit!—, twirling in streams of sweeter and sweeter light now... Finally, somehow, I touched the beautiful star, loved—loved, yes!—since it was dependant on Irene or Irene on it...

A form moved away. Was it Jeanne Stolz, all dressed up, believe it or not, in woven rays of the Sun? Was Jeanne dead or did her soul come to my rescue in the depths of the radiant oceans of sleep?

My intellectual depravity kept me from completely enjoying what surrounded me. I am sure that, in what little I might have tried to say, I was going to ridicule, diminish and materialize everything. In that strange and almost indescribable scenery, so superior to what I was normally able to see, I imagined—obviously an effect of my blind rudeness—that I came across things that faintly resembled the most beautiful things I had contemplated on the sublunary globe. I believed I saw a flower: I beheld something like large woods whose trees were only flowers; nothing but petals, corollas and calyces, fragrant and cradled by a breeze that itself was plainly perfumed with floral breaths—and just as sweet. All the nuances of the rose adorned these gigantic fluttering bouquets. Some of the roses, *brown-lipped roses*, were so unbelievably arousing and voluptuous—if I can speak like this—that I felt like they rejuvenated my soul. A flower often stood alone, as big as a tree—and with such a divine form, such an embracing scent— that's the only word that translates, a little ridiculously, what I felt—that the air wafting around it would kill a normal human being with excessive pleasure. Because I was disembodied, I could breath it in with no harm—and even blend myself, overcome by joy, with its intoxicating, incarnadine cloud. Large, flashy birds flew among the heights of the flower-trees where they sometimes alit like snuggling light. Their slow-noted songs evoked a magical past more enticing even than this splendid present. The sky was pink and gold. Pink fountains flowed there, flashing with gold—whose music could only be compared to harps that had—absurdly—crystal strings—and to go further in absurdity: living crystal. All this nature seemed enshrouded—and at the same time penetrated—with a tender cheerfulness. I floated in the pink perfumes of the woods, in the soothing radiance of the glades, in all that gentleness and beauty that felt like an infinite bounty manifested by transportive images and by an immaterial well being...

And even though I desperately did not want to leave this atmosphere of delights—which I can give no real idea of—I felt unbalanced, brutal and *out of place* among the ethereal sweetness. A charitable, sorrowful force (I felt it) chased me away almost in spite of itself in order to cut me off from these joys I was unworthy of.

But just as I was leaving the delightful star that seemed to grow pale before I had abandoned it, I suddenly saw even more diaphanous and more aerial than the rest of the supernatural scenery—marvelous, fantastic dream palaces and wondrous vegetation: these were the imaginary domains of my princess...

And a kind of grand Antillean villa, which was more sharply drawn (?), with verandas and pillars like white light, stood a little ways off. A flowing sea of Sun almost reached its wide, snowy stoop set in purple roses and it cast a glowing, rainbow shower on the forest of coconut trees that surrounded it and whose long golden green feathers brushed its high arcades.

I thought I had seen it before, but where? In a dream or in another existence?

And then, I woke up (?) at the sound of them calling the watch on the bridge of the *Augustine Bourdon*...

Now I was back on the sailing ship, a few hours after I had that strange dream (?). The blacks' boats, slender skiffs pointed at both ends, painted with all shades of blue, pink and green, formed long curves on the quiet harbor colored like a peacock's tail. Most of them were going fishing or coming back. A few carried white, black, copper, tan, citrine and amber ramblers, to whom the mooring of a sailing ship was a fascinating event that they rarely missed. Others were ridden by "Missié the dockhand," the carpenter, the caulker, the butcher or sellers of fruit—shiny yellow bananas and huge oranges that were sweet-smelling and tastily ripe despite their dark emerald shade, scaly pineapples, mangoes, sugar apples, avocadoes, sapotes, etc… And all the fruits—red, green, yellow, purple, corn-colored or ochre—were deliciously good in Martinique, maybe better than anywhere else, except for the wild strawberries that were magnificently shiny red, between ruby and garnet, but disgusting.

The little schooner of "Missié Dominique," the chief pilot, left us, gracefully slewing like a white gull, wings spread out and swollen with the breeze. Large barges crawled around on the waves in single file, loaded with barrels of rum and sugar and fantastic packages. Perched on the bundles or up on the large crates the sailors shouted—their skin a brilliant black like a break of licorice or dark tobacco, tonka bean, fresh chocolate, polished rosewood, very old tarnished oak, smoky—or like roasted coffee, café au lait, dark gold, amber yellow or flat yellow.

You could see many on and in the water here. Hundreds of swimmers, from six to 60 years old, were running on the beach, frolicking in the sea, galloping, lying on the waves, plunging into the water or wading like Newfoundlands, jumping and bumping into one another like pods of dolphins.

Under the large mooring trees, a crowd in Venetian colored clothes bustled about, hither and thither, apparently in procession, and with an unbelievably cheerful show of all that intense green, deep and mild.

Finally, the "Health" reached us. They boarded and inspected us and granted us permission to go ashore. We lowered the dinghy in the water and then dropped the "accommodation" ladder. The Captain and four sailors, of whom I was one, as Le Coatmabergastmelen had promised, sat in the dinghy, in that skiff and took off to the Mooring Market.

Under the high vault of greenery, the heat was heady, but wonderful with the scent of fruits and flowers. A fountain with a wide, tinkling basin sang a refreshing song and the sea breeze, still light, made the leafy arches gently flutter. Tall, slender and nonchalant women—dark caressing eyes, black carnations, golden brown, warmly pale or plain brown and delightfully pinkish, bulging bosoms and hips like lyres— dressed in long, multi-colored "gaules" that dragged around them and head-dresses of blazing madras, solar yellow or dyed the color of dawn or twilight—moved around, sinuous and graceful, between the displays of green limes and scarlet chilies, purple eggplants, tomatoes, bananas, all the West Indian fruits, colorful and polished—fish on which the light rippled, jewelry of red gold, silver, blue and pink mother-of-pearl. The light was filtered by the trees and sometimes became so alive, especially in the glowing halo that seemed to emanate from the blinding chilies and limes, that you would have thought that the displays were going to catch on fire.

On the other side, large palms swayed in the blue, powdery gold air.

A fat little black butcher, glistening like a blackberry, made a deafening music (?) on the stone tables with his knives, just to attract customers. A kind of sooty old dame haloed by a pumpkin and lilac madras, asked him bitterly for a 'ti bit o' meat that was missing, supposedly, from her measure the day before. The man with the big knives answered in magnificent Creole, mixed with the language of Montmartre[59]— see, the residents of Montmartre came all the way to the Antilles today[*]:

---

[*] This was written before the horrible catastrophe of May 8 last year[60] and the author would be very upset if anyone

"Don vex, ole cane chair: git long!"

He repeated this warning three or four times more and more threateningly. In the end the old dame lost heart and gave in to the advice that was so energetically expressed, but not before tossing this supreme Antillean insult at her enemy, a sexless insult that can be cast at man or woman alike:

"Fuckin' Bitch!"

Won over by so much courtesy, the butcher called her back and gave her a "ti bit o"—and laughed—and laughed—like his mouth was going to wrap around his head.

The heat was more and more sleep-inducing under the green archways, but the breeze picked up and its warm breath seemed exquisitely cool among all the scents of flowers and fruits that fought with the bitter, burning smells of the rum distilleries—where there was a kind of mix of caramel—of course!—Spanish leather and tan.

The long, hardy and supple women lounged around and seemed to glide and float—with their beautiful eyes half-closed—over the pink flagstones that were almost violet in the green shade where a drizzle of topaz seeped in.

There we were, four sailors loaded down as if with politicians' consciences. Le Coatmabergastmelen happily watched us sagging under our loads. Then he took pity on us, "Hang on, boys! There's plenty like that! The cook'll be laughing next if he sees us all coming back alive."

We did not have far to go to get back to the dinghy, but the sacks of bread, fruits and vegetables and the baskets of meat and fish really weighed us down. I was actually planning to take advantage of the comings and goings of buyers and sellers to disappear down that little green alley that opened up between two tall wooden cabins with frail balconies and verandas… Unfortunately, the Captain kept breathing down my neck. I do not think he meant anything by it. He was in a good mood and felt like talking and I was unlucky enough to be

---

thought he meant to make mean jokes about the people whom he admired and who deserved this admiration.

chosen as his listener... But, in fact, I now saw a little opportunity to get away more doable and much simpler than the first—needing neither hustling nor bustling nor desperate jogs. Just wait for the evening.

We went back on board and had lunch on the bridge under the sailcloth tent, which was neceassry under the ever-beautiful Sun of the Antilles. We were interested in what was happening on the poop decks and upper decks of the anchored ships around us. It was nice in the harbor on the blue sea with the enchanting vision of the neighboring island.

News soon came from the office of the consignee that pleased me more than you can imagine: since there was nothing, really, to gather in the port of Saint Pierre, the *Augustine Bourdon* would leave the Mooring tomorrow to head for Miragoâne (Haiti). A little after nightfall, I would surely find the opportunity I was looking for and tomorrow, while I was stretching my legs on the shady roads of mango and sandbox trees cheerfully mingled with waving palms, the crew of the three-master would have better things to do than search for me—unfurling sails, clueing up others, changing "the arms" in the wind, to the mad laughter of the azure sea.

I was not wrong. The suppliers were curious, and sportsmen besides, to whom the bridge of a sailing ship was an exercise field all marked out, and nightfall did not cool down their enthusiasm.

During dinner, around 7:30 p.m., before the rising of the Moon, the cry heard so often during the day rang out again, sent from the shore:

"*Ahgistine Bouhhdon*! Ho!"

As I was expecting, everyone complained this time, from the seamen sitting in front to the Captain who was finishing his plate of *cribiches* (big prawns like little crayfish) at a table near the mizzen and already minding his coffee, Russian... or other.

To the great surprise of Le Coatmabergastmelen, who knew I was lazy and an enemy of chores, I got up slowly but determinedly and—to those who criticized me for stirring up sh...trouble—I made this comment, unexpected of me:

"Yes, it's always like that: you don't want to answer the evening call—and then, the next day, you regret it. Maybe it's something really serious that they want to tell us about!"

"Mwhat? A simple vagabond who still doesn't have his little night life on shore in his collection..."

"Well, since you're not getting up what do you care! I think it's better to go see..."

"You're going to flop in the water or capsize the skiff."

"Not a chance! I'm a bad sailor, but I row like old Pants-on-Fire himself."

"That's true," grumbled Le Coatmabergastmelen, "those filthy Parisians, they're all the time flying in those damn soap boxes between the Morgue and the Opéra (!).[61]"

But this was not the time to point out *geographical* errors, even as glaring as this one. The Captain let me go—that's the main point; he can make his apologies to the Mayor of the 9th Arrondissement some other day.

The night was a splendid, dark, velvety blue; the stars looked like they were smiling at their reflections in the calm water.

I quickly went down the ladder, untied the dinghy and on a liquid sky of night where the starbeams zigzagged sharply like lightning in the shuddering swells I "swam" fast, fast, toward the balks. I made out my crier who repeated his tireless call until the stem of the boat actually touched land three feet away from him.

He was an old, very black gentleman with a respectable, paternal face. He smiled at me mildly in the starlight. I took off my hat and said to him with the utmost politeness:

"It would be infinitely kind of you, Monsieur, to wait five minutes for me. The Captain has sent me to get two liters of rum from Madame Cambyse, across from the police station of the Mooring."

"Go on, go on, but make it quick, boy. I have to see your Captain about a very serious matter. I am Missié Celinice Inzinor," sang the basso-cantante guttural of the good old man, the deep voice of a City Council orator.

After crossing Merchant's square and going up a road, I was in the green—a little choked by the warm and too sweet greenhouse odors… I thought no more about good old Monsieur Celinice Inzinor.

It was really beautiful to find myself free, on land, in the colony where my little princess had come for her convalescence, but I had only 100 *sous* and I did not know where I would sleep. There was no question of sleeping under the stars on an island where snakes—pitvipers—supposedly loved to stroll around on quiet nights. I walked for a long time, a little aimlessly, under the leafy vault, came out on a highway and, numbed by exhaustion, dreamed of nothing for the moment but asking to sleep in the corner of the first hut I came to.

And right there was one that looked inviting. The roof disappeared under the climbing plants now blued by the moon and the thin pillars that held up the awning of the low gallery were garlanded with large clusters of flowers.

The whole household—good blacks with open, smiling faces—welcomed me like an old friend. They are hospitable in Martinique and whoever would pour me a cup of coffee or a shot of rum would also serve me a big dish of court-bouillon fish or *zhabitant* soup of gumbo and pidgeon peas.

They never asked me what I was doing in their country or what I was planning to do. They set me up comfortably for the night and I slept while my hosts sang softly or talked together quietly.

In the morning, after insisting on making me breakfast, the master of the cabin eyed the knife hanging from my belt at the end of a hemp rope—and sticking out of my pocket. He had a weird look on his face and made a rather long-winded speech in Creole. Since I did not understand him very well, he took the trouble to fetch his festival day French and he said something like this:

"Knife there is chatty. It says you split a boat. Oho! Not too dangerous, you're not a State sailor, so de jack boot (!)

216

police won't run after you. But you have no *heap* o' money, no, my man? I'm not rich, me, but dere's always a ol' ten *sous* coin fo' pardners in trouble."

(He earned ten francs a day and had seven children).

And, after a little argument, like it or not, I had to pocket the 50 centimes. I pretended to laugh, but I think that I was never so grateful in my entire life. As they often say, motive is everything. And it was not over: before putting me on the road, I still had to "loose mabouya." The mabouya is a mysterious and also imaginary lizard that sometimes blocks the throat in the morning in the Antilles. This saurian is super mean and equipped with terrible claws—it clings onto the walls of its victims' pharynx; nothing can make it loosen its hold, nothing—except a strong drink of rum. When the mabouya is loosed, it is polite to "send the police." To "send the police" is to swallow a good shot of the aforementioned rum, then cool down the mouth with a gulp of water that should immediately follow the alcohol.

Finally, I was on the road after shaking the hand of Cicero Fanfan, my host.

I think there is no better population in the world than that of Martinique—black, white or mulatto.

Was I going to head to Fort de France or start asking around where the wife of the governor of Guadeloupe was to be found, which people should know? Both ideas were pretty much the same. It would have been useless for Irene to go as far as Fort de France to find fresh air. The whole colony was wonderfully healthy, except for two or three spots, and if I spoke about the spouse of a big wig in the colony—me, a decrepit vagabond—I might look suspicious. Then a dim intuition urged me to return to Saint Pierre. The wisest thing was to trust the luck that had served me so well up to then, wasn't it? Cicero Fanfan's little silver coin would certainly be a good luck charm. I flipped it in the air: if it landed heads, I would head North; if it landed tails, I would set off for the cape in the South. Heads! It was definitively toward Saint Pierre that I had to walk.

Just when I turned back on my tracks, the omen was con-firmed by a less strange event, but one in which I was happy to see, at the time, a mysterious encouragement. The road of bleakness, the *Trace*—on the spot where I had consulted Fate—overhung the lowlands so much that I could not see even the smallest bit of plain: nothing but the sea, the lumin-ous sapphire sea.

Now, exactly at the second when my eyes fell upon the blue waves, there seemed to come out of the huge wall of shining vegetation in front of me, the point of a mast, then the yardarm, two masts, three masts, then the entire hull, the hull of the *Augustine Bourdon*—of course!—the only one in the harbor that was painted—pretending to be gray—an almost pink mauve, recognizable miles away. The good sailboat was taking to sea without me. Hooray! Hooray! Saint Pierre was open for me now. I would cross the town—follow it rather, its entire length, and search in the North, always in the North, up to where the coast turned…

I went merrily down toward the beach by a shortcut—long enough!—covered the three main roads of the Mooring, the Center and the Fort, to the old and new wood houses, which were simple or fashionable but always clean, some without ornaments and others decorated with beautifully worked balconies; I saw the Bishop's Savannah, deeply green and intensely Creole, almost "Paul and Virginian," the Theater and the coconut trees, the Batterie d'Esnotz in the blue sha-dows, up to where the reflection of the sea's blue fire seemed to rise up—the Roxelane, called the River of the Fort, its stone bridge and all its leafy and flowery backdrop, the Marché du Fort, with its giant mango and sandbox trees—the church of Saint Peter and Paul perched on solid ground from where the white and smaragdine columns and the feathery shafts of palm trees rose straight up—then I passed the last houses of the town. Now the Habitation Périnelle whitened, once famous and still pretty with its high, airy and spindly palm trees. I walked for a long time again and then took a break to eat whatever they served me in a -K-* whose decoration was quite primitive and African.

There, the plumes of a forest of coconut trees swelled up all glistening with their sprays hurled by the big waves, by the foamy crests of a little cove—beryl, turquoise and silver froth. A grand villa, like white light, shimmered between the large feathers of green gold and purple roses that looked like they wanted to drench its snowy stoop in blood. It was the house that I had seen in the beautiful star. I could have sworn that Irene was very close to me, now that I was going to see her...

Servants of all known colors, from the clear ruddy of the Norman to the most satiny black of the Congo, came and went under the arcades and on the steps, under the greenery that surrounded the villa. I did not try to question anyone, but I was more and more certain that I had arrived in the right port. For a long time I hid behind a grove of orange trees as tall as cedars—and began to give up hope of seeing my princess that day, when my lucky star (?) suddenly presented Chapitel, the old servant of Roffieux, who was now, as he was going to tell me, the valet of the potentate Letellier:

"Oho! Monsieur Veuly! You here, and in that get-up of... of... a sailor!..."

And after exchanging explanations:

"Sure, then, Leonard, that guy from Vassetot, wasn't wrong when he said you'd fallen hard for Madame, 'cuz it's a lot of road and sickness from the lower Seine to here. But if a simple servant like me, who is all yours, is allowed... a way of thinking, I'll think that you that you didn't get bored: there was also t'other Madame, your cousin's, who had a crush on you, a hammer blow; and no offense, but you're no *sculture* or cowboy or zouave[62]. She talked to herself a lot, the Lady of Monsieur Roffieux and I heard'er going through a rosary one evening when there'd been a lot of people and a few drinks. When the people'd left, she stayed in the smoking room where

* K (barred K)—cabaret—graphic joke from over there; the -k- was used as a sign for many drinking spots of the Colony.

219

I came to pick up the cigars that were lying around—not smoked and also barely—she was talking and talking, but she kept coming back to saying the same thing: 'Oh! Philippe Veuly! Philippe Veuly! You don't love me after I *scarificed* myself for you! Oh well, I surrender you to all the *explotations* of creepy Elzear. But you did love me since you went on the lam one night from your Vassetot to disgrace me with your *sardistic* love and you went back to your cage after that!' She said it better than me, imagine! I do the best I can: she was talking *like a sailor*!"

(Chapitel knew very well that he could talk like a sailor.)

Kmôhoûn, who had not budged since the scene that he had made the night before our arrival in the Antilles, started giggling. Of course, it made no sound, but it shook my nerves worse than the crude laughter of a hundred alcoholics huddled together.

And while Chapitel kept feeding me with Raoula's confessions, the Tkoukrian confessed:

"OK! I didn't say anything about it, but you could have found out if you'd consulted my *memories. You never look into yourself! My man, it was deliriously funny! You know the smile—that annoyingly pretentious smile of Roffieux's wife... Well! You know—that thing, that thing that you almost never see except in these situations—when you see it!—Yes?—Well! The thing was almost... (here, he guffawed) ...the same smile, or I was imagining it! It was hilarious!"*

How hideously disgusting! Foul, revolting Tkoukrian! If only you had a body I could torture, lacerate, tear to pieces, and mash to a pulp!

But I could not let the horrified and savage look on my face chase away the kindly Chapitel. I had more important information to get from him. With great effort of will, I calmed myself down and politely interrupted his lecture on Raoula, asking him to give me some news of Irene:

"She's much better! There's no more of that craziness, no more of that! And she's the one who controls her husband as it is now. In the beginning, he was slapping her around and

220

calling her a bunch of awful names. He even threw things at her head; she's a mark or two from it. But now there's an old woman, kind of a witch, who says she's given her a potion to get the upper hand. Ha! He's really nice now with her trying to hide from him the fact that without holding a grudge—she's not mean, you know—she'd like to see him go far, far away… He's lost weight…"

I saw that I would only get stupid gossip from him after that and, again, assertively cut short the speech of the omnipotent satrap.

"And does she ever go out in the afternoon?"

"Sure, and probably pretty soon. Around now, when the breeze comes like double quick, she'll take a walk to the other end of the Fond Coré around Saint Pierre under the coconut and mango trees."

I got away from Chapitel telling him that I had to return to the ship before nightfall because I had had some bad luck —alas, a detail that was too true—and that I was emigrating (really, where could I emigrate?)—Hold on!—to Venezuela where they had just discovered gold mines in Guárico…

Then I made a long detour and went to post myself on the other side of the villa, on a narrow path where the tall, thick tropical foliage sifts the gorgeous shower of blonde flames and changes it into twilight green.

They would not surprise me here. I only had to slip into the tangle of lianas like the good black vagabonds, hunting wild turtles, or Hindu immigrants, cutting cabbage trees…

And I could see perfectly the surroundings of the beautiful, white, luminous cabin.

Hours—or unbelievably long minutes—passed:

Finally, a woman whom I recognized—and did not recognize—took away my breath! My heart pounded hard and dull, shook me and shattered me; a woman dressed in pale pink cotton came down the front steps, all alone.

Was it her? I no longer knew! Yes, it was *Her*! But what was it about *Her* that puzzled me? She was on the road that followed the sea; she moved toward my side; she came closer, closer...

Five feet from the path, she stopped—and remained there a long minute, as if attracted and repulsed by the darkened path under the drooping foliage. I saw her in full light and watched her greedily; yes, greedily! If I was not afraid of appearing grotesque, I would write that my eyes were hungry and thirsty for *Her*! But what was going on, my God! At a distance, after a second, I had recognized her. But looking at her up close, I did not experience any of that boundless joy that I was looking forward to and that I was afraid of—that made me painfully, exquisitely afraid while I was waiting for it...

It was Irene and it was no longer Irene! Would I be a brutally insensitive cur for loving her less because it was obvious that she had suffered—and suffered a lot?

She was still beautiful, but in a different way than when she had entered me not like the "stab of a knife," as the god-like Baudelaire had said[63], but like a sweet and strong perfume that invaded my whole being. Her eyes' magic night was as darkly radiant as before. If her skin was paler, faded a little, it had also become more delicate, gentle like a dying petal. Her face had the subtle, warm color of tea rose, velvety with almost unnoticeable golden pollen. Her mouth with its cruel and adorable pink arcs was still fresh. All her traits had kept their purity. I saw them again just as they had been before—was it more or less than a year ago?—yes, just the same, but why was the harmony of the whole different? There was nothing you could really see that had changed—yet, she was not the same woman. Even though her beauty had nothing sickly about it—far from it: Irene seemed stronger and more energetic; there was even a sparkle of pride in her eyes that I had never seen before—even though this beauty was blooming, triumphant and superb, in the Latin sense of the word, I could not help feeling, deep inside me, that she had, I repeat, suffered a lot and it had changed her. Consequently her innermost essence was completely altered. I was sure that it was her former reflection that I had seen in the beautiful star and not her present one.

She was still charming, but her charm was different and therefore *lesser* for me. I imagined that my love changed and I felt a new passion for her, but it was not the passion of the past that flooded me with the thrill of emotion—a pleasure that was so madly intoxicating and so exquisitely disturbing. And why fool myself? No, it was no longer this woman here that I loved, but really the Irene of past days—she who had disappeared! Yes, it was *an Irene* whom I was devouring, whom my eyes were drinking in, searching for anything in her at all that could bring back the old drunkenness, the only true one, but it was not *my Irene*!

So, it was over. I loved a woman who did not exist anymore. I could not even hope to find her again in another life since the subtle principle that emanated from *Her* like the scent of a flower had changed now. She was no longer *Her*! She would never be *Her*! And I, did I still have a reason to exist after this? It was not sorrow that I was experiencing; it was a kind of dreary apathy about everything. Nothing interested me anymore. Yes, it was over and I was done with too!

I started laughing so loudly that Irene was surprised—oh, not at all scared!—and walked straight up to the little path, lifted the curtain of drooping lianas and saw me. No, certainly not! She no longer looked the same. What was left of that little princess who was so shy and so divinely girly? (Oh! Not always so girly!) Her face looked severe, almost threatening; her voice was still sweet but deeper than before and sounded authoritative in the silence of the forest:

"Your little joke is stupid! You wanted to frighten me, didn't you? It didn't work, but I will hold it against you for the despicable intention. Go away and quick! You hear me!"

These words lit me up with an insane and furious anger immediately fueled by Kmôhoûn. Despite my emotion, I read, I was forced to read, the Tkoukrian's soul better than my own. He, too, was furious with this woman who got away with appearing different than herself, who could no longer give him

223

exactly the same joys as the night of... my imprisonment in the cell; with this woman who, after that, talked to us like dogs! Infuriated, we threw ourselves upon Irene; I grabbed her by the elbows and dragged her into the bush. Oh! It was not that I wanted her now. It would have been less painful for me to cheat with someone other than *Her*. No, I did not want *Her*. My frenzied desire was to murder her, to punish her in her lying flesh—yes, lying since she no longer fooled me in the same way—to beat her savagely like a Stone Age brute would do to punish his shifty female for a long-standing betrayal.

And even while I revolted against myself, I hit her and tortured her with expert savagery. And what I dimly anticipated, without wanting to admit it, happened: she recognized me—and did not let herself complain in case someone came running to her rescue and beat me like some rabid beast. Yes, at Vassetot, I had shamefully defiled her; today, I was martyring her, despicable executioner that I was! But because of my old rape, and the fact that she was submitting half-willingly... for... a few seconds... I became, in a way, a thing to her, I who thought I was taking her—and she defended me by her silence.

Hideous coward, I was glad to see her cry big tears and clench her jaws so as not to scream out. I twisted her wrists and bit them; I sank my nails into her throat. She tried to put up a little fight, but I took away all her desire by torturing her cheeks, kneading her breasts and ravaging elsewhere, claws out. Oh! What grim pleasure I got from her stifled whimpering! How much I suffered from her suffering, but how cruelly good it was! Ah! I was going to take my knife, carve her, bleed her a little, but not too much; I did not want to kill her too fast; I wanted to make the pleasure last! And I cried as much as she did... Oh! The wonderful torture of frightful pity vanquished! I cried, but I was elated!

Irene saw the blade glinting. There was a bottomless terror in her eyes—and suddenly, so much begging tenderness. Was she becoming crazy again? Now she put her arm around my neck, crushed me and burned my lips—what a kiss!

224

Ah! I understood: the wench wanted to save herself by prostituting herself. She was enjoying my violence down below; it was more fun! SoI bit her mouth until it bled!

But my frenzy died away suddenly. A real, delirious pity took hold of me, shook me up and broke me down with such a sharp pain that I almost shrieked...

Because the disastrous Kmôhoûn, the chilling phantom, redolent of the Red Star, that distant globe of puss, had just *shot out* of me, freeing me of him *forever*; he had crumbled—I believe that this time I heard him *physically*.

Did he leave happy to have brought me to where he had to bring me, to the infamy of infamies? Or had I horrified him by this nameless crime that he had wanted, and that I had just committed, trading murderous bites for kisses—maybe an unprecedented atrocity in the history of worlds?

VI

I barely have the force to write now after confessing what I perpetrated, which was, no doubt, the most dreadful experience in the course of my existence...

I think I threw myself on the body of Irene and covered her with tender, sobbing caresses...Yes, I'm sure of it. She even kissed my bloodthirsty mouth, which forgave the unforgivable.

Then, Irene passed out. I thought she was dead. And they were coming as well... They were looking for her... They had heard my cries. Desperation and terror threw me into a panic again. I was just a fleeing beast...

So, what happened? I think I crouched in the thickets of terrible forests and leapt through golden, green savannahs... After that, I must have lived a pretty long time under the savage, powerful foliage of fairyland, savage, powerful and graceful too, the most beautiful that I had seen in my life. I ate strange fruits, drank from streams and slept all night in the trees on the solid, tightly interwoven branches... One day, some people got hold of me in a clearing near the sea... Yes, I caught sight of something like a port, houses and a town... As far as I can remember, they tied me up and carried me like a monkey captured alive and threw me into a little black room. I must have been shut up again in a lunatic asylum because I heard a lot of women screaming, just like at Vassetot. How long did I stay there? I managed to escape again... but how? I have no idea... I got on a boat again, then on others, working automatically, more a moron than a madman: they would not have enlisted a mental case! But an imbecile, now that was different! I think I went to Guyana, La Plata, the Falklands and to the southernmost tip of Chile, then to Valparaiso where I did not think to ask of news of Magne and Nigeot...

I was able, however, to meet up again with the adventurous quacks in a hospital of a very hot little republic in Central or South America: a bout of fever with delirium (?) got me admitted into this "model hospital" where my two old friends from Vassetot—who had set it up—after being expelled from Chile for too noisy religious propaganda—were committed at the time. They were considered infinitely less dangerous, so they moved around everywhere, from garden to garden, from room to room, sowing in their wake—they believed— benedictions and miraculous cures, because they imagined that they had become gods—fortunate men! They were, of course, transformed into pure spirits and they preached it. The total neglect of their bodies made them almost unrecognizable because of their filth, but they seemed perfectly happy.

It was in this same Central or South American republic that I heard news that saddened me. The plenipotentiary French Minister, a certain Monsieur Letellier, ex-governor of Guadeloupe and its dependencies—official denomination— had left the colonial administration for a diplomatic career with that ease of adaptation that characterizes our politicians and was accused of having illegally confined his wife...

Now, after a few weeks of treatment and a serious medical exam, they said I had been "afflicted with *simple cretinism* (?), which was incurable, but harmless to anyone armed with a solid stick and a strong pair of boots" (sic). And here is what I saw one of the first days after I was released.

I left in the morning to go get a ship in the port of Majaderos. The road ran through the equatorial forest lit by emeralds and diamonds after the downpour, since we were in the middle of the rainy season. At a bend in the *carretera*[64], just when I was joyfully watching the big trees, like flowers of pink snow, and sensually breathing their truly paradisiacal perfumes—it was like a blissful mood was spread in the air— two men who looked like convicts or snitches came out of a bush two feet away from me carrying the naked corpse—and bloody in places—of a very beautiful, emaciated woman whose hair dragged on the soggy ground.

Was it another madness crossing my brain? I had the feeling that I had seen these men recently, that they were attendants at the hospital I had just left?

227

They tossed the dead woman into a kind of van that I had not seen and, before I got over my shock, the horse took off at a gallop down the muddy road. The muck flew up and splattered the left side of the chariot with big, yellow stains—and everything disappeared.

And I stayed there for hours and hours, sprawled in the mud in the grips of a crisis of wild desperation, because just when the body was passing by me—without being able to make a single movement or strike a single blow at the executioners—yes, executioners; I remembered my frightful vision of old!—I had—despite the muddy hair, despite the awful skinniness, despite everything—I had recognized the once so loved Irene—my little princess!

I do not know how I got back to France. I saw my brother again, but no matter what he said, I insisted on being brought back to Vassetot where I would never leave again. Now the large, white buildings and the deep gardens would be mine forever, haunted by the Exquisite of Exquisites, by Irene of yesteryear, who became like herself again—and came again to smile on me, haloed in solar rays and roses of pink light as she floated near the window where I had seen her for the first time.

Leonard asked to take charge of me again. He respected me after learning why I had escaped. I did not tell him the end of the dream!

He had now a light lilac bowler hat, the gift of a young patient from the Republic of Liberia. And my Leonard, right or wrong, no longer needed benzenes when it came to *delicate* marks. Now he took—I am inventing nothing, I swear to you!—watercolor lessons from a nice lunatic who was a former medalist at the Palais de l'Industrie[65], only so he could, if the opportunity arose, restore by himself his luxurious hat with the brush!

I no longer dreamt of Madame Robinet, who had remarried and this time to a schoolteacher! If she wanted to start writing on walls again, she would have a blackboard available—and mines of chalk.

Anyway, I pity her husband's students.

VII

LETTER FROM THE DOCTOR

Monsieur,

In making an inventory of the papers left in the room that was occupied for several years by your distant relative, Monsieur Eumolphe Gigon, recently deceased at Vassetot, I discovered a rather bulky manuscript (a rough draft) entitled *ENEMY FORCE.* To this manuscript was attached a letter signed by you, and which I have read. It concerns a work with the above title.

You were telling Monsieur Eumolphe Gigon that, as soon as you found a publisher, you were going to print this literary (?) work[*]—your common effort.

In case you carry out this project, allow me to make a few observations that are not threatening, believe me, but are accurate and essential:

1st: The hospital of Vassetot was not established by a Doctor Froin, but actually by the undersigned.

2nd: The said Doctor Froin, his assistant Bid'homme and Messieurs Le Lancier and Barrouge have never, in any capacity, been part of its administration. On the other hand, the patients Froin, Bid'homme, Le Lancier and Barrouge, *all four dead today, but all four completely cured beforehand*[**], received my diligent care during periods ranging from five to nine years.

---

[*] The question mark was put in by the Doctor, who obviously lacked any education.

[**] The italics are mine.

3rd: The names of the male and female guards are pure fantasy.

4th: The deeds that are attributed to them are impossible under the severe discipline that reigns at Vassetot. The female guards and patients have never, ever, thanks to the precautions taken by me, communicated with the male guards and patients. The hideous scenes of debauchery related in the course of this tale have therefore come from your imagination.

5th: I have never, at any time, had inmates here with the names of Veuly or Nigeot. Your collaborator, Monsieur Eumolphe Gigon, sometimes saddled himself unduly with these patronyms. Veuly, Nigeot and Monsieur Eumolphe Gigon are one and the same person, in different states of mental alienation. Doctor Magne is entirely unknown to me. The only doctor that I have had as a patient—I don't count the health officers Froin and Bid'homme—was named Trollman. *I have never had the pleasure of knowing Monsieur Kmôhoûn of Tkoukra*[*].

6th: The patients treated in my establishment have never, under any pretext whatsoever, suffered the water torture. The shower itself is used only in the rarest of cases. *(The devices dedicated to this practice are topnotch).*

7th: Monsieur Eumolphe Gigon is bragging when he says that he escaped from Vassetot. You don't escape from my hospital. He did, it's true, often ramble on about South America and the Antilles, places which he had visited in his youth, and with which he was obsessed to the point of raving about them.

8th: I have never bribed any country man-hunters.

9th: Madame Letellier was an old, very respectable resident with the face of an Algerian witch, whom Monsieur Gigon saw only from far, far away. The husband of this lady, far from "*being an honorable figure in our deliberating assemblies,*" far from "*presiding over the destiny of one of our oldest colonies*" or from "*making his fiercely peaceful but wisely*

_____

[*] The italics are mine.

patriotic warrior voice heard on the distant shore"*, instead cultivated the green banks of the Diahot River (New Caledonia[67]) for a long time *in his capacity*** as relegated by life.

10th: My guards, while I am alive, will at no time devote themselves to *useless* occupations—especially *artistic—such as working with string or coconuts, woodwork or painting, even if it was only watercolors.* Moreover, I do not allow them to wear any headwear of a *strange* or *unusual* color.

11th: Monsieur Elzear Roffieux has been unworthily slandered by you. The misappropriation of funds and forgery that he was formerly accused of were committed by him with the most humanitarian objectives in mind. He married, not a Raoula Fromage, but my daughter Gastonie. He bears no relation to the Gigon family and figures among the silent partners of the hospital of Vassetot. This last detail will keep me from praising him too much here.

12th: I have never sheltered arsonists under my roof.

I call upon you to print this letter at the end of your book, which I hope to see preceded by a few lines of preface edited by you to warn patient readers that they should not be disgusted by the grotesque and preposterous characters portrayed in this work, which is not a documentary but rather fantasy, of your *ENEMY FORCE*.

Monsieur Eumolphe Gigon deformed everything that he saw and his lucidity—intermittent at best—*wore tainted glasses most of the time.* He was not a maniac—oh, no! far from it!—if I can use a metaphor, he was like a *one-man band* of madness.

I am upset, Monsieur, for having to criticize you for treachery. You have taken advantage of the many visits that I allowed you to make to your relative to collaborate on this puerile book of lies. I will not, through blocking its publication,

---

* The Doctor has certainly attended some sessions at the Palais Mazarin[66].
** Quite nice.

try to gain for *this crooks' story* a success that it does not deserve.

Kindly respect, Monsieur, my very just demands and accept what you believe you should of my regards.

(signed) Doctor Le Joyeulx des Eypaves

I have obeyed you, Monsieur le Docteur.

ENDNOTES

1. André Le Nôtre (1613-1700), landscape architect of King Louis XIV, most famous for the park at the Palace of Versailles and Tuileries.

2. Grief, sorrow.

3. Port in Seine-Maritime in the Haute-Normandie region of Northern France.

4. In Eastern France. It is known for its passion for hunting.

5. A type of Russian cap trimmed with fur.

6. E. T. A. Hoffmann (1776-1822), German author of horror and fantasy.

7. Louis Marie Quicherat's (1799-1884) Latin-French dictionary was the standard during the 19th and early 20th centuries.

8. "And now...and now...and now!"

9. Cusenier, a black currant liqueur; Noilly-Prat, the original French Vermouth; Pernod, absinthe.

10. Honoré Daumier (1808-1879), French artist best known for his caricatures of political and social life.

11. In Northwestern Paris, one of the most densely populated municipalities in Europe.

12. A common name for a bear.

13. "Voilà l'racommodeur de faïence et d'purcelaî-no!" and "Rempailleu'd'chaises! Rempailleu'd'chaises!".

14. Solferino, Palestro, Palikao (Baliqiao) were battles in which French forces were victorious.

15. Napoleon III.

16. Félicité de Genlis (1746-1830), French writer and educator.

17. Faïence and ceramics.

18. *Les Fleurs du Mal*, "Recueillement".

19. Louis Hyacinthe Boulhet (1822-1869), French poet and playwright, born in Cany and a childhood friend of Gustave Flaubert (1821-1880), French writer most famous for *Madame Bovary*. Cany is a commune in the Haute-Normandie region of Northern France.

20. Odilon Redon (1840-1916), French Symbolist artist.

21. Urbain Le Verrier (1811-1877), French mathematician and astronomer famous for his discovery of Neptune.

22. A Parisian literary journal published between 1879 and 1914.

23. In *Ubu Roi* the first word is "merdre", i.e. "shit" or closer, "shitter."

24. Cayenne is the capital of French Guiana and was used as a penal colony from 1854 to 1938.

25. Coffee (or tea) with eau-de-vie or rum.

26. A civil law notary as opposed to a notary public.

27. "The Graphic" was a British illustrated newspaper and Le Monde Illustré a French illustrated newsmagazine.

28. Le Théâtre de l'Ambigu-Comique in Paris, perhaps the most famous, showing musicals, dramas, melodramas, mysteries, vaudeville acts, etc.

29. Bandits living in the mountains of Greece.

30. I.e. "Cheese,"

31. Similar to a pillory but the victim would have to carry around the device.

32. In the center of France.

33. Esna in Egypt. Mathura in India.

34. Nicolas Boileau-Despréaux (1636-1711), French satirist, friend of Molière and Racine.

35. I.e. of the beautiful buttocks.

36. Nana Sahib (Dhundu Pant 182?-1859), one of the leaders of the bloody Indian Mutiny or First Indian War of Independence of 1857-8. Faustin Soulouque (1782-1867) became president (1847) and then emperor (1849) of Haiti where he ruled with terror as a kind of parody of Napoleon.

37. "Et lassata viris necdum satiata recessit", Juvenal, Satires, VI, 130 (cited by Alfred Jarry after Rabelais): "Exhausted but unsated she withdrew."

38. Jean Richepin (1849-1926), bold and outrageous French poet, novelist, playwright.

39. Doubs in Franche-Comté in Eastern France; Saint Flour in Auvergne in Central France: like saying, "He was from the hills, you'd have thought he was from the country."

40. From *L'Histoire de veritable Gribouille* by George Sand (1850): he jumped in a river to escape the bees; or *La Soeur de Gribouille* by Comtesse de Ségur (1862): he jumped in the river to protect his new clothes from the rain.

41. The Sipahis were originally an elite Ottoman cavalry force that later served French forces in Algeria and elsewhere. French pronunciation changed their name to Spahi.

42. Monstrous swelling of the thyroid and cretinism were endemic in certain regions of the Alps due to iodine deficiency.

43. A character from the play *Le Malade Imaginaire* by Molière, portrayed as proud and pedantic giving complicated explanations with no concern for the patient.

44. From the opera *Don Giovanni* by Mozart, the cruelly deserted lover.

45. Suburban areas around Paris.

46. "Total Depravity of Inanimate Objects", *Atlantic Monthly*, Sept. 1864 by the American essayist and religious writer (1833-after 1869).

47. Said of a woman with no buttocks or breasts. The opposite would be a Venus Kallipygos (see note 35).

48. A term in voodoo relating to charms, amulets and talismans.

49. After Léon Ohnet (1813-1874), French architect or perhaps Georges Ohnet (1848-1918), French dramatist and novelist.

50. Joséphin Péladan (1858-1918), French writer and occultist who gave himself the Babylonian name for king, "le Sâr".

51. An insane asylum founded in 1645 perhaps best known for housing the Marquis de Sade from 1801 until his death in 1814.

52. French writer (1873-1907) most famous for his play *Ubu Roi* (see note 24).

53. The first French (perhaps World's) department store in the 7th arrondissement of Paris, it had a specially designed building constructed in 1869.

54. The westernmost French region located in Brittany.

55. Famous comedy acrobats from England.

56. Parisian music hall.

57. An industrial town in the Rhône-Alps region of southwestern France.

58. Main character of a French puppet show descended from Pulchinella, as Punch in England.

59. Area in Northern Paris famous for its bars, clubs and decadent entertainment.

60. The eruption of Mount Pelée claimed around 30,000 victims on May 8, 1902.

61. The Paris Morgue is situated on the banks of the Seine; the Opera is north of it, not on the river.

62. Zouave was the name of the French infantry serving in North Africa, famous for their distinctive, colorful dress.

63. *Les Fleurs du mal*, "Le Vampire" opens "Toi qui, comme un coup de couteau, / Dans mon cœur plaintif est entrée."

64. Road (Spanish).

65. A huge exhibition hall in Paris.

66. The Palais de l'Institut de France, seat of the Académie Français among others.

67. It was used as a French penal colony.

SF & FANTASY

Guy d'Armen. *Doc Ardan: The City of Gold and Lepers*
G.-J. Arnaud. *The Ice Company*
Aloysius Bertrand. *Gaspard de la Nuit*
Félix Bodin. *The Novel of the Future*
André Caroff. *The Terror of Madame Atomos*
Didier de Chousy. *Ignis*
C. I. Defontenay. *Star (Psi Cassiopeia)*
Charles Derennes. *The People of the Pole*
Harry Dickson. *The Heir of Dracula*
Sâr Dubnotal *vs. Jack the Ripper*
Alexandre Dumas. *The Return of Lord Ruthven*
J.-C. Dunyach. *The Night Orchid. The Thieves of Silence*
Henri Duvernois. *The Man Who Found Himself*
Henri Falk. *The Age of Lead*
Paul Féval. *Anne of the Isles. Knightshade. Revenants. Vampire City. The Vampire Countess. The Wandering Jew's Daughter*
Paul Féval, *fils. Felifax, the Tiger-Man*
Arnould Galopin. *Doctor Omega*
Nathalie Henneberg. *The Green Gods*
V. Hugo, Foucher & Meurice. *The Hunchback of Notre-Dame*
Michel Jeury. *Chronolysis*
O. Joncquel & Theo Varlet. *The Martian Epic*
Jean de La Hire. *Enter the Nyctalope. The Nyctalope on Mars. The Nyctalope vs. Lucifer*
G. Le Faure & H. de Graffigny. *The Extraordinary Adventures of a Russian Scientist Across the Solar System* (2 vols.)
Gustave Le Rouge. *The Vampires of Mars*
Jules Lermina. *Mysteryville. Panic in Paris. To-Ho and the Gold Destroyers*
Jean-Marc & Randy Lofficier. *Edgar Allan Poe on Mars. The Katrina Protocol. Pacifica. Robonocchio. Tales of the Shadowmen* (anthos.; 6 vols.)
Xavier Mauméjean. *The League of Heroes*
John-Antoine Nau. *Enemy Force*

Marie Nizet. *Captain Vampire*
C. Nodier, Beraud & Toussaint-Merle. *Frankenstein*
Henri de Parville. *An Inhabitant of the Planet Mars*
Polidori, C. Nodier, E. Scribe. *Lord Ruthven the Vampire*
P.-A. Ponson du Terrail. *The Vampire and the Devil's Son*
Maurice Renard. *The Blue Peril. Doctor Lerne. The Doctored Man . A Man Among the Microbes. The Master of Light*
Albert Robida. *The Adventures of Saturnin Farandoul. The Clock of the Centuries.*
J.-H. Rosny Aîné. *Helgvor of the Blue River. The Givreuse Enigma. The Mysterious Force. The Navigators of Space. Vamireh. The World of the Variants. The Young Vampire*
Brian Stableford. *The New Faust at the Tragicomique. Frankenstein and the Vampire Countess. The Shadow of Frankenstein. Sherlock Holmes & The Vampires of Eternity. The Stones of Camelot. The Wayward Muse.* (anthologist) *The Germans on Venus. News from the Moon*
Jacques Spitz. *The Eye of Purgatory*
Kurt Steiner. *Ortog*
Villiers de l'Isle-Adam. *The Scaffold. The Vampire Soul*
Philippe Ward. *Artahe*
Philippe Ward & Sylvie Miller. *The Song of Montségur*

MYSTERIES & THRILLERS

M. Allain & P. Souvestre. *The Daughter of Fantômas*
Anicet-Bourgeois, Lucien Dabril. *Rocambole*
A. Bisson & G. Livet. *Nick Carter vs. Fantômas*
V. Darlay & H. de Gorsse. *Lupin vs. Holmes: The Stage Play*
Paul Féval. *Gentlemen of the Night. John Devil. The Black Coats: The Cadet Gang. The Companions of the Treasure. Heart of Steel. The Invisible Weapon. The Parisian Jungle. 'Salem Street*
Emile Gaboriau. *Monsieur Lecoq*
Steve Leadley. *Sherlock Holmes: The Circle of Blood*

Maurice Leblanc. *Arsène Lupin vs. Countess Cagliostro. Lupin vs. Holmes: The Blonde Phantom. The Hollow Needle.*
Gaston Leroux. *Chéri-Bibi. The Phantom of the Opera. Roule-tabille & the Mystery of the Yellow Room*
William Patrick Maynard. *The Terror of Fu Manchu*
Frank J. Morlock. *Sherlock Holmes: The Grand Horizontals*
P. de Wattyne & Y. Walter. *Sherlock Holmes vs. Fantômas*
David White. *Fantômas in America*

SCREENPLAYS

Mike Baron. *The Iron Triangle*
Emma Bull & Will Shetterly. *Nightspeeder. War for the Oaks*
Gerry Conway & Roy Thomas. *Doc Dynamo*
Steve Englehart. *Majorca*
James Hudnall. *The Devastator*
Jean-Marc & Randy Lofficier. *Royal Flush*
J.-M. & R. Lofficier & Marc Agapit. *Despair*
Andrew Paquette. *Peripheral Vision*
R. Thomas, J. Hendler & L. Sprague de Camp. *Rivers of Time*

NON-FICTION

Stephen R. Bissette. *Blur 1-5. Green Mountain Cinema 1*
Win Scott Eckert. *Crossovers* (2 vols.)
Jean-Marc & Randy Lofficier. *Shadowmen* (2 vols.)
Randy Lofficier. *Over Here*

HEXAGON COMICS

Franco Frescura & Luciano Bernasconi. *Wampus 1*
Franco Frescura & Giorgio Trevisan. *CLASH*
Luciano Bernasconi, Jean-Marc Lofficier & Juan Roncagliolo Berger. *Phenix 1*